THE HATCHING OF EVIL

That night was the worst she had known.

The thing moved with a rapid clicking sound, as on tiny high heels, along the passage. It was cold: it was seeking heat. It found her electric blanket, pressing the bed down with its soft, intangible weight, and settling, content; until it found her warmer body beneath – but she was too sleepy to move, or even to register the gradual takeover. Now it was encroaching on her, an intelligence that calculated, and knew how to soothe, how to please, to invade, to divide and sip and conquer – pleasing when half-asleep . . . Then suddenly, frightening.

She was wide awake, and terrified. Something was with her. She curled her body cautiously away from it and crept out of bed. There was nothing to be seen in the curtained gloom except shadows and darker shadows . . .

Dark Runner

ROSALIND ASHE

SPHERE BOOKS LIMITED
London and Sydney

First published in Great Britain by
Century Publishing Co. Ltd 1984
Copyright © Rosalind Ashe 1984
Published by Sphere Books Ltd 1985
30–32 Gray's Inn Road, London WC1X 8JL

For George Harris

Printed and bound in Great Britain by
Cox & Wyman Ltd, Reading

Prologue

IT WAS SMALL and very heavy. It looked like an artifact, so elaborate, so pleasing was the interlacing of nickel-iron and black stone – all polished now, across a million years of reverent handling, to a mirror surface.

Palaeologists who have come across such stones – or rather, travelled far to see them, for only four are officially known and recorded – maintain they are further proof of the vast meteorite, six miles in diameter, that plunged into the North Pacific some sixty-five million years ago, and now lies wedged deep down under the Asiatic continental plate: the largest and most effectively buried treasure in the world.

The explosion of impact covered the earth with a black cloud. This was the long darkness that brought extinction to three quarters of all living things; and among the debris of mud and matter raining down through that lethal twilight were a few scattered crumbs of the meteorite itself.

Holding it, Sebastian knew that this small fragment was capable of re-enacting such destruction, its lethal force no longer a simple matter of mass and velocity, but the immanent power conferred by millenia of worship and dread. It had grown to such stature, this particular stone, that it had outstripped even the fanatics and tyrants who had used it; accumulating, throughout its long history of violence, massacre and domination, such a force of evil as might no longer be earthed. And it was said that this history might be observed, literally, in the simple clasping of the stone; the

1

submission of mind and spirit to that high-speed replay of its bloody pageant. It was as though such contact triggered a momentary release of energy so powerful that the human mind could not take more than a few seconds of exposure. However, with the correct preparation and discipline, an observer could attempt to sort and distinguish those images, and even relate them to the recorded sightings of the past five hundred years.

Theories about the actual power of these sacred ju-jus were many, colourful, and no more to be trusted than the individuals who had been ruled by them. But it was a simple fact, to which Sebastian would one day bear witness, that they bred a ruthless possessiveness in their keepers; indeed, there was no record of anyone having abandoned this particular stone, nor having been parted from it, except by *force majeur*. It had made mild men vicious and vicious men great.

Then there were the tales of encounters with its physical presence, the 'bodying forth' of its living evil. These were garbled and rambling at best; at worst, an obscene litany of man's oldest fears. The most interesting aspect of such tales, when the various and far-flung accounts were compared, was the timing. For, although there were sometimes gaps of a century or more between incidents, wise men who studied them in the past had formed the conclusion that the stone was not merely an amalgam of the elements – earth fused by air, fire and water – but seemed to have an organic life of its own, with periods of gestation followed by bursts of activity. This, they calculated – and Sebastian checked and double-checked – was not a matter of months or years, or of human generations, but of an exact number of days: 7777.

When the tumbling, bright digits of his pocket calculator first settled at this figure, it had shaken him. Foreknowledge was no real preparation. There it was, an abstraction transformed into a pattern: a neat row of small, luminous hooks. A figure to conjure with.

Now, confronting the thing itself, he tried to clear his mind. A stone and metal egg that conferred power on its obsessive guardians, its slaves, was sufficiently far-fetched an idea for the sceptic in him: any such power, surely, was imbued by the credulous themselves. (Why then is it growing *more* powerful? countered the voices of the sages; and what of its cyclical 'flowering'? What of the individuals, by no means all credulous, who had observed it at such times? What of those who had perished in its service, or the few that attempted resistance and were destroyed? And why should these deaths always coincide with the peak of its observed cycle?)

All these questions, and their multiplicity of answers too, he had known: in theory, from study, from travel, from wise men and mad ones; but it was only when he cradled it in his palm, and its memory, stored in the metal and stone like a battery charge, got through to him, that he began to understand.

The sensation was like standing two feet from a passing express train. During the ten seconds Bob Loren permitted him to hold it, the centuries of images roared by, flashing against his eyelids. And yet, after the first headlong fiery fall, all but the last few moments were black, dormant, locked deep in cool mud with the weight of a mountain above. Then sudden light and noise, crowds, blood, jewels, fragments of shattered cities, robes of saffron, indigo, red; jungles, skyscrapers, wings, waves, explosions, carnage, marching feet: all in shattering split-second tableaux, subliminal glimpses – a high-priest with red hands; peaked white hoods lit by a human bonfire; a shouting face, and the emblazon of a twisted black, broken-armed cross; the broken, twisted limbs of some mass grave – and all seemingly at once, unbearable as white noise; yet each image sharply focussed, and linked with a flow of hands and lips and eyes –

Then Bob took the stone from him, replaced it in its wash-leather bag round his neck, and poured a double brandy.

'Well? Getting quite physical in its old age – isn't it dear?' he said. 'Hey man – for a nigger you've gone ever so white…'

Chapter One

LONG BEFORE THE girl arrived in the nice warm flat, it was there.

It had found a good home, a hiding place in which to lie low and ripen. The natural cycle was in its last months, building up slowly towards the violent burst of activity, the birth of its next generation. A tepid English summer, that had only made it restless and hungry, was over. At last the old boiler just below in the basement had been fired. This was better: it was accustomed to tropical climes; and in this phase especially it needed warmth, more even than worship – quiet and darkness, not spotlights, nor roaring crowds. It had its store of food. Languid, tumescent, it had gone to earth.

But now it stirred, and took notice of a new presence that flowed strongly like clear cold water along the corridor, into the kitchen opposite, the drawing room and the two bedrooms, along the very wall of its lair, chilling it for a moment as she passed so near, so bright, so absolutely new – reminding it with a pang of Eve in the first days of the created world. It wrapped itself tighter round the hot black pipes, content for the time being with that warmth, and satisfied with its rations, its latest sacrifice.

She heard the suck and sigh, the low gurgle, of ancient heating. This served the whole block, she had been told, and, though eccentrically arranged with radiators only in the passage of each flat, effectively warmed the rooms on either side if you left the doors open. The three hearty girls upstairs – her sole contacts so far, apart from the agents who supplied the keys – planned to 'take a spur' off it into their sitting room. 'It *is* a bit noisy – like a giant digestive system at times!' they giggled, handing her a mug of coffee. 'And worst on the ground floor, probably; but it goes off at twelve – so it shouldn't keep you awake.'

She would grow used to the central heating; and to the cooling noises. At midnight the clicking-cooling started: rapid as a rattlesnake at first, and slowing down over the next hour to nothing more disturbing than a 'tick... tick... ' so far apart you might fall asleep waiting for the next.

But in the airing cupboard, it moved restlessly, disturbed by this loss of heat; and ventured out, reaching its infinite fingers through the cracks and along the passage, seeking a new source of warmth.

She was so lucky to find the flat.

As a paying guest with a friend of a friend of her parents, she had hoped this tenuous connection would have rendered her independent; but the four long weeks in St Johns Wood under the wing of Mrs Twining proved both isolated and smothering. In her late fifties this soft sweet lady – all powder and white gloves and small good causes – had been deserted by her husband for a younger woman; and her many children lived their own lives it seemed. The large house in which she had brought them up was now her only world: they could not persuade her to part with it; but they encouraged her to take in PGs, thus providing her with both pocket money and company.

At first, raw from home, Lucy felt grateful for the cosseting and interest; for the little lunchpacks with explanatory notes; even for the kidnapping and careful ironing of discarded skirts – and always the nosegay, of pansies and rosemary, on the dressing table. She found herself taking Mrs T to the cinema (not that Lucy really wanted to see *On Golden Pond*, especially with the latest *Rocky* just round the corner); or getting her out to the pub for a glass of sherry ('Ridiculous, really, when we've got oodles at home – but very sweet of you, dear.') On impulse one evening she decided to stay away after work and explore the Covent Garden cocktail bars, in the company of an engagingly neurotic copy-writer who needed diversion even more urgently than Mrs Twining did; and she telephoned 'home' to report her change of plan – only to learn that her devoted landlady had made a special dinner, 'to celebrate your twenty-first'. 'My *what*?' 'Your twenty-first day in St Johns Wood, Lucy!' She went back; and it was about then that she realised she must cut loose and concentrate on a life of her own: that she, too, was lonely.

She was so used to having friends around that she had always taken company for granted. She had none in London: her nearest contemporaries were in Reading and Oxford; promising to visit her, but soon involved in the excitements of their first term. As for the friendships made at her new job – her first in London, as a secretary with an advertising agency – these did not seem to follow through into the evenings. She knew things would improve; told herself it was up to her to get organised, go out, join groups, meet people. But for the time being, she found herself an outsider.

Lucinda Morland was nineteen, beautiful, bright, and – as her parents repeatedly told each other – sensible. 'It's not as if she'd blossomed suddenly,' said her mother; 'I mean, she's been pretty for so long – no, not just in our eyes – that she's used to it: it hasn't gone to her head. Has it? And I don't think she's ever been tempted to sleep around to prove something to herself – or anyone else.' 'No. And London won't change her. Not that side of her. Come on: we're both glad she's ambitious. She won't be a mere secretary for long, according to that supervisor of hers. Face it, m'dear, we're just missing the creature – last fledgling to fly the nest and all that – and particularly now we've got to get those ruddy apples picked.'

Letters from home still upset Lucy: about washing the dogs, and the golden autumn weather, the late raspberries, an abundance of figs, the difficulty of getting down the highest apples without her there to climb. ('Why are they always the biggest and best? If you come for a weekend soon, you can still catch the top Coxes from your favourite tennis-court tree.') She was suffering childishly from a home-sickness far worse than the boarding-school variety; for she had never been lonely before.

The other secretaries, Daphne, Esther, Sally and even Florence-with-the-ailing-mother, all seemed to have their own action-packed lives after work. Red-headed Daphne, and Esther, a plump, intensely pretty Jewish girl, were both engaged and worked just to fill the waiting. Sally was more Lucy's sort, laughing at the same catastrophes, exchanging lunches, magazines and nail-polish, biding their time and keeping sane only because they were confident of the Big Time ahead. But Sally was collected by a different sports car each evening, it seemed; and Lucy sometimes felt that Sal's smooth avoidance of introductions was quite intentional, springing from the same fierce possessiveness with which she monopolised the new young executive director's dictation time. It was some compensation knowing she was better-looking than Sally, and that at least Eddie, the brilliant neurotic copy-writer, found her more sympathetic; but Sally was smart, in both senses, and saw her perhaps as the new and only threat on a fiercely competitive scene. I'll become slick and aggressive too, thought Lucy. Yet when, after a fortnight of passing through, the young exec. asked her to stay on and have a drink with him (Sally was out of earshot using the photocopier), she heard herself decline before even taking time to consider.

'Why?' he asked sweetly.

He had such pretty eyes, narrow, sparkling, green: they were his best feature, and he knew it.

'I suppose I simply don't have drinks with married men,' she said.

'I see. But the other girl, Sally, said you were pretty ambitious – you know: keen to get ahead? Ah well, can't win 'em all.'

Afterwards, she was surprised at herself – my first invitation

7

in the big city: the start of my social career: great! – and tempted, also, to tell Sally about the incident. Sal would have been amused, impressed, and wildly envious; but would certainly have passed the verdict of 'wet' on Lucy's prim cop-out.

Lucy replayed the scene over and over again in her mind as she stood squashed and swaying in the tube back to St Johns Wood, with the evening stretching before her, of shampooing and tights-washing and Mrs T's choice of television – through which she would talk and dart about 'fixing a little salad', while Lucy furtively switched channels in her brief absences. She imagined how the evening might have been if she had simply said 'Yes': the drink in the city wine-bar expanding into oysters at Wheelers, his phone-call home to say he was working late, the dim nightclub, the reggae beat…

Pathetic! she thought: I don't even find him particularly attractive. Now if I had a place of my own, or sharing, and could ask Sal and her boyfriends round – and they'd bring someone for me. And a spare room, so I could ask Caroline, or Nell, or Jamie and Jenny, to come up for a show. I never could at Mrs Twinings.

She had promised to stay at 'base camp' – as she thought of it – for at least a month while she found her feet; but now she hardened her heart and started looking in *The Times* and *The Standard* for possible flats. Twice on her way home from work she had rung hopeful numbers, only to find she was too late. Then, one morning on the tube, she opened her *Times* and saw the advertisement, high on the list: 'A nice warm flat, small block in choice square, 2 bed, use of gardens, £40 per week inc., 4 months only, references please. Phone Mrs Maturin' and a Kensington number.

She was already late for work, so she rushed out to the phone box in her lunch hour. The number was engaged the first time. As she waited, she prayed. It was so astoundingly cheap for the area – and two bedrooms! There must be a catch somewhere; and anyway, at that price, it would have gone. Then she got through.

It was a long and rather extraordinary telephone

conversation. She ran out of fivepenny pieces and Mrs Maturin insisted on calling her back to continue. 'I feel you may be just the person – did you say Aquarius? Good. You must understand I'm in a dreadful hurry – leaving tonight for a stay in the sun – South Africa, actually: I'm a hot-blooded creature and for me the winter here... Of *course* you'd like to see it; this evening? Oh dear, but it's going to be such a rush – I really wanted to fix it up now – and the phone's been ringing all morning... Well yes, it's such good value – *so* many people wanting it sight unseen, I may say – but I didn't feel they were, well – really *me*. I mean: foreigners. Two were Pakistanis, I'm sure, though of course they tried to disguise their voices – but they couldn't fool me – and they'd be bringing in the whole family, cousins and aunts – *you* know... But you: you're from Wiltshire – lovely county: all those marvellous ley-lines, lines of power, you know, Avebury and so on. And you say you need somewhere as a base to look for something more permanent? So this would be perfect for you, dear. Now, let me describe it to you.'

Lucy felt her precious lunch-break melting away: nearly half an hour had passed telephoning, waiting to be phoned back, being cross-questioned – and sometimes quite personally – by this woman she had never met; waiting while she went to answer the doorbell. 'Are you still there? Oh good! The laundry, that was... ' She listened to her lovingly descriptive tour of the flat (it sounded quite large and rather grand), and shifted from foot to foot while Mrs Maturin expatiated on her fear of flying – 'though one hardly dare use the phrase since that dirty book came out by that Erica Wong... ' Lucy heard herself responding patiently in the brief pauses: it wasn't simply that she knew the flat must be a bargain – whatever was wrong with it – and that it seemed almost within her grasp, but that she had become too involved to ring off: the voice, the invisible woman herself, was hypnotic, somehow, with all her house pride and little refinements; her passé trendiness, doing her own thing, and how up-tight it made her leaving her little pad... And now Lucy was recommending good reads she might find on the airport bookstall, and even suggesting a small tube of moisturiser in the handbag (a tip she had just seen in a woman's magazine) to counteract the drying-out effect of the air-conditioning.

'Oh what a good idea! You are sweet.' The voice was a rich, over-expressive contralto – could she have trodden the boards? Or taught elocution? And the laugh was frequent and tinkling. 'Oh dear though – so much still to do… And then I simply can't make up my mind whether or not to take my *most* precious with me – you know how it is with things you really don't want to be parted from? Dearie me, decisions decisions … Look, I'll tell you what I'll do – just because I like you – your voice – oh, your whole background; *you* know, dear: it matters so much. You see, it's not that I want to make money – at that rent how could I? I mean, I just want someone to keep my dear flat warm for me and care for my things – mind you, I've locked all my treasures and most breakable pieces in the cupboard, the airing cupboard; but you won't miss it: all the sheets and towels are in the ottoman, and you'll find the radiators more than adequate for drying and airing and so forth. What was I… ? Yes, just someone sympathetic to enjoy – And I'll agree to let *you* have it – I'll inform the agents that you are to have the keys, if you'll agree – gentleman's agreement, you know – to take it – I just can't cope with the uncertainty, and all these calls. Then I can tell them all it's taken. I can't say fairer than that, can I? Oh, *good* – I think you're ever so wise. And if you drop by this evening early on I'll show you round. Lovely – I look forward – I'm so relieved, I feel better already. And Lucy – I may call you Lucy? Lucinda – light – such a lovely name – I'm convinced you won't regret it, my dear.'

But she never met Mrs Maturin.

That evening she got away from work as soon as she could and took the tube to Kensington. Ten minutes' walk along the High Street brought her to the turning that led to Clarence Square.

It was a large, pleasantly open space with fenced gardens in the centre; and she could see the glimmer of water beyond the shrubbery. Three sides of the square were handsome terraced Regency houses, red brick with bright doors and posh cars; but as she approached the squat thirties block of flats on the far side, her heart sank.

It was a mean grey building, streaked with soot and damp. Paler grey net curtains webbed the rows of windows, and the front door was set in a lumpy portico that tried and failed to be grand. Well, better to look out than in, she told herself; but she was already regretting her impulsive 'gentleman's agreement'. She crossed the road to the corner of the gardens nearest the flats; and, as she faced the portico, skirting the clammy evergreens that pressed between the railings, a dark figure like an ill omen loomed suddenly into the edge of her vision: a runner loping through the twilit black trees and disappearing round the corner beyond the street lamp.

Inside, the lobby was bright and warm. Firmly she rang the bell of No 2, and waited. There was no answer. She could see a light; she rang again; then she bent down and peered through the letter-box.

A dim, fringed wall-lamp was on at the end of the long passage, showing doors on either side. Nearer to her, by the first door, stood a bulky suitcase. There was no movement; no sound, apart from the rumble and hiss of the central heating. Yet she was suddenly sure someone, or something, was there (lying low and wouldn't answer? Or trapped – and couldn't answer?) Half-heartedly she rang again; then quickly crossed the lobby to No 1 to ask; and, finding it dark, with papers stuck in the door, she went upstairs to the first floor and rang the bell of the flat above 'hers'. Here there was music, then voices and footsteps. The door was opened by a girl of about her age in paint-splashed dungarees.

'Looking for Mrs Maturin? Well, we thought she was away – oh, more than a week now – Wait… Ah, someone saw her going in this morning. I reckoned she must be off on her hols: she usually goes away this time of year. Are you the sub-let? And you've missed her! What a shame – come on in and have a drink or some coffee or something. We're just cooking: 'scuse the frying smells. I'm Ella. And Diane – and Josie, on the ladder.'

11

They turned down the radio and found her a mug in the small crowded kitchen. The long corridor, dust-sheeted and half-painted, had the same arrangement of doorways and radiators Lucy had glimpsed through the letter-box downstairs; here, a bright tunnel with openings. No hint of concealment, or threat, from doors closed or ajar. A matter of lighting, surely…

'You've got that flat for three months, have you?' Diane was saying. 'Four? So it'll see you through till spring.'

'She agreed on the phone, yes. I suppose I won't really be sure till I get hold of the agents: I was going to ask you for their name.'

'Foss & Cornfield – I've even got the phone number. There. So you haven't seen the flat yet? Well… ' As Lucy looked up from her coffee she caught them exchanging glances. 'Well, you'll find it marvellously spacious and warm… '

'In fact,' said Ella quickly, standing up, 'it's a replica of this one, of course, but the rooms down there are higher, I think. Come and look round, since you can't see No 2. Here's the airing cupboard where the heating pipes come in – noisy but effective – and then there's a bedroom next door – bathroom here, and then the sitting room down here at the end, and the other bedroom. The sitting room's largest, you see, with the full width of the passage as well. We've just painted it white: Josie works in a poster shop and we're going to hang all her freebees.'

'It's lovely,' said Lucy: 'so bright and open-feeling.'

'Well, your downstairs will be like this. Won't it, Diane?'

'Yes, basically… '

'Not quite like this,' Josie cut in. She was busy scraping a paint spot off the floor, and she did not look up.

'Oh she's just got a thing about that flat: don't listen. OK, it's totally differently furnished, they say.'

'*You* haven't seen it?' asked Lucy.

'Not me, no. Mrs M. asked me in to a party or something once and Josie said it was spooky and I mustn't go if… '

'I said it had funny vibrations.'

' "Funny" – great! I could have just died laughing, right?

12

Anyway I didn't go. Something else came up... '

Diane, pink-cheeked peace-maker in a floral smock, said, 'I've been there – same time as Josie, just to look round – and it didn't bother *me*. It simply isn't our sort of decor: but with a few personal touches – well, a poster or two, some of your own things – and what-the-hell-it's-home, I say. Mind you, I'm not a sensitive plant like Jo here.'

'I don't think I'm all that sensitive either,' said Lucy.

Diane nodded emphatically. 'And for a few months until you find your own place – what are you paying? There you are: at forty quid a week, and room for a lodger, it's a palace.'

'I just hope Mrs Maturin remembered to ring the agents and tell them,' said Lucy, walking back to the front door; 'she was in a great flap when I talked to her earlier. She did *say* she'd see me: her plane didn't go till late.'

'Last minute shopping? Or just asleep, maybe,' said Ella. 'Let's try phoning – got the number? I'll dial it and, on your way out, you can hear it ringing and see if anyone answers.'

Standing in front of No 2 again, her ear close to the ripple-glass pane, Lucy could hear the empty brrr-brrr. She did not look through the letter-box this time; she did not want to remind herself of the fringed light, the bulging suitcase (why go and leave it?), the secretive doors and shadowy pictures that seemed to lean inwards... 'Thanks,' she called up the stairwell; 'but there's no one there – it seems. Thanks for everything. See you.'

Next morning on her way to the office she telephoned Foss & Cornfield. The secretary informed her Mr Cornfield who dealt with Clarence Court would not be available till 3.30, but she could leave her name.

Lucy felt unexpectedly let down, and had to battle with growing anxiety all morning. She worked through her lunch-hour to divert herself, and to justify leaving early – as she might need to, if... It was absurd how much more desirable the flat seemed now she was no longer sure of it. Any misgivings born of her encounters the previous evening – the twilight runner, the not-quite-empty flat, or Josie's hinted warning – died in the light of day. Now she felt perfectly confident of her ability to take it over, decor, vibes and all. It was big, in a good position looking on to an elegant square – and with all that lovely heating, however noisy, included in the price; if £40 a week made life hard, she could always share… All this – and only if scatty old Mrs M. had managed to ring Foss & Cornfield.

Permission was granted for her to use the office telephone for a personal call. This time the secretary seemed to know who she was: Mr Cornfield had said it was all arranged, and she must pick up the keys and pay a month's rent as deposit before five, or wait till Monday – but they didn't like the premises to be empty, especially ground floor apartments, so…

'I'll be there before five,' said Lucy. It was hers.

The late October day had turned warm and bright, an Indian summer; there was an orange sunset with the sun hanging on the horizon like a red balloon, and pink, woolly clouds strung out above Hyde Park, when Lucy reached the agents' office in Knightsbridge.

'The flat will be empty, won't it?' she asked the blonde Amazon who was busy tucking up the typewriter and assembling her shopping bags.

'Must be, mustn't it? If she was leaving yesterday. I shouldn't think the squatters move that quick, would you?'

'I mean, I was meant to meet her last evening, but she wasn't there.'

'Well you were too late then, weren't you? Just make certain you're there on Saturday when Mr Cornfield comes to check the inventory, that's all. Come along now: I've the locking up to do.'

On the doorstep Lucy said, 'I did try to phone her you see, but there was no answer.'

'So? She's gone. It's empty. You've paid your deposit. You've got your keys… ' through the closing door.

'But: suppose – suppose I don't like the flat… ' With the

14

money paid, and the key to that door in her hand, she had committed herself to – to what?

'Oh *no*.' The Amazon folded her arms and rolled her eyes heavenwards. 'You mean to say you haven't even seen over the property? Now: you've paid, you've signed a contract; if you don't fancy it, you can leave it – but don't think you'll get the money back, my girl. Lord help us – what next? Look, just be there on Saturday – that's tomorrow – when Mr Cornfield arrives, and *he'll* tell you what's what – OK?' The door banged.

Lucy took a taxi to St Johns Wood and made it wait.

'You're home early, aren't you?' said Mrs Twining. She was putting away the ironing board hastily. Lucy's laundry, still warm, lay on the sofa in a neat pile.

'Oh Mrs Twining – you shouldn't have – you make me feel so *awful*... You see, Mrs Twining, I've found a flat. Well, I found it yesterday; and I want to move in right away – they don't like it being empty. I've paid you up to the end of next week – so I can only apologise most sincerely for it being so sudden, for not being in to supper, and thank you: you've been so good to me. And I've loved it. But I must learn to cope on my own – and this is a chance I can't miss – Yes, I'll phone my parents – but I must rush, the taxi is waiting.' She had to do it like this, quickly, gathering up her clothes, carrying out her sewing machine; not looking.

Mrs Twining said little; she unpursed her lips for a brief 'goodbye'. 'I'll let you know my address and phone number,' Lucy called as they drew away from the curb. 'And thank you, for everything.'

There was only a dull glow in the western sky, darkness and street lamps in Clarence Square, as Lucy unloaded her suitcase and carrier bags onto the pavement. The taxi-driver helped her into the lobby. When he had gone she faced No 2 with her key. The light was still on. Superstitiously, she rang the bell and waited; then she unlocked the door and walked in.

Carrying through her belongings she nearly tripped over the large suitcase that stood near the door. She switched on another light and walked straight along to where the sitting room must be: the left hand door at the end. She was aware of

15

a nasty smell, sweet and rotten, overlaid with a strong whiff of incense. Another light; none of them were very powerful, and all were muffled by heavily fringed shades.

It must have been just as big as the room she had seen upstairs, but its height and its furnishings made it seem smaller. The plum-coloured flock walls and heavy damask curtains with swagged pelmets seemed to slope in, lit dustily by several pairs of gilt wall brackets. A three-piece-suite over-stuffed into the bulging rays of an art deco design, fat satin floor cushions, small stools and nests of coffee tables in multicoloured thirties geometry crowded the open space, their claustrophobic richness compounded by all the shawls and rugs, flounces and fringes, mats and scatter cushions that cluttered every line, and by the multiplicity of nicknacks and pictures that covered the tables, shelves and walls. Orange, black, purple and red seemed to appeal to Mrs Maturin.

Amazed, Lucy stood by the door, then picked her way over to a standard lamp, and on to a table lamp, illuminating the various areas with pools of murky light, and finally switching on the 'Queen Anne' two-bar electric fire in the hearth. Above her, over the mantlepiece, hung the sort of hunting trophy one might buy at Harrods: a pair of huge curving ibex horns, gilded, and tipped with crystal, springing from a sliver of pale skull – forehead, eye-sockets, upper jaw – and all mounted on a leopard-skin targe. 'That's got to go, for a start,' she said out loud in the empty flat, and was answered only by the gobble of the central heating.

Nothing could be changed, of course, until the inventory, she thought, switching on the light in the bedroom across the corridor. This was clearly Mrs Maturin's own; aggressively feminine and predominantly mauve, with a draped four-poster bed, a great complication of net and lace and slub-silk curtains over the window, and flounces round the kidney dressing-table. Off-white cherubs held the wall lights in here, and two large plate-glass shelves were filled with cute porcelain figures of wide-eyed little boys in lederhosen and little girls with short frocks that showed their bottoms. Perhaps the other bedroom is better, thought Lucy.

It was different, certainly. The chest of drawers and the high single bed were good old mahogany. There were long black velvet curtains and dark orange wallpaper, Regency striped with funerary urns, upon which hung a set of Indian masks; they were both beautiful and sinister, the eyes long and heavy-lidded, with wide, leering, red mouths and fantastic crowns. The wall by which she stood seemed warm, and when she put her hand on it she felt the warmth, and a faint buzzing sensation. Stepping back into the corridor, she could see that this was the wall along which the airing cupboard ran. Its door was fastened with a neat Yale lock; inside it must be not only all Mrs M.'s valuables, but the hot-water cylinder and ganglion of central heating pipes that branched out into the passage under the floorboards to feed the large old-fashioned radiators. Leaning her ear to the panel, it seemed momentarily quieter; that pumping noise, the suck and sigh, had ceased, and only a gurgle from the nearest radiator, and the throb of the boiler beneath her feet, broke the silence. It was almost as though it had stopped to listen too... Then she moved back into the spare bedroom, running her hand along the tingling warmth of the wall; and went across to pull back the curtains, and look out on the square gardens. This clearly had a better view than Mrs Maturin's room, and would, moreover, be the warmest place of all, so close to that cupboard – but the persistent smell was even stronger in here; and though it would be simple to take down the masks and brighten things up, somehow even the mauve love-nest seemed preferable. She pulled the curtains back, switched off the light, and took her suitcase along the passage.

The bathroom, tiled in shiny dark-green, was a tall tank of a room, but warm, with a huge bath that stood on handsome claws. The bathmat was black and curly, in the shape of a giant footprint. Now only the kitchen remained to be seen; and she would make herself a cup of tea before unpacking.

It was the half-open door opposite the cupboard; she knew it would be what the agencies call 'compact', maybe 'well-planned'. But the range of easy-care work-surfaces were not immediately visible. Piles of encrusted plates and cups

17

filled the small sink and draining board; a pan of some glue-like sauce had boiled over and welded it to the top of the cooker. A clogged frying pan and two trays of half-eaten meals, clearly dating from different periods, covered the table and work-top, the older trayful including a plate of furry stew, probably a helping from the casserole that stank of corruption when she lifted the lid. This and unemptied rubbish were explanation enough of that smell: it looked as though Mrs Maturin had been out of the flat for the last week, returned briefly to arrange the letting, and left in one hell of a hurry: no time even for a note of apology... Without further thoughts of tea – much less of supper – Lucy flung open the window, ran the hot water, tied a plastic apron round her waist and got to work.

It took her most of the evening. She threw away the casserole and the saucepan; also the box of sprouting potatoes under the sink. It was not just her country-born disgust at such crying waste that upset her. There had been something desperate about those blind, groping tendrils and matted roots; and a remark of her father's came back to her – 'Dreadful, somehow: like womb cancer in spinsters... '

Her radio kept her company, and stopped her thinking viciously of Mrs Bloody Maturin, so caring, so house proud, now baking in the heat of some far-flung coral strand – no, living it up in the cocktail bar by now – while her sub-let humped black plastic bagfuls of her rubbish down to the dustbins by the area steps. By ten o'clock she had wiped all the cleared surfaces a second time, and set out her own teapot and honey and home-made jam. Her geraniums were on the window ledge, her own tea caddy by the kettle, the pint of milk she had brought with her sitting alone in a spotless refrigerator; her chinese mug and a small jug from home, Souvenir of Polperro, stood on the well-scrubbed tray. She filled the kettle, plugged it in – and got a small tingling shock from the switch. I'll deal with that tomorrow, she thought wearily; and unpacked her nightdress and slippers while it boiled.

It was strange to take her tray – Mrs M.'s tray – through to

Mrs M.'s sitting room, and look round for the right place to sit: nothing was hers; nothing was right. She had no chosen place, no routine. Rather than settling into the slick maw of one of those huge, richly-cushioned easy chairs, she perched at the table in the bay window: she could not feel the electric fire from here, but she was still warm enough from her labours; and she had a need to be upright, alert, in a good position to see the whole room, and the open door. That smell persisted in the corridor and the spare room. She had closed the door on the Indian masks and left all the others open to circulate the fresh air from the kitchen window.

She had done well. But still she could not relax. In here the personality and eccentric magpie tastes of the woman she had never met made her feel like an interloper... She got up abruptly, mouth full of toast, went to the bedroom and dug in her suitcase for a length of bright cotton print she had bought to make a summer dress. She spread it over the table: her own cheerful pool of primary colours; and set the tray back on its crisp, new surface: a little stronghold, a safe circle, in the underlit, overfurnished room. She poured her tea and thought, perhaps it will grow on me.

She went to bed early. There were only satin sheets, black or brown, in the ottoman, and they felt and smelt alien; but she was so tired she fell asleep long before the clicking started.

Chapter Two

HALF AWAKE, LUCY lay very still, struggling to find herself, to identify the huge cobweb that filled her one-eyed view towards the light. I'm still asleep; I'm a nightmare fly. I'm caught. There is a huge spider in a cupboard, and if I don't –

She sat up with a jerk. The layers of net curtains backed off into focus; then she saw her dressing gown on the end of the strange four-poster bed, and knew she was in her flat, and it was Saturday. And Mrs Twining would not be tapping on the door with a cup of too-strong Lapsang... Poor Mrs T.; she must be rung, and visited. But now it was still early: 6.15; and she lay back, pulling the brown satin sheet and the fat mauve quilt up to her chin.

There *was* a spider up in the corner of the canopy. For some reason she had never liked spiders, or octopuses, or crabs – perhaps because one never knew which way they were going to move. This was a very small spider; she might have seen it when she was half asleep, unco-ordinated, and read it as huge and further away. Why in a cupboard? The airing cupboard? It must have been the central heating that woke her and she had mixed up the spider and the locked cupboard in her muddled brain.

The bed was comfortable: rubbery and firm, moving all in one piece – and slightly seasick-making after Mrs T.'s old-fashioned horsehair. At least it wasn't the alien landscape it might have been, of humps and hollows created by another body. The pillows were very soft ('morbid' in Italian, she thought – a horrid stifling word), and smelt faintly of the sort of dark Eastern perfume people went mad about a few years ago in the ethnic boom. Those masks in the spare room were an odd collection for old Mrs M. Lucy was trying to build up a picture of her absent landlady. She must have spent quite a lot of money on doing up the flat – and some years ago, judging by the grey shading of the ceilings and the grubby, faded tawdriness of the valances and trimmings as the morning light strengthened. Yet Mrs Maturin presumably loved it all; had chosen and treasured each ornament and picture, pondered over the placing of a cushion, the width of a flounce; rearranged and admired the effect even of those porcelain tots – Perhaps I can find some drawer where I could put them away safely, she thought; and I'll bring up my egg-cup collection and my little chinese horses from home. But nothing could be touched till after the inventory.

Pulling back the drawing room curtains, she saw the runner again, black threading the black leafless trees on the far side of the gardens. Mesmerised by that even pace, the long, easy, almost leisurely, stride, she watched him until he started along the nearest railings; then drew back, and smiled to herself as she visualised all the grey net curtains in the block twitching in unison. Perhaps the cold weather would bring out a track suit – so much less disturbing and more in tone with the prim Georgian terraces. That was it: disturbing, rather than menacing, by the morning light. After all, every open space in London must have its joggers; yet this one seemed positively exotic, bringing a jungly wildness, a sort of heat and freedom, to the wintry London square.

Mr Cornfield was an altogether different animal, from another jungle: his was of glass and chrome. His hair was as yellow as his name; he wore sharp, pale-grey suiting and a cloud of classy aftershave, and he arrived promptly at 9.30. He declined coffee, observed himself in the big looking-glass, unzipped his pigskin briefcase and laid two copies of Mrs Maturin's inventory on the table in the bow window.

'I hope you appreciate that a sublet is trusted to make no alterations,' he said, looking round the room suspiciously; 'in any shape or form,' he said, fingering Lucy's impromptu tablecloth and clearly marking it down as sale goods. She was glad now that she had overcome her impulse to remove the photographs and the more off-putting nick-nacks. He went on; 'Our client, Mrs Maturin, is very proud and fond of her effects' – it made her sound like a stage magician – 'and we don't want her upset, do we?' A baring of many even white teeth. Mr Cornfield wore the ring of confidence with great awareness; but his eyes, twin pools of blue like any romantic hero's – the cold official blue of tiles and chlorine – did not alter by a ripple. Lucy wondered if he were wearing turquoise contact lenses: the rims were pink; that was so often the flaw in beautiful blond men. Then she realised he was waiting for an answer.

'Oh no: she'll find it just as she left it, Mr Cornfield,' she said; 'except perhaps for the kitchen.' And briefly, as matter-of-factly as she could, she described what she had been faced with, and the fate of the saucepan and casserole. 'I still can't get rid of that smell,' she concluded.

'I see. You will of course replace those items,' he said. 'But I hasten to point out that this is a handover situation totally untypical of our client. As you suggest, she must have left in a hurry – had to make an earlier flight, no doubt. And as for the suitcase, you may simply arrange for the caretaker, Mrs Dortmund in No 8, to take charge of it. No: we do not have a key to the airing cupboard; and that would be overstepping the bounds of our client's privacy. Now, we will start in here, and tick both lists, one for yourself and one for the Agency. So: a circular limed-oak table, slightly marked, I believe… '

It took well over an hour. The only light relief was the pseudo-Sotheby's jargon of the definitions; nor, it seemed, was anything deemed safe from the concupiscence of a sub-let, not even the Regency-style plaster ceiling-rose, the onyx vase in shape of praying hands containing artificial floral arrangement, nor the Rosenthal porcelain figure of a Madonna, faceless and hooded. The variety of ashtrays – bats' wings, or art deco cottages, or cupped palms (Mrs M. was clearly into hands) were listed, identified and duly ticked. To be fair to Mr Cornfield, he showed something of the distaste she herself felt for the weirder items in the Maturin museum; he began to flag towards the end of the fifth typed page, and merely counted the cute tots on the bedroom shelf, murmuring 'Our client would seem to have added to her collection.'

Passing the airing cupboard, Lucy observed 'One can't help wondering what on earth she's got in there and how she arranged them all: there hardly seems room for more.'

The twin swimming-pools looked chillier than ever. 'Perhaps I need to emphasise that any secured entity of our client's premises is sacrosanct.'

'Of course,' she said brightly. 'Really, Mr Cornfield, I've got enough to dust right here without wanting to…'

'And I trust,' he interrupted, zipping up the briefcase, 'that you appreciate the quality of the accommodation. This apartment is ridiculous at the price, as I told her; but she was set on having the right class of person.' He shifted his blue gaze from his image in the mirror to look her up and down: new jeans and red sweatshirt, long pale hair brushed neatly back and held by a band: the good tenant look.

'What sort of person did she say?' asked the sub-let disarmingly.

He went on looking, then turned away and gathered up his camel coat. 'Oh, nicely brought-up, quiet, no attachments: that sort of thing. No wild parties; last year's tenant proved highly unsuitable: actually cohabiting, I believe. And insisting on her own curtains; moving the pictures – a chipped frame, one broken glass. No end of trouble; she left quite soon, rather suddenly.' He observed her again, closely, by the front door. 'She said you were different. I trust she was right; it makes our responsibilities much less onerous… What was this business about the possibility of your not liking the place or something? My secretary…'

'Oh, it was just I hadn't seen over it and I was afraid that…'

'A somewhat cavalier way, if I may say so, to take on the care of another person's home, was it not?' He tilted her chin with one finger the better to talk down to her. 'But I feel sure you will enjoy it and look after it,' he said dismissively – and patted her bottom as she turned to unlock the door. 'I'll be keeping an eye on you' – heavy jocularity now – 'to make certain you do – OK? Goodbye, Miss – er… '

'Morland,' she said frostily, and slammed it behind him. She was so angry she had to laugh; she kicked the dustbin hard enough to dent it while she waited for the kettle to boil; 'fair wear and tear, that is,' she said out loud. It would seem that according to the blond god (passably Aryan?), the first law of property established that a sub-let is by definition a vagrant, to be admonished and, where appropriate, groped. Now: away with all the creepy statues and praying hands, the ju-jus and the pierrots! And first, those horns.

She set a chair in the hearth, and tried to lift down the leopard-skin mount; but it was fastened with strong pins driven deep into the wall. All she could do in the end was drape a large silk scarf over it. Pictures next: there were several sub-Beardsley drawings – ladies with bare bosoms and crinolines attended by naked black page-boys, or dark woods fringed by tall, sickly trees and peopled with half-seen monsters. These, and hollow-eyed waifs in the corridor, all fitted into the back of the wardrobe. She put up two posters: one to cover the space the 'Beardsleys' had filled in the sitting room; the other, of a great summer beechwood like the one where she walked the dogs at home, she pinned firmly to the warm door of the airing cupboard. She had found it nagging at her, that locked door; her eyes were always drawn to it as she moved about the kitchen or passed along the corridor. Now it was sterilised by the power of those bright sloping shelves of green and the good brown earth beneath.

Two other pictures she considered removing, then decided against it: the muscular Fuseli angel by the front door, and a reproduction of Blake's Flea in the bedroom. She left them in their places, partly out of deference to the artists, and partly because one small corner of her liked them. Moreover (though she did not quite admit this to herself) she felt it was, well – sophisticated to appreciate them. 'Oh, don't you rather admire

Fuseli?' she could hear herself saying to Sal and her chinless wonder as she took their coats...

By the time she got round to the multiple tot problem in the bedroom, Lucy was hungry. She would go out shopping, and explore the neighbourhood. As she moved about the nice warm flat, dabbing make-up on her eyes, collecting her anorak, shopping bags and purse, she thought: I'm moving about my nice warm flat – and Mr Sodding Cornfield is going to be disappointed if he thinks *I'm* going to run away suddenly like last season's unsuitable sub-let.

Clarence Square turned out to be in one of those mixed areas of London where banks, chain stores and smart flower-shops flourish in the main shopping street, while Eastern takeaways and West Indian grocers, cleaners run by Pakistanis and delicatessens run by Poles, bloom in the side roads. The ready-heated golden pasties by the cash-desk of the small supermarket were too much for Lucy: she bought two for supper and ate one on the pavement outside.

Nearby was a small scuffed park with roundabouts and swings where the multicoloured children of the area played, a threadbare tapestry of Utopia; and Lucy sat on a bench in the weak sunlight and ate the other pasty, and one of the expensive peaches she had bought. She was suddenly, marvellously, independent and free, doing her own thing (like Mrs M? She it was who had used the expression); and, heading back to her flat, she felt it held no dread this time. What a pleasant square to look out on, she thought as she came into it, with its Regency terraces and its own pub on the corner. That had been a bit noisy last night around bed-time – but cheerful noises; now at 2.30 there were a few brave late drinkers sitting outside on benches in the chill sun, and a carful of people about her own age pulling away from the kerb. It was a smart, brightly-painted pub, its handsome brick shape in keeping with the square. Looking again at the terraced houses – all the different coloured doors, several flanked by bay trees in tubs, or well-clipped rosemary – and at the rows of gleaming cars,

Jags and Porches, filling the residents' parking, she got the impression that Clarence Square had only recently come up in the world. Walking round it she saw two or three houses on the far side still badly in need of paint and repointing, with the beer-cans, the rusting pram, the overgrown front gardens that proclaimed them 'ripe for modernisation'.

But the grey block of flats gave nothing away, except perhaps a faint breath of genteel poverty, like a sigh of resignation, echoed by the wheezing heating pipes as Lucy closed her front door behind her.

Home again – it had begun to feel like that – she set up a shelf of her own food, putting all the exotica, the tins of okra and jars of braised ortolans, into the back of the saucepan cupboard. She chose a tough plastic tray that would fit on the sitting room window sill for the two potted plants she had bought herself; and Mrs M.'s wilting Dragon's Blood joined them: to save it would be a challenge.

Carrying through her tray of tea and biscuits and setting it down on the table in the window she thought smugly: that's almost a little routine already. But with her second cup, sitting and surveying her new domain in the last of the daylight, she found herself still uneasy, perching on the edge of her upright chair; self-conscious, almost nervous, as though she were playing a part – and observed doing so. She got up and closed the curtains on the deep blue dusk, switched on all the lamps. The draped horns that had made an eerie shape in the twilit room now cast a cloaked and pointed shadow on the ceiling; shifting the standard lamp only lengthened that menacing cloud, whose edges stirred in the updraught from the electric fire. Better to bare the thing. She took down the scarf and turned her back on the mournful eye-sockets, thinking, I must remember to get stronger bulbs: that might help. And still she felt she was not alone.

Surely it was just the overwhelming personality of her absent landlady, present in every carefully chosen fringe and bauble, tuck and flounce, in the astrology manuals and carved black figures with elongated necks and protruding navels. Her taste in colours, in the pictures and objects she had elected to live among, was more than eccentric; and, though Lucy was discovering a way to cope with it in trying to understand what she must be like, an exercise both of imagination and detection, she still found the most informative corner of the drawing room positively disturbing.

This was what she called 'the shrine': a small intricate brass table on which stood a red-shaded lamp and a large gilt-framed photograph of – presumably – Mrs Maturin and a beautiful young man, young enough to be her son. But this was no family snap; the large glossy colour print suggested a press photo, or perhaps a tourist souvenir, flash-frozen after some special party. And the setting reinforced this impression: glimpses of a curly velvet sofa, a palm tree, a low glass table with magazines and fancy drinks. They sat close together, her arm round him, his hand lying on her satin knee – so, not her son maybe. She was fat and jolly, with a bright red mouth, bouffant beehive hair and glasses swept up into spangled points; a flowing Kaftan masked the bulky figure. She looked about forty-five. He was less than twenty-five; a black shirt unbuttoned nearly to the waist showed off the even brown-suede tan and fine gold chain. She was smiling up at him; he smiling into the camera.

On the table in front of the gilt frame was an elaborately carved ebony stand, a small quilted black velvet pad contained by its upper rim; but the 'object of vertu', as the catalogue might have described it, was absent: locked away, no doubt.

It was an odd little group: a strange thing to set up; and already Lucy had furtively taken down the photograph and put it in a drawer – then as furtively replaced it. Now she gazed at it trying to discover why it made her so uneasy...

'What I need is live people,' she said out loud at six o'clock.

She dressed carefully, and more than once, in the deliberately casual way she felt would be right for her new image, her new life: none of the good cardigans and skirts, the mix-'n'-match designed for work, or for drinks on Wiltshire Sundays. She surveyed herself in the glass: the newly acquired baggy trousers looked good with her old striped pullover, but the scarf was too sober. Mrs Maturin's bottom drawerful tempted her – that purple silk with polka dots, perhaps – but she resisted, and tied the arms of her denim jacket round her neck instead. She let her hair out of its elastic band, brushed it well and pulled it over one shoulder to make its shiny straightness less symmetrical. A one-sided bunch like that girl in the typing pool? Or pigtails? – so fashionable; but they would make her look even younger. Eye make-up, some of her new blusher on her cheeks; then she carried out her tray, collected her purse and left, glad to get away from the vacant, watching flat.

The Clarence Arms was an oasis of light in the dark corner of the square. Cars were parked half on the pavement in front of it, and a few hearties in anoraks were at the small outside tables. Chatter and smoke hit her as she pushed open the door; the bar itself was two deep all round, and the benches and chairs were full: mostly young people like herself, but got up in a sort of stage motley of furs and flying-suits and spiky hair and space boots – both male and female. Those were the ones you noticed; there was also a solid base of men in tweeds or cords, city bods relaxing with each other, with only one or two obvious wives to be seen.

The young peacocks and cockatoos barely turned their heads when the pretty girl walked in alone; the older men's glances lingered, and they made room for her to order her drink; but, from her smooth shiny hair to her hush-puppies, the new talent proclaimed 'I'm a nice girl'. They turned back to their man-talk and away from anything so patently too young and too neat to meddle with. No one said, 'You on your own then?' or even 'Do you come here often?'; and Lucy carried her lager-and-lime through the crowd and into the lounge bar beyond.

This was quieter and better lit. Two tables were taken up with four large motorcyclists, crash-helmets couched beside them, monosyllabic over their shepherd's pie; a couple and two men stood by the bar. The rest of the room was dotted about with lone drinkers, two behind newspapers, one playing patience; and two elderly ladies sat at one table, not speaking.

Near them in the corner was a free table, and Lucy set down her drink and edged in on to the banquette, wishing she had thought of bringing a paper or a book.

She took out her packet of cigarettes, especially bought for sharing or ego-boosting; twenty usually lasted her a fortnight. Now she lit one carefully and looked around. She found she was observed. She raised her eyes to the warming pans and old photographs, and the glazed tan ceiling above; then looked down and sipped her half pint. She had taken in the separation, and the similarity, of the lone drinkers, and why the crowd in the public bar might prefer standing room only. Here sad regulars had staked their claim, and spun their web of silence. If you spoke in here everyone might look round. She couldn't just get up and go. She was feeling in her bag for her diary or a shopping list to keep her company when someone did speak to her; and everyone looked round.

'Haven't seen *you* before, have we?' It was the elderly blue-rinsed lady leaning across from the next table.

'No, actually,' said Lucy. 'I'm – I've just moved into a flat nearby.'

'Ooh? How nice. Would that be Clarence Mansions? We know Clarence Mansions – don't we, Estelle?' The skinny, faded lady beside her sipped her sherry, nodding and swivelling her eyes round to study Lucy. 'Well that *is* nice. What number, dear?'

Lucy glanced round. The balding man with the newspaper was gazing at his shoes; the solitaire player was gazing at hers, and the sandy-haired man in the grey mac got up with his glass to peer at a group photo.

'Well it's not – it's just temporary, you see – and I don't really...'

'Not on the ground floor is it?' asked Blue-rinse leaning closer. 'Not Maisie Maturin's by any chance?' – a thrilled stage-whisper – 'not that lovely warm flat! Ooh, did you *hear*, Estelle, dear? She's got Maisie's lovely flat! Oh, we know that flat ever so well – don't we?' She picked up her drink and her handbag and shifted along the banquette closer to Lucy; the sandy-haired man was there with a chair, leaning on it and beaming down at the charming newcomer.

'Couldn't help but overhear, my dear young lady: Maisie was such a friend, you see.'

'Oh, she did up that flat of hers so beautifully,' said Blue-rinse laying her small beringed paw on Lucy's arm. 'Took no end of trouble about it.'

'Didn't think she'd take a lodger though,' said Estelle, edging along the bench to be in on the action.

'No, she's gone orf – hasn't she, dear? Gone on her hols, to South Africa again – isn't that right? So: tell us about *you* dear.'

Lucy suddenly found herself the centre of an odd little group as the solitaire player pocketed his cards and joined them. 'This is the Colonel,' said Blue-rinse. 'I'm Mrs Villiers; Cecil here writes for the newspapers. And Estelle of course – she's my companion, as it were' – a mouthed aside – 'fallen on hard wotsits… '

It seemed they all had known and visited Mrs Maturin; all congratulated Lucy on her good fortune in taking over No 2 Clarence Mansions. Someone bought a round of drinks, and they raised their glasses to 'dear Maisie' – how they missed her, her warm hospitality, her jolly company.

'Always laughing, she was.'

'You make her sound as if she'd passed on, Mrs V!'

'Well she's my great friend, you know, and I miss her when she goes orf in the winter. You didn't actually meet her you say, dear? What a shame – you'd have got on together – ooh yes, I can tell! What a shame you just missed her… Everything all right, though? In the flat?'

Estelle, swigging her schooner of sherry, chipped in rather loud: 'Has it quieted down then? Doesn't bother you at all?'

Mrs Villiers quelled her. 'Never mind her: she's referring to – to the central heating, my dear. So noisy always; and then cooling orf, at night… But it's so nice and cosy, isn't it? And if you leave the doors open it warms up the whole flat. I miss it, really I do – and all the good times we had there… '

'Well, you must come round some time and have a cup of coffee.'

'Ooh thanks! We will, won't we? When, dear?'

'Well.' Lucy had finished her drink; her outing was over. 'Well, why not later this evening?'

The two men together up at the bar had been eyeing Lucy since she came in; one was youngish, bluff and fair-haired, in a sheepskin jacket; the other older, well-set-up, good-looking, casual in a camel cardigan, was more what her mother would laughingly call Our Class Darling. Now they came across, and the older man shook her by the hand – not as she expected, for the grip was both limp and prolonged.

'Might we join you, fair lady?' The voice was right. 'With my friend – Maisie's friend – Dermot, and a bottle? Drink to Maisie? Absent friends – all that?'

'Well I'm not sure that I... '

'No harm in us, m'dear,' said Dermot, bowing stiffly. He was almost the sort of young man her family might like – although, close to, his coat was too new and he smelled of whisky. 'We can show you how the TV works – always was a bit dicey what ha ha? and help you feel at home.'

'That's right,' said his friend: 'a little flat-warming.'

Mrs Villiers and the Colonel seemed somewhat put out by the takeover bid.

'We were just popping over to see Lucy – I may call you Lucy, dear? – later on, as a matter of fact, so I don't suppose you two will still... '

'*He*'s meant to be taking home the tonic water – that right Mr Wotsyername?' crowed Estelle. 'That's what he *said* – remember? when we asked him to join us.'

'She'll be after you, squire!' said the journalist, wagging his finger.

The colonel was chortling. 'She Who Must Be Obeyed, what?'

Under cover of this exchange, and feeling rather sorry for the handsome man with the limp handshake, Lucy had edged out from her seat. 'Never mind,' she said as the men regrouped round her offering her one for the road. 'No thanks – but I may see some of you later.' She waved at Estelle and Mrs Villiers, and escaped into the crowd.

So that evening Lucy entertained. It was an eccentric but flatteringly interested little band of new acquaintances: not quite the cast she had projected for her flat-warming, but easy enough to entertain. They knew each other, they knew the flat, and filled her with the cosy feeling of spreading sunshine that she remembered from helping her mother with the pensioners' Christmas lunch.

Not that all her guests were of pensionable age; Dermot was about thirty, a salesman from Godalming, driving back down to 'the lady wife' – 'and sharpish, as a matter of fact – but couldn't say no to a jar in Maisie Maturin's lovely place. Bit of a laugh, poor old Charlie Vesey, eh? Glad to say my better half doesn't keep me on such a tight rein.' He seemed as harmless as he had promised, sparing no pains to get the record player going, and persisting with the TV until he had a shock from it, and the jumping picture disappeared altogether.

Cecil the journalist was harder to put an age to; he had the ferrety sort of old-young face that probably hadn't changed much since he was a sharp lad of fourteen, and the reddish sandy hair that would simply fade rather than turn grey. A nervous fast-talker who tended to cap people's bon mots, he had shifty, rodent's eyes that Lucy did not take to; nor did she like him knowing the flat so well – though this did not bother her in Mrs Villiers. It was discomfiting to watch him rootle in drawers she had not explored and come up with 'Maisie's classy chocs' – a little stale – which he handed round. 'Maisie wouldn't mind – "Feel *chez vous*," she'd say – "so long as you save the strawberry cup for little me." '

'And anyway,' said Dermot starting on the second layer, 'If It Shrinks, We Replace, eh? Sorry Colonel – I missed you out.'

The Colonel was the quietest, and possibly the most 'respectable', of them. (God, I must be lonely – as lonely as them? – she thought suddenly: to fill my sitting room with these funnies... No: be positive. I'm seeing life; takes all types – but I suppose he's the only type one might just find at a Wiltshire drinks party.) He had a fringe of white hair and a strawberry nose supported on a small moustache; he was very gallant with the ladies, and Lucy herself he treated with the sort of dogged admiration that, if encouraged, might become dependence. When they questioned her about her job, her home, her interests, even her birthday and her love-life – her chief interrogators were Cecil and Mrs Villiers – he contributed little cries of indignation: 'Oh come now!' 'Oh I say now;' siding with Lucy, and glancing towards her for approval – but actually making it harder for her to object. 'Not at all – I don't mind,' she heard herself carrying it off lightly; and thought, another limp hand-shake at heart, bless him, as he chortled with embarrassment over Lucy's staunch denial that she was 'going steady': just a nice old boy who has had to sing for his supper since his better half passed on.

He beamed up at her and tapped his foot to the popular tunes on 'Golden Strings – always one of Maisie's faves,' said Mrs Villiers sipping a small glass of Cointreau (Cecil had produced this from the high shelf of the wardrobe). 'How she did love it.'

'And will again, Mrs V. She's lying on some sunny beach no doubt...'

'Oh, and she's here too – can't you feel her? Joining in? Here's to you, Maisie dear.'

They all toasted the photograph, and Lucy was going to ask them about the young man when Estelle said: 'It's not there, I see. Funny: you know, I could *feel* it wasn't there when I came in.'

'She means the stone, dear,' said Mrs Villiers: 'Maisie Maturin's "touch-stone". Not that it was a stone – too heavy.'

'An artifact,' said Cecil. 'Very precious. On special evenings she'd put it out on that stand under the lamp – wait now, that's been shifted.'

'Ah – probably when I dusted it,' said Lucy.

'Here, this way round, you see. The lampshade's got this circle cut out of it: a sort of spotlight; and feel: it's warm. Special bulb, the kind they sell to heat the "smallest room", eh? Had to be kept warm, she always said: It must have warmth.'

'Probably took it with her,' said Estelle.

'About her person, ha ha – in its little bag. There,' said

33

Dermot, pointing to the mantlepiece, 'the one in the snap, hanging round young Bob Loren's neck: that bag.'

'No, dear, she made a new one for it, don't you remember? To make it really hers? And embroidered it... ' Mrs Villiers' tone was admonishing.

'But who was he?' asked Lucy. 'Her son?'

'A drummer, dear. That's him and his pop group in the snap. They'd been touring in the Far East.'

'Yes, but she met him in Joberg, didn't she?' said Cecil. 'That's where the Encounter took place, and that photo. Goodness gracious me! Is that the time?'

'Ooh! Yes, Estelle, it's well after eleven-thirty! We must be running along.'

There was general movement, a hasty gathering of glasses and coffee cups.

'You won't mind if we leave you with the washing up, dear, this time?' said Mrs Villiers half way into her fur coat and moving towards the door.

'Of course not,' said Lucy. She had began to wonder how she was going to get rid of them; but within five minutes they were gone, with hurried goodbyes and a parting aside from Mrs Villiers, a promise to tell her more.

The flat seemed suddenly very empty and oppressive. She decided to leave the clearing up till the morning, and got quickly into bed. But she could not sleep. The street light made the room eerie; when she drew the fusty curtains across, the dark was worse. Then she heard the boiler cut out, the clicking of the cooling pipes; and as she dozed fitfully she kept dreaming someone was coming along the passage – or rather some thing: not really footsteps; just an approaching. Feeling foolish, she got up to close the bedroom door; but it seemed to be warped – had always been left open, probably, to let in the warmth. She wedged it shut as best she could with her suitcase, pulled back the curtains and opened the window on a gentle Indian-summer night: the weather seemed to be turning warmer. Back in bed, she started counting sheep; but she was still thinking, I must get the window catches fixed in all the rooms so I won't be afraid of intruders... and I suppose I

34

must get an electrician in – for the telly – and the kettle...

Not intruders, but some nameless dread edged into her dreams. Waking with a start and a slow tingle of terror, Lucy reminded herself she was not a 'spooky' person: she used to laugh at ghost talk in the dorm at school; and had sometimes even wished, watching a horror movie, that she could be deliciously scared like her friends round her. It was cold comfort now, as her scalp crawled, and she lay waiting for the slow clicking to cease.

Chapter Three

MORNING AND WARM sunshine melted away her night fears. She only remembered them when she found her suitcase against the door, and realised why the room had seemed so much colder than yesterday. The bright day outside and, inside, the now familiar ugliness, even the grotesques and excesses of her big warm flat as she padded round it in her dressing gown, mocked that darkling disquiet. She did remember now, and clearly, her half-waking dreams. She was not one for nightmares, except as a child, and found she could always explain them, find a good reason for such journeying back into childhood. It had, after all, been only her second night in a strange place – strange in both senses, she thought, reaching down a cobweb from the gilded horns – and the first night she had been too weary for fancies. Obviously the cooling noises had bothered her: they would soon become part of the background, familiar as the gurgle and sigh of the pipes by day.

Careful not to ridicule herself, as she would have treated anyone who'd had a bad night, Lucy remembered, explained, dismissed – and rather liked herself for being so sensible.

Now the whole of Sunday was before her. She opened the sitting room windows wide to let out Cecil's cigar smoke and the smells of stale drink, watered her plants, and carried the tray of dirty cups and glasses to the kitchen. She heard music faintly from upstairs and turned on her own radio while she washed up. I'm not really alone, she thought. Not that I *need* anyone; but I might ask them down for coffee or something later: they wouldn't be spooked by this flat on a sunny day. In the evening she was having supper with Mrs Twining in St Johns Wood – 'Please come,' she had said on the phone: 'just to show there are no hard feelings, Lucy.' But this morning she was going to set up her sewing machine and cut out a wraparound winter skirt she had been planning: a length of tartan wool that her brother James had brought her from Edinburgh – so soft it was almost like cashmere. With care there'd be enough for a big scarf as well.

After breakfast she strode out to buy the papers. These she decided to save for later, or the morning might disappear. She got out her sewing things and looked round for the best place to work.

It seemed a pity to take over the table in the sitting room: only next door, after all, was a whole spare room unused. It would exorcise her dislike of that room to set up her gleaming Singer there and spread the bright new length of worsted over the carpet for pinning and cutting. The table by the window seemed sturdy enough; she unfolded the tartan on the floor and got to work with scissors, a mouthful of pins, and the radio beside her.

She was so absorbed in calculations that she hardly noticed the crackling over the music at first, bursts of interference as if there were a thunderstorm brewing. All the other stations and wavebands were just as bad; yet outside there was not a cloud in sight. She tried the aerial, opened the back to check the batteries were clean and making contact, turned down the tone button in an attempt to cut out some of the crackle, then gave up and switched it off. Odd that it seemed to work better when she was actually handling it, as if *she* were an aerial, or some sort of filter…

Then she started losing her pins.

She opened the tin and took some more out; she finished pinning and marking, and started cutting. With nothing to divert her through the long dull tacking stage, her mind wandered back to last evening, to Mrs Villiers and Estelle, Cecil, Dermot and the Colonel. She wondered if having a big warm flat so near the pub might not have its drawbacks: she would have to learn to say no. But it would be nice to see Mrs Villiers again. She might be inquisitive, pushy and eccentric, yet she seemed kind-hearted; and she had told Lucy of a nice girl called Alma who had been very friendly with Mrs Maturin and had painted her portrait. 'More your age, dear; pity she wasn't in the Clarence this time, but she is busy I know: getting married, it seems – to a rather dull man – Oh dear, I *am* a gossip!' There was also the unfinished tale of Maisie and her beautiful drummer-boy: Lucy wanted the next instalment...

It was not until she got up to make a cup of coffee that she saw the pins.

They were clinging to that warm wall, the side of the airing cupboard. They clustered there, a glinting silver swarm, in little whorls and irregular starbursts, just above the skirting board; and as she picked them off she felt again that minute buzz through her finger tips. Intrigued, and wondering how strong the magnetic source might be that could pull her pins off the carpet from an arm's length away, she reached for her small scissors and tried those. With a click they took hold, slithered down a little and stayed.

Could central heating pipes be magnetic? she wondered: had the electrics got mixed up in them somehow, making them live? It was more than likely the whole block needed rewiring, if the dodginess of the points and gadgets around this flat were anything to go by; but something there was, she remembered vaguely from elementary physics classes, that had linked household electricity with magnetic pull. If only she could get in there and see what was doing it.

With her head close up against the warm tingling wall, she squinted along the skirting board where it disappeared behind the heavy mahogany chest of drawers. There seemed to be a ridge or break further along: if she just shifted it out a little...

It took a good deal of heaving and inching to move it far enough for her to reach along behind it. Now she could see there was a gap in the wainscot, a botched join. What she was hoping to discover she did not stop to think: she just wanted to get her hand in and feel along the back of the warm wall to discover what was there. She edged the chest of drawers another couple of inches to allow a better angle, crouched down and slid her hand into the slit, stretched out her fingers cautiously in warm emptiness – nothing else. Then it happened, and she leapt back in pain and shock.

Afterwards she thought of it as 'the razor-blade effect': a swift, slicing sensation, no more painful than a sudden deep cut – but many cuts: a multiple blade – and just as shocking. Like a deep cut, the pain came afterwards. She crouched on the floor shivering violently, eyes tight shut, clutching her wounded hand with all her strength, unable to look at it; her mind registering only fear and pain, her whole being wrapped round her hand – her right hand. That registered first; and then she started to think again. Casualty. Stitches. But realised she couldn't feel any blood – gripping it too tight – and that she was aching with the intensity of that grip, that she felt faint, that she must tie it up or something before she passed out.

She opened her eyes. No blood. Slowly she released her hand. It was blotched and dented with pressure, but there was no other mark on it.

Brewing strong sweet tea, good for shock, and huddled on the kitchen stool sipping it, Lucy knew that she was unhurt, that the agonising pain had quite gone; and thought, I will simply have to ring the agents about these electrical problems. Yet it had not felt like an electric shock: it had been exactly like a razor-blade attack.

Weak and sick as an accident victim, she took her tea and the papers to the big soft sofa in the sitting room and fell asleep before she had finished the colour supplements. She woke still stiff and tired with the western sun on her face; she made herself return to the spare room to push back the chest of drawers and tidy up – not that there was any real need to: she firmly intended to go on sewing in there. But patiently and meticulously she picked the enchanted pins off the wall, shut them in their tin, and covered her sewing machine: insulating it from – what? She could not resist fetching a small torch and shining it under the chest as straight into the gap in the wainscot as possible. It showed her nothing, of course; and, forcing her mind back into the moments before the – the attack, she knew there had been only empty space. Out of which something had come. Slicing. Leaving no mark.

So how could she tell anyone, or get help in investigating it? Persuade a friendly sceptic to put in a hand and see? It was like that stone mouth in Rome or somewhere, the Mouth of Truth, that bit off your hand if you told a lie; or that old rotten tree stump in the beech wood her brothers had dared her to reach into…

Mrs Twining did not think Lucy looked well, and said so. 'A big flat of your own is too much for you to cope with, surely. I mean, it sounds lovely, and I do understand why you – but working and running a place like that, all on your ownsome…'

'Oh, it doesn't take much running now I've cleared it up and organised things,' said Lucy. 'But you're right: it's a working day tomorrow and I mustn't get back late.' She was thinking of the clicking. As soon as she had finished her coffee and helped with the washing up, she said no to the interesting TV programme Mrs Twining had planned for them, thanked her, promised to keep in touch, and set off for home.

In bed by 11.30, she lay dreading wakefulness; and slept, and dreamed of the black runner. She was leaning on the window sill as he ran towards her along the side of the square gardens and she thought, I've never seen his face. Then, before he was close enough, she was frantically dragging the huge curtains, now heavy as sandbags, back across the window – for she knew that he had no face. She woke with a thud, half-heard the clicking, covered her ears and slept again.

Lucy walked to the underground and squeezed into a full train, the fastest way to work in the city; but she promised herself the long gentle bus ride home, almost door to door. London lighting up in the evening still enchanted her; to sit back and watch the neon and shop-window show unrolling was like a childhood treat; and so luxurious after the stifling train.

That evening she managed to get her favourite seat right from the start, on top at the front. Creeping along the Strand past the glories of the Savoy and the new Coutts bank, she was already looking forward to the warm flat; to high tea with the cream slices she had bought, and the rest of the Sunday papers: no one else to bother about. It would be fun to have people in, soon: real people, not just Mrs M's old buddies... Sally had sounded keen. She was clearly impressed by the idea of a spacious flat in Kensington.

Lucy had not described it too closely. 'It's rather splendidly awful,' she said: 'bizarre – but all the comforts. One of my landlady's old chums said it was totally "Biba" – the shop that used to be Derry & Toms, as I dimly recall.'

'That's right: all art deco and nouveau and stuff – satin cushions and curly lamps and rather mad fashions. Went bust.'

'That's it; and Mrs Maturin bought most of the furnishings in their closing down sale, I gather: amazing, the colours – well, you'll see. We must make a date...'

Eddie Symes, the highly-strung copy-writer, had questioned her more closely about it, but halted her when she started on the state of the kitchen.

'Don't!' he cried: 'I'm a fastidious soul. Did you look into that casserole you threw away? Eye of newt and toe of frog, I'll be bound – and the *thought* of some old hag you've never met still *living* there, as it were: all her belongings, I mean – her actual dressing gown, you say?' He shuddered expressively and closed his eyes, then opened them, wide and dramatic: 'Even worse: what is locked up, I wonder? Steaming away in that hot, dark cupboard? No, darling, I'm being naughty now – but you know *me*: just the thought of people's used things, not even sent to the cleaners... Well I paid more simply to get a totally sterilised box in Ealing, a brand-new conversion in colours of my choice.'

So there did not seem to be any immediate possibility of Eddie dropping in, and Lucy was tired enough now to be more relieved than sorry. She knew he wouldn't be able to

41

resist if asked; that she must make the effort to invite friends properly – but wondered vaguely how she could amuse them. At home there had always been ping pong and billiards and tennis and the big kitchen table to sit round talking while her mother cooked. Here she did not even have TV; she must arrange for a local repairs shop to call on a Saturday.

As the top of the bus emptied a little towards Knightsbridge, and she had the whole seat to herself, she noticed the occupant of the other front seat, masked before by the two bodies between. It was a strikingly handsome black man, as much as she could see of him behind the turned-up collar. Once glimpsed he was impossible to ignore; she looked across again, casually – she must not stare – and saw the proud aristocratic profile, the noble lines of forehead, nose and cheek-bone, hewn in ebony and superimposed on the passing lights. No Harry Belafonte this, but the pure African source; and so composed, so withdrawn, so separate and above it all. Then, without a movement of the carved image, the eyes slewed suddenly sideways to take her in, a glance that transformed an impassive face into a sinister mask.

Lucy dropped her eyes, turned away and pressed her hot forehead against the side window, staring blindly at the floodlit Albert Memorial. She knew she had looked too long at him, unable to pull her gaze away. She opened the newspaper on her lap, but became aware as she straightened it out that she could still see his reflection in the glass near her; and, however hard she concentrated her wits on getting as many words as possible out of LIVESTOCK, her eyes travelled back to the dark profile floating across the lights of the Hypermarket and Woolworths, Church Street and the Arab Bank; brightly outlined by the windows of Safeway, C & A – and remote from them all; as totally still as a jaguar looking down from a branch...

It was nearly her stop. While she was gathering herself together (half-glad she would be free of him, half-promising herself a parting glance), he stood up, very tall in his dark belted mac, and turned down the gangway ahead of her. So – it was his stop too. She looked up as he passed; and that was

42

when she saw his dog collar, stark white against the black throat and black upstanding lapels. Following, Lucy almost stumbled: it was like a step that wasn't there.

During the next few days she kept glimpsing him – sometimes she felt it was only her fevered imagination – across a street, or passing by when she was inside a shop. Once he was coming out of the West Indian grocer's as she went in; he passed quite close, but he was calling something back to the cashier, a snatch of richly accented back-chat about feeling up the mangoes next time, that raised general laughter; and she did not have to meet his eyes. When she emerged he was on the pavement outside talking to a thin, poorly dressed woman, with a bag of shopping and two small brown children leaning against her legs. She was in her mid-thirties, as far as it was possible to guess from her lightless hair and defeated shoulders. The parson was talking quietly to her, a low comfortable rumble; and as he talked he put out his hand and smoothed back a wisp of her hair. The woman turned her head a little, almost flirtatiously, and Lucy saw such a look of adoration she felt intrusive even witnessing it. When she stopped in front of a shop window and glanced back, the man was carrying the woman's shopping with his free hand, and she was leading the two children, as they turned off down a side street. Could it be his wife? His children? And why should it matter?

Saturday in the launderette; and she saw the woman again, on her own. It was not difficult to get talking to her. Lucy said she had just moved into the area and didn't even know which day to put out her dustbin. Soon she had heard about the refuse collection, the bottle bank, the Thursday market three blocks south but worth the walk for the rock-bottom prices, and about the party there'd been in the playground for the royal wedding. As they talked, Lucy was uncomfortably aware of the woman's eyes taking in her bright skiing anorak and soft boots; and she thought: You'd never guess how I envy *you* – knowing him, having him carry your shopping... But she

43

couldn't just ask straight out, 'Was that your husband?'

The woman was saying, 'My Wayne is almost a twin of the royal baby, you know.'

'Really?' said Lucy. 'And – and did you have a christening?'

'Oh yes: at St Mary's. Lovely, it was.'

'And is that the church... Is that where... You know the parson you were talking to the other day...'

'Yes indeed, that's his church. Mind you, he didn't baptise our Wayne: he's only been here a while. Not staying neither' – wistfully – 'on an exchange, like... Oh he's a good man, that one... There now: my lot's dry and finished and I must be moving along. Don't want to! Lovely and warm in here, isn't it?'

'Lovely,' said Lucy. 'Well, thanks for all the helpful tips. See you again.'

So he wasn't her husband, and he was only here for a short time, it seemed. Lucy asked the man in charge of the launderette where she could find St Mary's church.

'Know the playground? Other side of that and you'll see it further on down that road: big church – can't miss it.'

Hugging the unwieldy plastic sack of washing, Lucy set off towards the playground. I'm being very silly, she thought. I should be getting back in case the television mender arrives – and here I am, walking in the opposite direction, just in case I might get a glimpse of that beautiful black parson laying out the hymn sheets... Or maybe I'm just going to take a look at the times of Sunday services so I can sit at his feet and have him lecture me about hell fire.

The church was big and ugly, built of dirty yellow brick, with offshoots from its squat steeple like ears. It was not the grim looming exterior that chilled her so much as the gilt letters of its full name:- The Church of Saint Mary the Blessed Virgin: the question of denomination simply had not occurred to her. But inside there was no doubt; even in the gloom she could smell the incense, see the garish saints and the candles. Not bigotry but shock made her back out into the sunlight: her obsession, it transpired, was with a Catholic priest.

She walked home fast, looking neither to right nor left. Her sense of shock was now at herself, for she had dreamed of that man twice. The first time, after seeing him outside the grocer's with the woman, she seemed to be at some party, and suddenly he was there on the other side of the room, looking at her: they knew each other; he was coming across to her; everything was wonderful. That was all, though she tried to dream again; and, even waking, or travelling to work, or moving round the flat, she found herself extending the dream, imagining his voice, his concentration on her, as he smoothed back a wisp of her hair … Then last night she had dreamed again – so God-given and inevitable and right compared with her laboured, freeze-frame fantasies. Again it was nothing spectacular: they were leaning on a gate looking over fields; the dogs were there with them. And he and she were close, had known each other long. And he laid his black hand on her white wrist, and stroked her slowly right up to her neck – The violence of her response woke her. She had lain awake burning with simple lust; angry with herself, pathetic little virgin that she was – and he hadn't so much as touched her breast. She contemplated a cold shower, but suddenly felt she could not face the tall gloomy passage, the locked cupboard; and had made do with splashing a handful of water from the glass over her face… So! she thought, trudging up the steps of Clarence Mansions with her laundry bag; so: now I'm having sexy dreams about a lover who is black, celibate and holy. I sure do pick 'em…

Lucy knew she had been dreaming a great deal since she moved into the flat, more than she had ever done before. Her two fantasy encounters with the beautiful black man had not only been thrilling in themselves, and all too brief, but had been a welcome diversion from the nightmares she had almost come to expect.

Through these nightmares another figure moved: the runner. Superficially the two were alike; but this was a creature from the dark substrata of her mind, and as menacing as that peripheral vision on her very first visit to Clarence Square; always naked in her brief, hastily-buried dreams. She could not – nor did she try to – recall them; sometimes they came back to her when it began to grow dark; sometimes when she was sliding into sleep, and then she would wake herself deliberately, switch on the light and read.

Their common denominator was a sense of creeping threat, a vague fear, often without images. But often, too, the images had been obscene, startlingly so: glimpses of horror and beastliness she could never have imagined; and she strained to forget them. She realised she had begun to dread her dreams, however effectively they might be dispelled by her busy working hours; also, that a new feeling of fatigue was becoming part of her daily life. Getting up in the morning unrefreshed seemed unsurprising, something merely to be coped with: showing the need for a holiday, perhaps. But summer had not long gone, and she could not hope to take a break from her new job in the advertising firm until some time in the spring, at the earliest.

It was Esther at work who first said, 'That's not mascara, is it, Lucy? I'd say you were a bit blue under the eyes – wouldn't you, Daphne? Maybe you're working too hard, love.'

'Or missing the country air,' said Daphne, buffing her nails.

'Yes; d'you get home for weekends ever? Your folks live in the country, don't they?'

'But London's such *fun* at weekends,' cried Sally. 'And if you do go off for a couple of days, it's only one night really – and all the bore of the traffic coming back on top of the Sunday evening blues.'

'I suppose so,' said Lucy. 'And with this big flat...'

'Right: you just want to dig in and relax in your own space – lucky old you.'

'What does your mum think of it then?' said Esther. 'Mine's too possessive, I'm afraid; but she'd never let me just find a place for myself like that. Or she'd be in and out all the time, worrying.'

Lucy stopped drawing circles and spirals on the cover of her shorthand pad and tried to be animated. 'Oh, my mother's working, you see: she's a teacher, and now she's pretty well tied up until the Christmas hols. But I think she's rather impressed by me striking out on my own: she's all for it. Mind you, she'd love to come up and stay – I've got a spare room – and she will, maybe during the sales. But what with the dogs and the chickens and piles of correcting, and producing the school play, it's quite complicated for her to. I must say, it will be good to get down there for Christmas.'

'You're taking two weeks, aren't you, Lucy?' Sally said turning back to her typing. 'That'll bring back the roses to your cheeks. Don't worry, Esther. The good Loamshire rain will wash away those mascara stains – right?'

'Oh, those! I just don't get enough sleep,' said Lucy, laughing and stretching. 'You know how it is.'

'Ah! It's this gigantic West Indian of hers, you see,' said Sally.

And Lucy once more regretted babbling about her morning glimpses of the black runner. Teasing office gossip was obligatory: even Florence-with-the-ailing-mother got her leg pulled about the Irish VAT man.

'Nice work if you can get it,' Daphne was saying.

'And talking about work, girlies… ' Jerry the Whizz Kid was back from his executive luncheon.

Mrs Villiers, entertaining Lucy to cocktails, was the next to cross-question her. Last evening, in her pretty, frilly, bijou maisonette, before a gas fire in the form of imitation logs, with Estelle bringing in a dainty tray of sherry and biscuits, Mrs Villiers peered at Lucy through a pair of old-fashioned lorgnettes, stroked the chihuahua on her lap and said: 'You're looking peaky, dear: tell me, have you been sleeping badly?'

Lucy admitted she had. Nothing about the dreams: those were entirely private; and, however well-meaning Mrs Villiers might be, she was by nature a gossip.

'I'm sure it's just a matter of getting used to the flat: I have these silly night fears. I've hardly been away from home before, you see, except at boarding school… But I'm so lucky to have that flat.'

'So, nothing is really disturbing you – is it, dear?'

'What sort of thing d'you mean, Mrs Villiers?' asked Lucy,

facing her squarely and trying to hold the butterfly gaze.

'Oh, I don't know, dear. Anything that might – well, be disturbing your – your "aura", as Maisie – ah, Estelle! Finished your little chores, dear? Come and have a sherry then. Did you know, Lucy, that Estelle used to be a dancer? Yes, proper ballroom dancing: that was her *métier*; she was in the formation once on *Come Dancing* – weren't you, Estelle?'

Lucy sensed that her hostess had been somewhat flustered by the direct question – though her normal delivery was so punctuated by little gasps and cries that one could not be certain. She clearly preferred to ask the questions rather than to answer them. Why did she want to know about Lucy's state of mind? Was it simply kindness? Had Maisie Maturin also been troubled, perhaps, by night fears?

When Estelle had put away the press photos of her shining hour, Mrs Villiers turned her flickering gaze and puckish smile back to Lucy. 'Now, dear, we should do something about these bad nights.'

'Please don't worry about me, Mrs Villiers: I'm sure it's all in my imagination. As I said, I'm sure it's just a question of getting used to my surroundings.'

'Ah!' said Estelle.

'Estelle!' said Mrs Villiers: 'shouldn't you be seeing to our supper? *No*, child! Sit down! Please. No, you haven't stayed too long – I just didn't want that silly old spinster filling your head with her nonsense. Now then, I know some very good sleeping pills. And they're the same sort dear Maisie uses; she wouldn't mind one bit if you tried a couple. They're in her bathroom cabinet, dear, unless of course she's taken them on her hols!'

'Has she gone to South Africa to see that Mr Loren?'

'Oh no, dear.' She wasn't laughing now. 'Don't you know about him?' She sipped her sherry and absent-mindedly topped it up. 'They were ever so close – oh, he was almost like a son, in a way. Closer than a son of course. Or so I gathered... Yes, they met in South Africa: they were staying at the same hotel in Johannesberg – very posh you know – the whole pop group, to do a concert – and Bob had some sort of fit, epilepsy

48

or something, *petit mal*. She did auxiliary nursing once, and she took charge of him. That was the beginning; and there was some trouble with the police out there, too… Anyway she saw him again in London; he wanted her to read his future – she's quite famous for that, you know? Ooh yes! Quite well respected: she's been consulted by a well-known opera singer … oh, and a Member of Parliament.'

'And a racing driver,' Estelle contributed, leaning her thin frame through the doorway, '*and* a TV personality.'

'Yes, dear. And then afterwards, she got this stone, his ju-ju, sort of, in a package through the letter-box, just a couple of weeks later, I remember: she came across to the Clarence and said he must have passed on – and then of course we heard he had: it was in all the papers! But she treasured it ever after – didn't she, Estelle? And she set up that little table, and made a bag for it, and a little velvet cushion – that's right, Estelle: the same time as the guest room curtains… '

Sorting the clean laundry in that room, Lucy laid the things for ironing on the high bed, and fetched the iron and board from the kitchen. To imagine Mrs Maturin saving the scraps from those curtains, and stitching them into a little bag – an embroidered bag – and a cushion to show off her precious ju-ju, somehow made the smiling comedy-monster of the photograph much more real to Lucy. In her search for a rounded personality, something more than the laughing hostess that her cronies offered, she found these contradictory fragments convincing: a house-proud lady who left her kitchen in a mess; an extravagant purchaser of pricy junk who wouldn't lay out money to get her bedspread cleaned; fortune-teller to the famous saving the off-cuts from the guest-room curtains…

Lucy had taken Estelle's darting in and out as a signal their supper was spoiling, and firmly made her adieux; but not before Mrs Villiers extracted the promise of another get-together in the Clarence – 'and maybe just a little cup of coffee with you, dear, afterwards? I do so want you to meet Dr

Max. Such a good friend of Maisie's: *such* a fascinating man.'

So this evening would be a replay of last Saturday. She must not let it become a routine, and decided that, even if it meant going out to a film on her own, she would be otherwise engaged next time. As she drew across the curtains and set out ash-trays, she was thinking that, in spite of what she said to Mrs Villiers, she was getting used to the flat. It *was* growing on her. Now she hardly noticed the ornaments and pictures that had made her so uneasy a week ago: they were just part of the colourful, cluttered background. Her complaints to the agents about faulty electricity had met with little success: they would try to send someone round when he was in her area, but it had all been checked out less than a year ago and could not have etc, etc – so she simply avoided the gadgets and plugs that seemed faulty, and made a firm date with the TV engineer for next Saturday.

Only the spare room disturbed her; and it wasn't just the stuffy-sweet smell that still lingered; she could neither explain nor come to terms with the attack she had suffered in there. She could swear she had not been hysterical, or under stress – yet could show no scar from that blinding pain: it could only have been psychosomatic, self-induced. She sewed and ironed in there, hoovered the carpet from a perfectly sound power-point, and nothing had happened to her. She had even gone in there in the dark and crouched down to peer through the gap in the skirting board (anticipating a mysterious glow? Sparks? Movement in the blackness?) then retreated, shutting the door behind her; satisfied only that she had made herself do it.

Otherwise she was adapting to her surroundings, as though she had accepted how little she could affect them. She spent the £10 her mother had sent her as a moving-in present on a pot of flaming orange lilies, heavily scented – and not really her sort of thing – because it went so well with the satin cushions in the drawing room. She had started using Mrs Maturin's silver snake-handled teapot (from the Far East, according to Dermot), instead of her homely blue pottery one; and found that joss-sticks were better than spring-fresh aerosol for drowning out that smell she still noticed on coming home. She had not replaced the light bulbs: proper illumination made the colours more garish, and showed up the shabbiness, the cobweb grey of the multiple net curtains, the dun of the high ceilings. It wasn't perfect, but it was spacious, and warm. Almost too warm, certainly for her own winter dressing-gown: the purple silk one left hanging behind the door was enormous but very handsome; so much part of her flat it hardly felt like borrowing. And she even learned to sleep through the clicking-cooling. It was now only her dreams that retained that initial unease: images boiling up from her subconscious – the black runner moving naked down the corridor, oiled and gleaming, his gilt horn tipped with crystal... Some warm animal – a big dog perhaps – curled on her eiderdown, licking her feet, her legs...

Mrs Villiers watched for Lucy's arrival. Dr Max, whom she particularly wanted to meet the girl, could not be expected yet. A pity: Mrs V. had meant to fill him in a little more fully before he saw the new 'acolyte' – his word, when he heard someone had taken Maisie Maturin's flat. He had been not a little disgusted by Maisie's 'turning windy' – a turn of phrase the ladies felt to be unfairly harsh and rather coarse. The Doctor was good with words as a rule, the prime articulator of their little group, with Cecil running a close second; so, as Mrs Villiers explained later to Estelle when she commented on Dr Max's rough judgement, 'He must have been disturbed, dear. By Maisie's going orf like that, you know. He feels it breaks the chain, I suppose. That's why I so want him to see our lovely Lucy.' And Estelle had smiled knowingly.

The new acolyte was looking good. She strode into the lounge bar in the black flying-suit Sally had persuaded her to buy during their lunch hour. ('But I never *used* to be a size ten.' 'Well, you are now, ducks. Didn't you know you'd lost weight?') The new slenderness made her look taller in her freshly-dyed silver boots; and elegant cheek bones showed between the artfully touselled curtains of fair hair.

'The milkmaid look is all *passé*,' Cecil whispered reaching across for the peanuts. 'Enter The Avengers, what? And very nice too, I must say.'

'Yes indeed,' said Villiers. 'And I think the dear Doctor will approve.'

'The black makes such sweetness and innocence shine out,' said Estelle, and craned round to watch Lucy waiting at the bar for her drink.

' "A veritable Penthisilea", the Doctor will say. Don't worry, Mrs V.'

Even in passing through the crowded public bar, Lucy was aware that her attempts at self-improvement were not going unnoticed. Double takes from the older men; 'Hey, sweetheart, what's the rush? Join the party,' from the younger, rougher set by the slot machine; and a long hard look from two punky girls waiting for their dates – all told her she was on the right track; and she walked tall.

The impulse to update her image had come about the same time as an invitation to a party in Oxford from Peter, Nell's brother, and Alex, a friend of his she had not met. What'll I wear? she thought. Not any of my old stuff. Maybe the long skirt I'm making! 'No one sweeps the ground these days,' said Sally; and she had dragged Lucy along to the flash-tawdry little boutique in Holborn that appeared to be holding a permanent closing-down sale, and picked out the flying-suit first go. 'But it's got silver threads in it, Sal!'

Sally had been so right: 'If you want to get out of a rut, my dear, you've got to *feel* different.' Really she should have been cleaning and rearranging the flat, she thought, glancing past the new tendrils of hair – not spending time and money on tarting herself up. But one had to start somewhere. Now it was rewarding to see that people who had only glanced before were turning their heads. And she was pleased to note several new faces in the lounge bar.

She went across to Mrs Villiers and was given the place at her right hand on the banquette. There was a young man she had not seen before; the girl called Alma came over to their table – 'taking a break from wedding preparations,' she said smiling round at them. But she would not sit down.

'Walter's parents are giving us dinner somewhere grand, you see. Oh no: Walter wouldn't come for a drink – he's not really a pub person.' Her smile was quick, nervous and sweet, lighting up a thin, fey prettiness. It made her look young, but her mane of curly brown hair showed grey threads at the temples. 'So you're in Maisie's flat; do you like it?'

Lucy had never been asked this; only 'Isn't it lovely?' or 'Aren't you lucky?' 'Well, not at first,' she answered. 'Now, yes: it's certainly growing on me. Why don't you drop in?'

'Ah – I'd adore to – and I will – Lord knows when... Can I just come? Impulsively?'

Lucy said 'Of course.' It was hard to imagine Alma doing things any other way. 'I gather you painted a portrait of Mrs Maturin,' she went on.

'Yes. I don't think she liked it.' Again the quick smile. 'Help – I must go. Goodbye Mrs Villiers, Estelle.'

'See you,' said Lucy.

Dr Max came in later, a good-looking man with thick, wavy iron-grey hair, receding at the front, but collar-length and luxuriant. He was short and lithe (Lucy felt immediately that was the word he would have liked), and moved with the energy of one who is consciously in good shape. He seemed to fill his immaculate three-piece suit completely, as though it had been sprayed on; and she was momentarily reminded of waltzing with some host, father of a schoolfriend, and finding herself both impressed and repelled by the play of his shoulder-muscles under her hand. Trying to describe it later she had said: 'I know it's unfair; but for his age he was *indecently* fit.'

'I'm Dr Max,' he said lifting a chair with one hand and shifting Estelle's with the other. 'I'm a trickcyclist: psychiatrist, you know. And you're Lucinda. Lucy. Well well: and somewhat different from dear Maisie Maturin, I observe – a veritable Penthisiea... '

There was also the young man – Lucy did not catch his name – whom Mrs Villiers simply introduced as 'the gentleman from the magic shop – you know: just off Church Street.' He looked poetic and interesting, with a wing of dark floppy hair, dark eyes and a pale round face. He did not talk much; but when Dr Max leaned across the table and needled him about selling spells and love potions to the innocent rich of W8, he simply said: 'I hope for your sake they are not wiser and poorer round Harley Street,' and made everyone laugh.

Lucy left them early in order to receive them with hot coffee and freshly laid-out biscuits. She was expecting six of them with Dr Max, and the young man from the magic shop; she hoped he would come. But between her hearing them on the steps and the ring of the bell, some incident occurred. All she caught was the sound of raised voices, then laughter, and the Doctor's voice from the steps again, calling out: 'If your magic's so damn white you should – oh, let him go.'

They came in, Mrs Villiers, Estelle, the Colonel, Cecil and Dr Max. As they took off their coats, the Colonel said, 'That young man, m'dear: had to go off. Sent his apologies.'

Soon they were well dug in, with coffee and the liqueurs they had brought, and Herb Alpert on the turntable. Dr Max caught Lucy in the kitchen and asked her if she didn't have a nip of something stronger: 'Ah! Just the remedy,' he said bringing her Glenlivet out of the cupboard. She had bought it because she knew it was the right thing, the one they had at home, but put it away when she was told they were packing their own nightcaps, as the Colonel put it. Now the Doctor half-filled a tumbler and leaned across her as she stood at the sink to top it up with water.

'May I say,' he confided, 'you are a great improvement on that over-blown *virgo intacta* with her youth-fixation?' He tried his whisky. 'Mm – ah… I refer of course to your revered landlady.' He raised his glass. 'To Maisie! God bless her and all that sail in her!'

The man who waters his malt is not a man to trust, her father used to say; and back in the drawing room, playing the unobtrusive hostess, Lucy studied the psychiatrist more closely. She had seen in the bright kitchen that the closely-fitting suit of his choice was thin, hard, off-the-peg: not (said the sleuth in her) quite the thing to expect on a successful psychiatrist, or even a simply ambitious one. Listening to him addressing the assembled cronies on the significance of virginity in the history of ritual – he seemed to have virgins on the brain – she decided she did not like him. When he talked to her he stood too close ('I see you move away. Interesting: do you feel threatened?') and all his conversation was spiced up with the Latin-bes-prinkled smut that some of the younger medics she had met seemed convinced they were licenced, almost expected, to use in company. Dr Max was old enough to know better.

She also judged he was not 'harmless', like Dermot, the old Colonel and the ladies. About Cecil she had not decided, as she watched him playing up to Dr Max, feeding him his punch lines. Her disapproval made her feel she was prim: no one else appeared to be bothered, though Estelle gasped before she giggled, and the Colonel glanced anxiously once or twice at Lucy, and muttered something about 'pardoning his French'. She found herself having to be polite, as hostess, and forced thereby into the role of bland, uncomprehending innocence that they seemed to impose on her. Their attention, their admiration, was flattering; and on a lonely Saturday evening in November any company was better than none. But their overheard approval ('So white!' said Estelle, 'with that golden hair... ' 'Oh, in very good shape – lovely,' said the Colonel; 'And *such* a sweet nature,' cooed Mrs Villiers) made her feel like a turkey with Christmas coming; and she longed for peers she could answer back, be one of. Sally of course had been going away for the weekend, and Nell in Reading had not rung back – she may not have had the message. But there was the forwarded invitation from Oxford: a party in a fortnight's time; Eddie might be coming to supper next week; and Alma would be dropping in, impulsively...

Suddenly they were all going. It was a quarter to twelve. 'My, we have stayed late. Come along Dr Max dear: she must be tired out.'

'You were far away, weren't you?' The Doctor was holding Lucy's hand in both of his, and in no hurry to go. 'I wonder what you were thinking about – eh? All right, Mrs Villiers, all right: I'm coming! You know why *they* are in such a rush? They

55

don't like to be here when the heating goes off… But I feel sure it doesn't bother you, Lucy. Au revoir.'

She was locking up after they had gone, when, pulling back the curtains in the drawing room to check the windows, she froze in alarm: there was a large dark shape, a dim figure, standing on the pavement opposite – and the most shocking thing about it was that it was wearing a big white smile set far too low, like a member of some alien species. As she looked, her eyes adapting to the dark, another smile appeared higher up, and the tall figure moved away down the street: the priest, she realised, had been standing there looking up at the flats.

She dreamed of him again that night, and it was quite different from her other dreams. He was wearing only his dog-collar, and a pair of dark shorts. And all her pins were clinging in bright clusters to his smooth black legs… This time when she woke, she did not try to dream again; for now at last she saw that the priest and the runner were one.

In the morning, remembering her dream, she pulled on the purple dressing gown and went through to the sitting room. She peeped out between the curtains at the square gardens and the ornamental pond; and, sure enough, there he was, running like blue-black oil through the morning sunlight. He turned the corner towards her, and she closed the chink quickly.

Then, all at once, and quite naturally, they met.

Chapter Four

LUCY HAD ONLY gone into the Clarence for a packet of cigarettes from the machine – she seemed to be smoking more these days – but was caught, as she was getting change at the bar, by the Colonel waiting on the lounge side of it.

'Just a quick one, m'dear? The good ladies are so anxious about having kept you up so late – said you hadn't been sleeping well.'

It would be better to stay than be talked of *in absentia*. She was wearing an old track suit and no make-up, but they were too busy with their thanks and apologies to notice. A retired actor, Mr Winslow, who usually sat alone in a corner, joined them; Dr Max and Cecil were talking at the bar and came over. But Lucy did not feel bright and sociable; she would chat up, drink up and go.

Then he came in.

He walked in the lounge bar of the Clarence Arms: pre-prandial and post mass, tall and columnar in full length soutane and double smile. The pop-eyed bachelor with him, another fringe member of what the publican referred to as 'the spooky set', was also, it transpired, a regular worshipper at St Mary's. Cecil hailed him as 'Basil', and he waved back; then the priest said something to him, and they both came over.

'This is Father Sebastian,' said Basil.

Cecil took over the introductions. The priest nodded easily

to them all, and to Lucy last, holding her gaze.

'Sorry if I scared you last evening, Miss Morland: I was casing the flats for an empty one.'

'Father Sebastian is looking for a "pad",' said Basil.

'That's right: somewhere I can be near my parishioners. You see, I'm officially attached to the Jesuits, but I feel out of touch – insulated by those cool brethren from the thousand natural shocks that flesh is heir to. To coin a phrase.' The accent was almost entirely English now; but his voice was dark and warm, and the way he paused before the word 'cool', and pursed his lips a little in pronouncing it, accentuated this.

'*She* has a room,' Estelle was saying. 'Don't you, dear? You remarked only last evening that you'd like a lodger to keep you company.'

'Just to help pay the rent,' said Lucy quickly, on the defensive, and aware of it; hating him because she wasn't looking her best. The big moment, so long awaited: and she could only mumble, 'But this room wouldn't do at all – and I'm only there for two more months.'

'That would see me out,' he said pulling up a chair and leaning on the back of it.

'But it's – it's too hot – and it smells funny.'

'Might really suit a humble West Indian: sounds a bit like home… But not if you are unwilling, of course.'

'Priest's just what you need, love,' said the friendly tarty girl from the bar, gathering the empties, 'you and all those bad vibes alone in there.'

Lucy looked up in surprise, and laughed defensively, her cheeks hot. 'Me and my vibes are doing fine, thanks,' she said.

'That's right, m'dear,' said the Colonel. Dr Max and Mrs Villiers exchanged meaningful glances, and the priest standing above them watched the interplay.

Lucy was acutely aware of him and his observing eye. But now he leaned into the circle. 'Basil and I are on our feet, and will get the next round. Mrs – er – Villiers? What was yours? Miss Estelle?'

While he was gone, Lucy was able to reassemble herself. It had not been a good start, with everyone's attention suddenly upon her. All she had wanted was to be able to watch him and listen, to meet his eyes every now and then; to take it in: never again would she see him across the street and yearn to know him. He was here. He had talked to her.

While Estelle and Mrs Villiers whispered, smiled and glanced across at his tall figure dominating the bar, the Colonel muttered 'Fine-looking chap – make a good soldier' and Dr Max rejoined 'Oh indeed: some of my best friends...' Lucy lit a cigarette to steady herself: it made her feel more adult; gave her something to do with her hands.

Last evening, as Estelle so vociferously recalled, Lucy had mentioned, over the coffee, that she was thinking of getting a lodger. Clearly none of *them* needed a bedsit – but only later did it occur to her, as a sort of revelation, that however frequently and caringly they inquired about her wellbeing, and dwelt on her good fortune in getting such a lovely place, not one of Maisie Maturin's old friends would want to live there. Even if one of her 'lame dogs', as Mrs Villiers called them – the gracious old actor, or the penniless Colonel himself – should find himself without a bed for the night, he would rather doss down on a bare floor, Lucy suspected, than sleep in Maisie's nice warm flat.

Now it seemed that all the spooky set, and even the bar maid, knew of her night fears; and, under the encouraging advice, there was a fresh excitement, as though they were intrigued by the notion of stirring a black priest into the brew.

Dr Max was expanding on the concept of togetherness. 'It's a question of symbiosis, isn't it?' He paused for them to ask what it meant; but Estelle, who may have decided by now that the Doctor's longer words were usually rude, said brightly:

'Quite: a man about the house is always such a comfort.' And Father Sebastian moved in and set the tray of drinks down on the table.

He seemed to take charge. Although it was transparent to Lucy that he was leading the conversation away from her and her spare room, he did it so smoothly, handing out the drinks as he talked, that she felt absurdly grateful, receiving her glass of lager from him as though it were a chalice.

'Well, I'm wondering,' he said, 'if this togetherness isn't something of a drug: habit-forming, perhaps. For me, anyway. You see, West Indian family life (And yours was the scotch, Doctor?) like any good family scene, can spoil you for real life in a way (That OK, Mrs Villiers?) Oh yes: security – a great start for any youngster – but no sort of preparation for the hard old world outside. I mean, looking back, childhood – for me – seems all warmth and good cooking smells and a good broad lap to bury my face in when I hurt... Discipline? Indeed, Colonel: and beatings and chastisement – mostly from my mother, that was.' He laughed. 'Father was a lovely man but weaker than she, and no saint – oh no! Running ganja when he wanted the money – but love? Lord, that man could love!' His West Indian accent was strong now. 'As kids we were never cold or hungry or lonely. And then the big bad world hit us – and now, somehow, everything seems to slope away from that heaven... Lay folk can recreate it, or try to, in their own families, I suppose. But not me. Look – someone stop me from preaching, I beg you – or I'll be weeping over my own celibacy!'

They all laughed; and Lucy looked round and saw they were hanging on his words. Cecil, always ready to take over, said, 'Surely the Jesuits are a kind of family? Loyal, tightly knit.'

'Ah!' Doctor Max weighed in: 'but did they catch him at the tender age? "Give us a child until he's seven..." '

'No: actually I came late to my calling – after a wild and varied career travelling the world in the guise of a philosophy student: the cast-iron excuse for every excess, and – do you really want to listen to this stuff? Well, I've been a mercenary, a playboy, a not very good boxer. I've even sung for my supper – yes, Mrs Villiers, with a jazz band. And somewhere along the line I got hooked on comparative theology: started seeking out the local wise man or guru wherever I found myself; and finally joined a Jesuit order when I was – oh, twenty-five... Yes, back in Grenada; and later, Brazil.'

'Tell us,' said Estelle in a thrilling voice, leaning her sharp elbows in among the glasses and fixing him with her beady mouse's eye: 'Living in the West Indies, and all that, well –

searching for truth – did you come in contact with any strange-goings-on? You know: black magic, voodoo, that sort of thing?'

Cecil, half up to get another gin for his tonic, eased himself back on to the bench, moistening his lips.

'I didn't exactly "come in contact" with it. No: I simply grew up with it and carry it always with me. I think you mean the older religions, Miss Estelle: and they are in my blood. You know, Brazil is the spot where you can see most clearly the new Christianity – in the form of Catholicism – grafted onto the old African stock; and that is where I began to appreciate the importance of my heritage. And to be proud of it.'

'Ooh yes,' chirped Mrs Villiers: 'it's a fascinating thought – one can see why you would be! By the way, I do hope you didn't mind Estelle here calling it "Black Magic".'

'Why should I? Black magic, white magic, physics, medicine – they are only ways and means of coping with natural forces, aren't they? I think, we are all walking through a mystery, meeting things we cannot explain. Even you; even here. And that world, my world, has remained closer to the mystery; so we take it more for granted. But I'll tell you a story – against myself, as it happens – when I thought I was about to encounter the most bizarre and frightening voodooism – and ended up with egg on my face. You see, the very first dead man I ever had to bury – to officiate as a young priest at his funeral – had, as I discovered half way through the ceremony, no head.' There was a general intake of breath, and conversation ceased at the nearest tables.

'So. What do I do? For a moment I considered halting the service for a proper inquiry: some very black magic was clearly involved; but no one seemed concerned, not even the local constable who was there in his best rig. Well, I took him aside afterwards and said: "It may not concern the police department that the deceased was buried with a bunch of zinnias in place of a head, my friend, but as a priest I must root out whatever Obeah nastiness is going on."

'The constable laughed aloud. "Drink you Mannish Water, father" – this was at the party afterwards – "an' don' bodder

61

yourself: is pure practicality that make him lose him head." It seems that two men had been robbing a Post Office at night. One was shot dead by the post-mistress's neighbour, and the other ran off. When the neighbour came back from phoning the police, he found the body where he had left it, but without a head. Next day they caught the other thief in the rum-shop of a nearby village, trying to pay for his drinks with postal orders; and he confessed he had come back and chopped off his friend's head with his machete to prevent anyone from recognising him: "For him was a fine Godfearing churchgoing somebody, you understand, and only steal the once – and me just feel *boun'* fe save him face –"

'So you see,' said the priest looking round his captive congregation: 'not voodoo: just a kindly thought for his friend. Unfortunately they identified the body easily enough by other means, and it was buried by the parish in style. The head? No: his mate had taken it out in his fishing boat, wrapped it in a net with a stone and dropped it deep. And all my dark fears were misguided – that time... But of course there is magic, Miss Estelle, many kinds: the stuff for the tourist circuit and the humble everyday ceremonies and the all-night drumming and dancing – yes, Doctor: as you say, cathartic in effect – and a few bad hats who cash in on all this.'

Father Sebastian talked well: he came across as both knowledgeable and riveting. There was an exotic authority about him as he talked, like Othello's; and, like Desdemona, Lucy listened and admired. He looked at his watch and rose to go – 'The good brethren eat promptly' – long before she had had enough; and left her wondering, as always, when she would see him again. The sensible part of her had hoped, and quietly believed, that a meeting with the obscure object of desire – a simple fourth-form crush, after all – would cure her. But the cure had failed.

Between the farewells and the exit there was silence. Then Estelle said in an odd, singsong voice: 'The dark light has been removed from our midst.'

Lucy looked at her, rather struck with this gnomic utterance; but Mrs Villiers laughed merrily and shook her companion's shoulder as though to wake her: 'Mercy on us!' she cried, rolling her eyes; 'I think she's gone soft on him!'

The Doctor cleared his throat. 'A very charismatic gentleman,' he announced. 'No wonder the ladies are impressed. But I would take his travellers' tales with a pinch of salt, myself.'

'Just enough of a pinch for the M1 over an average January, at a rough estimate,' said Cecil, with a short laugh; he downed his drink and made a grimace – whether over the neat tonic or the black priest was not clear. 'But an interesting sort of flat-mate, dear girl,' poking his ferrety face at Lucy.

'Oh, I don't think that room would be right for him,' she said.

'Parents wouldn't like it, perhaps?' he pressed. 'That it?'

'Goodness, no: it's entirely up to me. But I'd rather imagined another girl.'

'Aha!' the Doctor weighed in with heavy joviality: 'so here we have both racism *and* sexism combined! – a rare example, and worthy, surely, of further examination.'

Lucy stood up, smiling, to show there was no offence. 'Well, I shall leave you examining it, Dr Max, and get back to my womanly chores.'

On her return, she opened the spare room door and looked round at the dark mahogany, the black velvet curtains and rust-coloured walls.

The suggestion of that beautiful man, whom she had, until an hour ago, only glimpsed and dreamed of, physically moving into Mrs Maturin's flat with her, was so extraordinary, such a violent reversal of fortune, that she had somehow expected the room to look different: everything else did – and especially her own face in the glass. It was, of course, impossible: not just too way-out, she told herself, for her conventionally brought-up little mind to contemplate seriously, but in practical terms, surely, no less than traumatic. She had fallen for a married man before; but this time she was taking on the Holy Catholic Church herself as a rival.

She closed the door, crossed to the kitchen and started mechanically to get some scraps of lunch together. The real problem, of course – and the giveaway – was her dreams: good sense did not rule her subconscious. Could you share a flat with a man you had encountered – had indeed *cast* – in such a role? Fiercely she turned her attention to the Sunday papers. But her mind kept wandering off; and later, as it started to grow dark, she gazed out past the film reviews and special offers to where the lights were coming on in the square. She thought, I suppose I'm simply not – I'm not adventurous enough – to face a challenge like that: I'm a safe little lady; and he's a tyger burning bright...

Self-disgust was not a sensation familiar to Lucy Morland. She had hated herself for not working as hard as she might over some exam, or developing unsightly spots on the morning of a party. This was different. Advice columns in women's mags are compulsive reading: Lucy had always identified far more with the agony aunt herself than with 'Painfully Shy' of Amersham or 'Jilted' of North Shields. But now, just as those sad maidens were so often exhorted to do, she stood in front of the bedroom mirror trying to evaluate the bad points and the good, subtract one from the other, and come to terms with the answer.

She found it difficult to take a fresh look at herself; she was so accustomed to – almost unconcerned with – that face, and the thick fair hair: useful stuff, as her mother said, that could be worn long or short, up or down. There were grey eyes with dark lashes, watching her suspiciously now from under straight dark brows; the best thing about them was that contrast, the mingling of a fair father and a brunette mother. The mouth – she attempted a smile, but it came out both false and tentative. The mouth, actually, was OK: 'curly and sweet – deceptively so,' (as one rejected admirer had described it) with a full lower lip; rather childish, and bracketed by dimples if she smiled too broadly. It was hard to play sophisticated-and-mysterious with a smile like that; nor, she felt, did she look really exciting or adventurous, a taker-on of challenges, ready to try anything...

She leaned forward and peered at the blue shadows under

the eyes. Esther and Mrs Villiers were right: those were something new; so were the heavy, slightly puffy lids; and when she opened them wide, and looked closely, she observed that the thick fringe of lashes concealed muddy whites, a sort of dim wetness that could not be mistaken for sparkle or even starlight. She half-closed them, mussed up her hair and pulled it over one cheek: maybe this was the moment for that debauched and sultry *alter ego*. No: the face was too round; even last night, tarted up, she would never have got the part of the bad girl. She would have to get a lot thinner and paler – or frightfully tanned, maybe, at one of those sun parlours – to play the *femme fatale*.

But did people like her? And why? These were the questions she should be asking. There had always been heaps of little girls with crushes on her at school; boys had always been around, her brothers' friends, and she could not even remember how long ago she had realised her attraction, her power to get what she wanted. Later she recognised, and disliked, her tendency to lose interest in a male as soon as she knew he was hooked. Only twice had she fallen painfully in love, both times with older men: one was married and unattainable; the other, all too eligible, loved her as a kid sister. Now she was nineteen; she was five-foot-six; there was the good figure, good job, good flat; and there was her precious independence.

Lucy was lonely. It did not help to know it was her own fault for doing nothing about it. So many times she thought, I must ring Nell again and get her to come to stay; or, why not an impromptu party, with everyone bringing a friend and a bottle? or, I'll just get away for a break – to Oxford for the weekend: see who's around, explore, have fun.

But every time, weariness or sloth seemed to intervene: the thought that she would have to get organised – wash her hair *now* – find her boots – go to the bank – or simply face people. Anyway, why should they want to see *her*? And did she want to see them? Wasn't 'independence' all about being complete on one's own? Later on, perhaps – before Christmas; and she would put up some decorations, make mulled wine or something ... Meanwhile, there was that party in Oxford. Then she remembered she had not answered the invitation yet. Some time she must do that.

It was nearly ten o'clock when Father Sebastian finished with his pastoral duties and turned his steps towards Clarence Square. He observed chinks of light between the heavy curtains of Flat No 2, then looked into the crowded pub just long enough to check on the spooky set. The hard core was there, heads together. One thing the girl had done for those lone regulars was to re-unite them: they had something to talk about. Before, without the dominating Mrs Maturin, there was no real centre – a period of some ten days during which her flat had been mysteriously empty: even Basil, who knew all the gossip, seemed put out.

Sebastian had seen the lady only twice in the pub before she disappeared; she clearly preferred to entertain in her flat. He had never even met her face to face, yet he had surprised himself with the strength of his instant antipathy. He always disclaimed psychic powers, having encountered enough gifted seers to know he was a mere novice; even across a crowded room, however, Maisie Maturin had scared him. At least he had tracked her down and knew where she lived. Now he had met the girl, her substitute – a somewhat different sort of lady, as Basil had remarked – and he was determined not to lose her too.

When the bell rang, Lucy was lying in front of the electric fire in the sitting room, her head on a pouf, a glass of Glenlivet beside her (she had quite taken to it as a small nightcap: it suited the new image), while the melodious pessimism of Leonard Cohen lulled her in the half-dark.

At the second ring she got up slowly, pushed back her hair, and tightened the sash of the purple dressing gown. If it was Mrs M.'s cronies again, she would send them away: she'd be perfectly polite, excusing herself with a headache – which

66

would be true enough after an hour of entertaining them. For this evening she was past even loneliness: she could not face seeing anyone.

'Don't worry,' he said quickly: 'I'm not pressing you for that empty room, Miss Morland.'

One look at the heavy eyes and the déshabillé told him he had caught her off her guard, quite unprepared. In a different girl it might have spelt out the scenario for seduction; but Lucy Morland was transparently unaware just how appealing she looked with the thick ashen mane all rumpled round her face, bare feet below that lush, imperially-purple gown – surely not hers – and a bright silk scarf knotted round her waist; depressed, he judged, and maybe a little tipsy: he could smell whisky under the heavy layer of joss-sticks. She started back, and her hand went up to her throat, clutching the purple borders together: the picture of a Victorian maiden surprised.

The priest stepped into the doorway as he continued, more slowly now, and keeping his eyes on her face so as not to discomfit her further. 'I hope you won't mind me calling in like this: but at the Clarence today, and even before, you see, I got this strong feeling you were in trouble of some sort – worried and distressed. And that maybe I could help. It's a trouble I recognise, deep down, you understand; and I am a sort of trouble-shooter...' Giving her time and space like some nervous animal, he looked past her down the corridor, then took a pace forward to study the drawing of a muscular angel beside the coat-rack. 'Fuseli?' he asked; she nodded. 'But not yours?' She shook her head, keeping her eyes on him. He stepped back, closing the door behind him: he was in the flat; then ambled past her and stopped by the kitchen door. 'Could I have a cup of coffee with you?' he said.

She hurried ahead of him into the kitchen, suddenly self-conscious: flustered as much by her rudeness as by her state of undress. 'I'll do it,' she said. It was the first time she had spoken.

He seemed to fill the small kitchen, looming even larger over her than that first heart-stopping moment when she opened the door. This morning (so long ago, it seemed), in the lounge of the Clarence, she had been stunned, reduced to silence, by the switch from daydream to reality: the contrast between the imagined man – so carefully arranged and lighted, speaking the lines you want to hear – and the three-dimensional body and face of that man suddenly confronting you. The warmth, the smell, that you could not conjure up, the eyes holding yours only three feet away, and your body responding as it never did to the ideal. Sometimes those night visitations – random, startling, out of her control – had been almost as real as this; but then her own body had woken her, and ended the dream, as her spoken words did now, waking her from her dazed vision of him standing in her doorway. Now she heard her voice, nervous and ungracious: 'I'll do it,' and even with her back to him as she filled the kettle, she realised this was no dream: he was really there. She could feel that.

'I know how to deal with this kettle, you see,' she went on quickly, pulling on her rubber glove; 'it can give you a shock if you're not careful.'

He nodded, watching her set it on the table and plug it in; then he laid his hand on its metal curve, like an absent-minded caress, and kept it there even while it murmured and crackled with heat. He was saying: 'You're new in London, aren't you? And new here. I judge you're lonely, too – or you wouldn't be congregating with that bunch of ghouls... '

She pulled her eyes away from the black hand on the silver mettle – a sort of party trick, of course, like swallowing lighted cigarettes or tearing phone books in half. She measured out the coffee, and said evenly, ' "Ghouls" is a bit strong, isn't it? They're fairly harmless. How do you want it? Black? Or –' and stopped, hand over mouth; and then they both laughed.

In the drawing room, he did not sit down. He asked her about her job; and while she talked he paced, switching on lights to look at the pictures, the shrine; opening books and flipping through them. 'And your family?'

'They live in Wiltshire,' she said. 'My father is a solicitor, and my mother teaches at Godolphin – the Girls' School, you know. Then I've two older brothers: one's in Canada, married, and the other is at Edinburgh University.' She didn't mind his questioning; she answered easily now, telling him about home, and content to watch him moving about on her territory; liking what she saw.

'So you're the baby: they must be missing you. Have they been up to see you here?'

'Not yet: I've specifically asked them not to, while I found my feet. Anyway, I think they rather hate London. But my mother will come in the school holidays. And I'll be going home for Christmas.'

He was holding the snap from the mantlepiece of the band on tour; silent now. He put it back, picked out a shell from the tray of *objets trouvés*, and held it to his ear; ran his finger along a piece of smooth, bleached driftwood, then reached past the dried flowers, the compass, the kaleidoscope – she knew them all from her attempts to dust them – to the infra-red spectacles at the back. These he put on, as she had done, and looked around the room. Lucy had not liked the scarlet twilight; but he seemed intrigued by the altered view, gazing slowly round the walls and down on the garish carpet at his feet. Then he bent over and pulled aside the shaggy goat-skin rug on the hearth, all without speaking.

He took off the glasses, tucked them away on the mantle-shelf, rearranged the rug and turned to her.

'You happy here? You like this flat?'

'Quite,' she said; 'it's growing on me. I found it a bit overpowering at first.'

'But now it's growing on you.' He nodded. 'Tell me something else: are you a virgin?'

Lucy was too surprised and outraged to speak – and the priest simply nodded again, finished his coffee and went on smoothly: 'Yes. My opinion, Miss Lucy Morland, is that you may need a guardian angel... OK,' he silenced her with a raised hand: 'you're full of your new independence, and loneliness is a small price to pay for it – I know the feeling. But if you ever want help, come to me – and this is my private number, if I'm not with the Jesuits. Thanks for the coffee. I'm going along now, so good night. Sleep well.' He paused by the

front door: 'But maybe you have some trouble sleeping...
Well remember: if you need help – So long. God bless you.'

On the steps outside he passed three of the 'ghouls'; Lucy
heard him greet them, and the excitement in their twittering
replies. She reached for the comb in her coat pocket and tidied
her hair, smoothed the dressing gown and adjusted its
drooping neckline, before she answered the bell.

They hurried in: Dr Max, the ladies, and with them the
handsome tweedy man Cecil had referred to as Charlie Vesey,
from her first visit to the Clarence.

'Well! You must tell all!' cried Mrs Villiers. 'That lovely
man! Was he after the room, then? What did he *say*?'

'He didn't come about the room,' said Lucy. Her voice felt
hoarse and shaky. 'He was only here a few minutes: just a
friendly call, you know – on one of his parishioners, as it were.'

'Friendly indeed,' said Dr Max leaning back against the door
and surveying her. 'We too are privileged to have you receive
us in your *robe de salon*. Confess, dear girl: were you expecting a
visit from your pastoral leader? And I did not even realise you
were of the Roman... '

'Really, Lucy,' Estelle cut in tartly: 'it's just not suitable at
all! Very lovely, of course – one of Maisie's, isn't it? But I
mean, things may be different nowadays. – '

'Oh for goodness sake!' cried Mrs Villiers: 'let's hear what
he *said*.'

For Lucy, still trembling from her encounter – the
overwhelming presence of the man, as well as the questions he
had fired at her – this sudden influx of Maisie's cronies came as
unexpected and welcome light relief. She found herself sitting
on the drawing room sofa sipping their brandy, surrounded by
their curiosity and concern; and heard herself confiding in
them.

'Are you sure that's all he said to you?' Estelle pressed her,
bright-eyed and eager.

'He asked if I was – if I had – had been visited here – by my
parents.'

'How very odd,' said Mrs Villiers. 'Anything else, dear?'

'Ah! but let us look just a little deeper into these innocent questions,' said the Doctor taking up a commanding position on the hearth and studying the tip of his cigar. 'Or, even more germane, perhaps, into his rejoinders. "You may need a guardian angel": now that's a curious thing to say to a young woman on her own; and I ask myself, is he trying to undermine her self-confidence? To make her turn to him, perhaps?'

Charles Vesey, perching on the arm of the sofa, stood up and said, 'Oh come now, my dear Doctor: he is a priest, after all.'

'But he was rather, well – imposing his presence on her,' said Mrs Villiers; 'cross-questioning her, and all that... '

'Well, you may be right,' said Mr Vesey. He patted Lucy on the shoulder. 'Must absolutely run along now, actually: only meant to be getting myself a packet of fags before closing time; wouldn't be too clever if my better half searched the Clarence and found me not.'

He left; and Lucy reflected, through the haze of whisky and brandy, that he was a nice man who probably didn't quite think she was a nice girl. It was chilling, as though she had slipped through the social mesh into some limbo, some infinite lounge bar dotted with lone drinkers and wilting watches like a Dali landscape... She pulled herself together. Estelle and Mrs Villiers were laughing at some *double entendre* of the Doctor's, whose interpretations seemed to have grown broader in the absence of the tweedy Charles.

' "Sleep well" – remember? Then, "But perhaps you find it hard to get to sleep" – that right, dear girl? "So if you need any help... " ' And she felt herself giggling weakly along with their laughter, and dipped into her brandy to dull the small ache of betrayal.

But later, after they had left, she went back to the sitting room. Two things she had not told them; the first because it was too personal: she might have repeated it to any one of them, and laughed it off – but not to all four. No: and not to Dr Max... The second thing had slipped her mind till now. Naturally enough: 'What did he *say*?' they kept asking; but on this point he had not uttered.

71

She put on the infra-red spectacles, crouched down and pulled back the goat-skin rug. Now she could see, drawn out on the patterned carpet in a shiny trail like slug-slime, the five-points of a pentacle.

Chapter Five

IT HAD NOT been in its place. But now the priest believed, as surely as he felt that *was* its place, under the heat-and-light lamp on the brass table, that it was still in the flat. Hidden somewhere. Somewhere warm.

Maisie Maturin could not have taken it with her: would hardly dare, after all that had happened. However little she knew about it – Bob Loren would have told her the absolute minimum, and he knew little of its long history; none of the records – still she must have begun to guess at its power, and felt it growing in her care.

What had made her take fright and leave it there? Had its physical manifestations, its 'body' as the wise men called it, appeared to her? Had it started spreading, exploring its new hiding place, and, maybe, finding her? But according to the dates, and if the time-honoured calculations were right, it should be going into hibernation; turned in upon itself, conserving and building its strength towards the moment of violent renewal. Only if it were subjected to cold... then it might well grow restless.

Whatever had taken place in the musty, neo-deco splendour of No 2 Clarence Mansions, Maisie Maturin had left. What a decision that must have been, Sebastian mused; and what wrenching pain, what sacrifice, to hide it away; to turn and go without it after some eighteen months of caring for it, letting it dominate her life – and having within her grasp, in that heavy, warm, smooth stone, all the kingdoms of the earth, its principalities and powers... Had she held it too long, perhaps, and been crazed by its images?

But not so crazy that she simply abandoned it: her last day in England, as he gathered from Basil's third-hand report, had been devoted to finding it a suitable keeper. Naturally enough, dear innocent Basil hadn't put it quite like that: along with his friends who sat so securely on the boundary fence of what they could not understand, but still determined to get a good view, Basil equated the sub-let's responsibilities with the upkeep of 'Maisie's lovely flat'. If the word 'acolyte' were ever used, it would be by Mrs Maturin in a grotesquely fanciful reference to herself; and Dr Max, indeed – whom the priest had encountered for the first time that day – would probably adorn it with adjectives for the new talent in their midst.

How much real danger was Lucy Morland facing, all unknowing? he wondered, closing the door of the Jesuit seminary gently behind him. He was late, the last in, according to the board; he deadlocked the latch and went through to the small chapel. A dim light was on over the altar, and the familiar smell of wax polish and incense wrapped round him, warming him in spite of the chill, and the severe, post-war ugliness of the furnishing.

The black priest sat down and put his head in his hands. Perhaps he had been too abrupt with her, cross-questioning her without offering explanations. That had been in her interest; now he wondered if he had antagonised her beyond reach. But it was clear to him now she had been deliberately chosen; and his evening call had only reinforced the impression that, even since his first face-to-face encounter with her on the bus, she had slipped downhill. Maisie Maturin's flat, its warm dark hiding place, was taking hold of her; and the presence of the stone was disturbing her sleep.

That night was the worst she had known.

The weather had turned cold; she plugged in her new electric blanket, and now, with dutch courage, opened wide her bedroom door to capture all the heat she could. She fell asleep quickly, and dreamed of the thing that moved with a rapid clicking sound, as on tiny high heels, along the passage. It was cold: it was seeking heat. It found her electric blanket, pressing the bed down with its soft, intangible weight, and settling, content; until it found her warmer body beneath – but she was too sleepy to move, or even to register the gradual takeover. Now it was encroaching on her, an intelligence that calculated, and knew how to soothe, how to please, to invade, to divide and sip and conquer – pleasing when half-asleep... Then suddenly, frightening.

She was wide awake, and terrified. Something was with her. She curled her body cautiously away from it and crept out of bed. There was nothing to be seen in the curtained gloom except shadows and darker shadows – and she could not switch on the light, too fearful she might really see something. She could not take the eiderdown with her: that weight was on it – but also, as she knew, underneath it. She made her way round the bed and tiptoed out, pulling the door shut behind her as best she could. There was a rug in the ottoman. She took refuge in the sitting room, with a table pushed up against the door, and curled up on a chair in the window as far as she could get from the pentacle. She dozed uneasily until the heating woke her at six; then slept again in fits and starts, peering at her watch, until she heard her alarm go off in the distance.

The prospect of getting smart and in to work was like staring down an impossible race-course: she could not face it. 'Close your eyes and let the horse get on with it,' brother Jamie used to tell her. Somehow her well-drilled reflexes took her there, dreamlike in the underground as live people bumped against her rubber shoulders and stepped on her wooden feet; and walking was just a slow scene-change accompanied by a repeated jarring sensation. This isn't a hangover, she thought: I haven't really got a headache. Perhaps I'm very tired.

The morning passed by over her low profile; she volunteered for nothing, took no challenges. Sally was busy seizing the chance of monopolising the married whizz-kid; she did not notice till lunch-time just how low Lucy was, when the

Kid, on his way out, took one look at her and told her to have the afternoon off.

'Thanks, Jerry.' He had insisted on first names, and now she tried to depersonalise it with a brisk smile: 'But really I feel better if I'm busy.'

Sally insisted on bringing back hot soup and rolls. 'What on earth have you been doing?' she said.

'Nothing really, that's what's so silly... No, it's not precisely a hangover, except from – well, nightmares – if you'll believe that! I seem to be sleeping badly, and feel – just terribly tired. Yes: I will take a sleeping pill tonight: I've got some.'

'Would it help if I came round? Made you some supper? I could easily cancel old Robin Thing.'

'No, honestly – thanks. I'll just get home and crash out. Catch up on the backlog. I'll be fine.'

Lucy left half an hour early and the phone was ringing in the flat as she put her key in the door. It was the TV engineer – 'I'm on my way past you – south of the High Street, right? – a bit late today; and I could pop in and have a look at your faulty set.'

It was so lucky: a good omen surely; she made coffee to keep herself awake, found him a lager, and by six-thirty she had a new plug and a picture to look at.

'There you are, then – magic!' he said gathering up his tools. 'It's an old set, mind you, and that dodgy power point must have been giving it the on-off for weeks – can't have done it any good. I've gunned up the blue, but it will fade: it can't last for ever. Then you'll need a new tube, though for my money I'd rather... '

'That's great,' she said: 'I'm only here for a couple of months.'

'Of course – you're a sub-let... OK: if you could pay me now, in cash, I'll be off... '

Then she was blissfully alone, free to stretch out on the big sofa and gaze at the moving pictures. She turned down the sound, and watched a prize bull, an air balloon, a picket line, the weather – and woke up to a detective drama, and slept again.

A blank shivering screen and the sound of the clicking-cooling roused her after midnight. She found half a pork pie in the fridge, and drank some milk. The locked cupboard looked back at her, and she saw that her beech-wood poster was discolouring in the heat, curling at the edges between the drawing pins. She took a sleeping pill from Mrs Maturin's comprehensive medication store and swallowed it with the last of the milk.

The unmade bed looked harmless enough; but memories of the night were strong now. She took the eiderdown and a pillow, and went back to the sofa. Her awareness of that pentacle shape – invisible, only a couple of yards away – forced her to get up and push the sofa back as far as it would go; and she put on her winter dressing gown over her nightdress: it made her feel more prepared, less vulnerable. Then she curled up and thought about the black priest; and she slept.

Over the days and nights that followed, the combination of television and sleeping pills seemed to impose a new order on her life. When the working day was over, she did not really need much more. The large sliced loaf seemed to keep indefinitely and she ate toast and marmite when she was hungry; she drank a lot of coffee, forgot to buy milk and decided she preferred it black. The lager was finished so she sipped her malt whisky and smoked and dozed in the flickering light of the TV: she switched off the others so people might think she was out. There was no need nor desire to visit the pub: Lucy found she was self-sufficient.

When Mrs Villiers and Estelle rang her bell one evening in the middle of an old spy movie, she told them apologetically she was just going to bed. They peered at her anxiously: 'We haven't seen you for days.'

'I'm sure we'll get together at the weekend,' said Lucy; 'OK? I'll look forward to that.' She was back in her seat and witnessing the shootout before the ladies were down the steps of Clarence Mansions.

Now that Lucy knew she could rely on sleep, she moved back

into the bedroom. No large invisible creature troubled her half-sleep: there was no half-sleep, for the Mogodon knocked her out cold between eleven-thirty and her alarm bell. But she knew also that she still had dreams; everybody did, after all, and most people forgot them. So, gratefully, did she. When she made herself review this change, she got the impression that her dreams now came from a lower level, and lay embedded in deep, drugged sleep. Occasionally the odd image or sensation would reach her, like a bubble breaking on the smooth surface of her days: razor blades in the deep silken pocket of a dressing gown... a black stallion above her, its penis as long as a machete... Mrs M.'s Dragon's Blood with suckers like little red mouths along its broad leaves... a hot weight on her chest, velvety and hard... a fat pale man with a peaked cap, dark glasses, no face... a twisted corpse praying and clutching a handbag... a black labrador waddling along the passage, its nails clicking on the floor – but the floor was carpeted, and the carpet criss-crossed with slug trails – and the slugs must have crawled up into the bed, slick and black, for she had felt them on her legs, on her breasts and oozing in between her thighs...

Yet she never woke in terror now. She seemed to be more relaxed. She noticed that her voices were back. These two voices had always come to her when she had a fever, or overworked at school; one was hysterical and high: 'Quick! Quick! You'll be too late!' and the other pitched low and sensible: 'Don't worry – nothing's wrong – everything's just fine.' But now she could hardly hear the high one except as a background bat-squeak; the other she thought of as Morpheus, or sometimes 'the great god Mogodon' because that sounded like the name of one of Father Sebastian's ancient deities. It talked her down; and, with a touch of its velvet glove, it enforced sleep.

She did not see the priest all week; not even in his running shorts: she left the drawing room curtains closed now since she did not eat breakfast – just a cup of black coffee in the kitchen – and it was dark long before she got home in the evenings. On

Saturday morning – nearly twelve: too late for any runner –
she pulled them back and discovered her forgotten pot plants.
The geranium was past hope, the pretty succulent nearly dead;
but Mrs M.'s wretched Dragon's Blood had straightened up
and put out a new leaf.

Sleeping late seemed to have given her a headache; blearily
she thought: I must shop – even the coffee jar's empty. And I
must have a sociable day... Which she did, in a manner of
speaking.

First she saw Alma with a nice-looking solid young man in a
hat, walking up the square. 'Hullo! What about that impulsive
visit?' Lucy called. Alma waved and smiled but seemed not to
have heard, deep in conversation with her man; and Lucy
decided she could be impulsive too. She crossed over and ran
after them.

'I say, Alma, would you both like to come in for a drink
before lunch?'

'Oh how kind – Lucy. Walter, this is Lucy... ?'

'Morland,' said Lucy.

'Yes. Who I met the other day, you know. In the Clarence
Arms.'

Walter studied Lucy with concentration both bright and
solemn. He had short brown hair and a furrow between his
thick brows. He said to Alma: 'Something to do with Mrs
Maisie Maturin?'

'That's right,' said Lucy; but he went on looking at his
fiancée for a reply.

'Yes, dear: living in her flat, that's all. Lucy, we are in rather
a rush today, I'm afraid. No, alas: tomorrow we'll be away.
You see it's only – golly! only a week to countdown. So –
maybe some other time? Fine.' Walter tilted his smug tweed
hat at Lucy and they went on their way. He had not smiled at
all, and Alma had done nothing but smile.

On her return from the shops Lucy left her bags outside the
door of No 2 and went up to ring the bell of the flat above: she
would give the girls a drink, then, if nervous Alma and glum
Walter were so busy.

'Hi there!' said Diane. She was wearing a suit. 'Come in and have a cup of coffee.'

'Well, I was going to ask you down to a drink: I've just been stocking up, so I can give you a choice.'

'How sweet of you. Actually I'm just off – I'm late already. Ella! Josie! Lucy from the flat downstairs is here.'

'Hi!' said Lucy: 'want to come down for a quick drink? I meant to ask you on a good sunny day, really, but I'm sure you wouldn't be spooked in the daytime… '

'Of course not! Well – fine! Thanks,' said Ella.

'Come as you are,' said Lucy; 'I'm just going to sort out my shopping. See you down there.'

She set out glasses on a tray, then put them away, not knowing what people would be drinking. She put peanuts and crisps into bowls. Ten minutes later Ella arrived alone: smiling, but a little flustered, her big loose Pre-Raphaelite bun escaping in wisps round her ears. She was clutching a bundle of leaflets.

'Just me, I'm afraid! Josie apologises: she genuinely doesn't feel great, and she has to go out this evening… Well, how *are* you? I say, you've lost weight, haven't you? Are you on a diet? – not as though you needed to.'

'No, I think I just got overtired or something, and haven't felt much like – why, do I look awful?'

'Oh no – not a bit! Here: I brought these – a sort of catalogue from Josie's poster shop; something about the antiques fair, lectures on art, all that sort of thing. Keep them: we've got others… So – can I look round? I haven't been before, remember. Goodness, it's so much higher than ours… I say, the decor *is* pretty amazing, isn't it? But it looks very comfortable… Are you getting fond of it?'

'I am rather. I'd love to change it all to suit me, but any such notion was very firmly jumped on by our Mr Cornfield. What will you drink?'

'Just a coke if you have one – well, just tonic then. Thanks.'

There was a ring at the bell. 'Josie, maybe, feeling better?' suggested Lucy going to the door.

It was Josie, but she looked fraught, and she did not come in; she did not even say hello. 'Ella! *Please!*' she called.

Ella hurried out to her, and Lucy went and got herself a cigarette while they whispered urgently together in the lobby. Then Josie ran off upstairs.

Ella said, 'I'm sorry about all this, Lucy, but I'll just have to go up and sort her out. It isn't like her at all – something very mixed-up about a horoscope. No, mine. Honestly, she *must* be ill to – I'll just finish my drink.'

On her way back to the kitchen she stopped and tilted her head to listen, as though she were afraid Josie might be up to something desperate. Lucy, following her, noticed her hair-clip fly out. 'You're really bothered about her, aren't you?' she said. 'Go on up, Ella: forget the drink.' She stooped to pick up the clip from where it lay by the airing-cupboard door; but before her unbelieving eyes it slid three inches across the carpet, through the narrow gap, and disappeared.

'Your hair-clip!' she said. And then wished she hadn't.

'Where did it go to?' said Ella. 'I thought it was just there. Perhaps it skittered under –'

'*Don't*!' said Lucy.

But Ella had her fingers in the gap beneath the door. 'I think I can just –' Then with a sharp cry she clutched her hand to her mouth, gave a little moan, and fainted.

Desperately dabbing water on her face and patting her hands, Lucy was relieved to see Josie and Diane in the open doorway.

'What have you done to her?' Josie cried out. 'I *knew* it – I *felt* it!' and fell on her knees beside Ella.

'She's coming to,' said Diane. 'Get her head down.'

They helped her up on to a chair and put her head between her knees. 'I knew it would happen – I *knew* – I *told* her,' Josie kept muttering.

'It's – OK… I'm fine.' Ella's voice was weak. 'What – what actually happened to me?'

'Quite,' said Diane, straightening up and turning to Lucy: 'what *did* happen?'

'I really don't know. She was looking for her hair-clip – then she let out a cry and fainted.'

'Well – let's get her upstairs, anyway. I've missed my train by

81

now. It's all right, thanks: we can manage.'

They took Ella away up the stairs almost without a backward glance. Lucy, appalled and dumbfounded, stood at the bottom saying, 'I'm so sorry – Really, I feel awful about it all – but I don't know what... ' She heard the upper door close.

Lucy's sociable day did not seem to have got off to a good start. She sat hunched on the kitchen stool, her back to that door and her dehydrated beechwood, and smoked, sipping at her gin and tonic. She felt sore from rejection, and scared by what she had witnessed. Yet she knew – and her good sense insisted – that the soreness was only a form of self-pity; and the fear was just plain silly: if she had really seen the hair clip creep across the carpet, and not just skitter under that door, then there would be a perfectly good explanation – the only real problem being the fact that there was still no way she could begin to find one. When the TV engineer was around on Monday evening, she had been tempted to show him what happened to her pins and ask him to – but that was it: how could she say 'Look, just tell me what you think is causing it but *don't* go putting your hand into that gap'? And now it was the same story with the locked door, and the narrow crack beneath.

We are all walking through a mystery, meeting things we can't explain... The priest's words kept coming back to her. Perhaps she should ask *him*. Go to confession, even. Or should she, as those words seemed to assume, accept the mystery and live with it? Busying herself round the flat, washing up a week's ash-trays and glasses (just as well, perhaps, Alma and Walter hadn't accepted her impulsive invitation), she wondered whether old Mother Maturin, not content with a Yale lock, might have rigged up some sort of electric fence, like the sinister force-field in a space movie, to guard her valuables – and Lucy realised that, eccentric as such measures might be – even perhaps illegal – she herself found them far easier to accept than Father Sebastian's vague 'mystery'.

She was dressing herself that evening for an expedition to the Clarence, and eager – she had to admit – at the prospect of being with people, when her mother telephoned. They had been wondering if she was all right.

'Why, yes: I'm fine,' said Lucy, 'flourishing. Yes, I meant to ring you this evening – sorry, Mum, it must be over a week… Oh, the flat is great: marvellously warm; and I'm getting used to the decorations. Oh, and I've got a working telly now: not the most brilliant of pictures – it's old but rather fun to be able to… No, I won't get glued, Mum. Actually I was just dressing to go out when you rang – meeting some friends at the pub… Oh no – it's not *all* go! I mean, I find during the week I don't feel like doing a lot… Oh, just tired… No Mum, it's really *not* too much, the flat and the job – But work is quite demanding, you know. Tell me about you.'

She heard that Jamie was coming down from Edinburgh for Christmas and bringing his girlfriend; that all the ruddy apples had been put away at last, a bumper crop; that Nell had phoned to say she had lost track of Lucy – 'I wasn't sure I'd got your number right, darling: I've tried once or twice and got a dead sort of noise – so I said you'd be in touch with her'; that cards and Christmas parcels by surface to Canada must go off this week…

Listening there in the tall, dim, overfurnished room with its oppressive oranges and blacks and horns and hands and hooded madonnas, Lucy felt dreadfully homesick. She could imagine exactly where her mother was in the kitchen of the big flint-and-brick farmhouse. She would be sitting on the window seat, with the high white shutters closed and barred, the Jack Russell up beside her; and her view would be across the broad table and the jug of 'last flowers', rosehips and coloured leaves, to the cooking range, the blue-and-white tiles, the convenient strings of onions and garlic; and half-listening to the music on the gramophone – Lucy could hear it filtering through from the sitting room…

She could not say, I've been scared – I haven't been sleeping – I'm taking Mogodon – this flat is creepy – funny things happen – people seem to be avoiding me/it and I think my landlady might be a sort of amateur witch and incidentally my jolly assignation in the local is with a gang of oldies known affectionately as the spooky set… She said, 'Oh Mum – it'll be good getting back for Christmas… Yes, *really* I'm flourishing… OK, yes: I'll ring you. Love to Dad – heaps. Bye.'

The prospect of the Clarence and Mrs Maturin's chums had lost its allure: that vision of home – square, clean and totally familiar – made her sick at heart. She stayed sitting, half-dressed in smart trousers and scruffy top, and reached for the TV button. There was nothing on, but she watched it numbly; and thought: some time I must organise my sewing – maybe start some knitting – so I don't just sit and smoke…

At about ten-thirty, as she must have expected, the bell rang. Mrs Villiers, the Colonel, Cecil, and Mr Winslow, the retired actor, trouped in.

'Long time no see, dear girl!' said Cecil, waving a bottle. 'You never showed! So we've come to you.'

'The mountain to Mahomet, what?' said the Colonel.

'*Are* you all right, dear?' Mrs Villiers clutched her arm. 'Poor Estelle is feeling a bit dicky and I wondered if there was a bug going round. But you do look a little more rested, I think.'

'Oh I am; and I've been trying those sleeping pills.'

'Wonderful, aren't they? So many people these days are against drugs – even the doctors, it seems: I had quite a tussle with him last time – "no repeat prescriptions", all that nonsense. But goodness me, if the help is there, why not make use of it I say. In moderation of course… '

'Aha!' said Cecil from the drawing room; 'the goggle-box rules OK – here's why she's been neglecting her admirers.'

'Not fair!' she called, setting out the coffee cups. She carried them through. 'I really am too tired to go out during the week.'

'That's right!' cried Mrs Villiers. 'She *works*, you know – unlike certain so-called reporters I could mention! When did you last do any news-reporting or whatever, I'd like to know?'

'Ah, but I am freelance, dear lady, for my sins; and we independent spirits have to wait weeks maybe for the coup, the inside info, the big one, the exclusive. No, Colonel: not that one – try channel three… '

The men, standing or sitting, watched the moving pictures; Mrs Villiers shook her head: 'They don't grow up, do they!'

and took Lucy away to the table in the bow window. She poured them both a tot of Cecil's Drambuie. 'And how are you *really*, dear? And tell me, have you seen that nice Father Sebastian at all? Oh? And he hasn't called in again? You'll laugh, dear, but you know when we dropped by the other evening – Thursday, wasn't it? and you didn't really want us to stay – Oh we weren't hurt, Lucy: absolutely no hard feelings among pals: with us, you know you can always – but naughty Estelle said: "I wonder if she's entertaining that lovely Father Sebastian!" Of *course* you weren't – Well, *I* knew you weren't, dear; and this very evening he was in the Clarence, early on: off duty, so to speak, casual clothes you know – with a *very* smart coloured lady. Oh, they do know how to dress, the smart ones do... And her husband, I think, though he was white... Anyway the good father came over to our table – yes! And was so charming; and he asked after you; said he hadn't seen you for some time; wondered how you were – and asked after "Miss Estelle", too. Oh no: they didn't sit with us. I think they were going on somewhere.'

Next morning Lucy was woken by the alarm she had forgotten to turn off. She felt she could go on sleeping all day; but she had decided the night before, after her guests had gone, that she must take herself in hand: give the flat a proper clean right through, tidy herself up, go for a long walk. So the rude awakening turned into a 'good start'. She had a bath, ate some toast with her coffee, hoovered all the carpets. Later on, fetching the papers, striding hard, breathing deep and feeling the cold air infiltrate her body like icy roots, she knew the timing of her walk was not accidental, and that she could reach St Mary's in time for eleven o'clock mass. She was even dressed decently, having forced herself to fold away the baggy trousers and put on a skirt. Not that they minded about such details in Catholic churches: she had never been to a service but had heard that people wore anything, came and went with babies on their hips, or bags of shopping, popping in for a prayer – not at all like the C of E's twin-sets, pearls and welded hats.

She sat at the back and followed the drill, the sudden kneeling or standing or responding, with one eye on the order of service and the other on her neighbours. She could not be sure Father Sebastian was even there: her view was blocked by a family of tall, broad Italians, two of whom she had seen shaking out tablecloths from the doorway of an ultra-smart restaurant in Abingdon Road. Then everyone sat down, and he was there in the pulpit giving out his text. ' "Father forgive them, for they know not what they do." '

She had not expected that seeing him, hearing him, would upset her so. Her blood bumped heavily against her chest and skull as though she were in mortal danger, and she prayed not to faint and give her presence away. She had tried so hard to avoid thinking about him over one long week. His brief and pointed cross-questioning had left her feeling angry, hurt, absurd – that was the worst. But still his image came to her before sleep; it was an indulgence she had allowed herself when she dreaded the bad dreams, and it had become a habit. Luckily sleep came fast, and the great god Mogodon snuffed her out before she had time to fantasise.

Now that voice (that velvet voice saying so evenly: 'Tell me another thing: are you a virgin?') was filling the big ugly crowded church. The shuffling and coughing ceased.

'I want to talk about sin,' he said, very confident, very relaxed, looking round his congregation. 'But you'll notice the word "sin" is not in my text. Did the people around Our Lord at that moment commit a sin – those soldiers and spectators? For the soldiers, a job, a routine crucifixion; for the onlookers, a show: something you watched on a Friday afternoon off. They knew not what they did... Which of the ten commandments were they breaking? None – and yet those people were implicated in the slaying of God's Son, and they needed His forgiveness. "For they know not what they do": and *that*, friends, was their sin! Yes: Jesus wasn't just naming a good reason for forgiving them. He was naming their sin – just like he might have said "Forgive them for they cheat"; "Forgive them for they murder me". Their sin was ignorance. Neglect. The sin of omission.

'Of doing nothing. Like the Auschwitz personnel obeying orders or the good citizens outside who simply took in their washing when the smoke blew that way... Like you lot' – the pointing black finger raked the congregation – 'when you pass by on the other side. As you do – don't fool yourselves! – every day of the week: you who don't want to meddle – feel you shouldn't stick your noses in – no business of yours... *You* know – and *I* know. Because I do it: too busy right now, I tell myself. Too tired, too many other things on my plate.

'But our sin does not end there; for, let's face it, we actually get a sort of kick (in our nice, neat semi-detachment) – yes, we get a buzz from the rather-him-than-me situation. "There but for the grace of God go I." Now, that's a saying which is always used to imply a realisation, an imaginative sympathy with the plight of another. If you've got *that* much imagination, brothers and sisters – don't kid yourselves: you should be in there *helping* the guy.

'You see, this detachment, this I-keep-my-nose-clean thing, is only possible because of the mess and suffering round us. And it's not just cosy, and smug: it is what I call "vicarious living" – and I think it is one of the most dangerous, most modern, and most neglected sins of all. Now, about this "vicarious living": I must say something about in self-defence, as I am after all a species of "vicar of Christ"; and it does *not* mean "living like a vicar" ' – titters – 'or "*with* a vicar" ' – laughter – 'it means living at second hand: treating experience as a spectator sport. And it's particularly modern, I maintain, because of media and communications: we can now watch everything from boxing to the Beirut massacres – think about that: actually watch it *live*, but from a great distance; from a nice safe position in our public house, in our homes; and discuss it all profoundly with our mates – then switch over to Toxteth or a western or a documentary on saving whales – or even, nowadays, a video of ourselves (big thing in the States, that: watching what you did yesterday, even if it's only yourself sitting in front of the video!)' More laughter; he could get it when he wanted it. 'But we give them all the same consideration; and we can switch over to something else when it gets too heavy.

'And we'd much rather do this than cross the road to break up a fight, or check that the lonely newcomer is settling in, or that the old witch upstairs has a bob for the meter... I know someone – who is here today,' no one looked round: it could turn out to be them, 'the so-called friends of this character are all very attentive and well-meaning. Know what? They're sticking around to see what happens. They're fascinated. Living vicariously; getting their kicks from watching someone else moving towards the edge... And they'll be terribly upset when something nasty happens. But their hands will be clean. Like the centurion's, going about his business; like those spectators. Two centre stalls, please, for the Friday show at Golgotha.

' "Father forgive them... " '

As he turned towards the altar, two hundred people rustled and shuffled to their feet; and Lucy played her Sicilian gambit, using the wall of Italians to mask her move to the door. Then she was outside, safe and sane again under the cold impersonal grey sky.

Chapter Six

TWO WEEKS LATER, Charles Vesey was standing at the long window of his elegant first floor drawing room when he saw the girl cross the corner of Clarence Square and disappear into the block of flats where she lived.

Attractive creature, he thought. Three or four times, now, he'd seen her in the Clarence, and had gone along that once with the others to her flat, to visit her. Pity he had to leave early. Very attractive. Beautiful? Big word: but now that she seemed to be shedding the puppy fat, there were clearly good bones underneath, and also there was a new, fascinatingly, well – vulnerable look. In the three weeks or so since he first spotted her, she'd lost a good deal of that depressingly hearty, apple-cheeked, striding quality – almost strident: so aggressively young and healthy had he found it, like bright sunlight hitting a hangover. Funny how she'd ganged up with those old biddies in the lounge bar.

But Charley Vesey was no fool: he'd noticed the younger, more swinging crowd virtually close ranks when she first appeared: her wholesome beauty (yes, OK: she was a beauty, marching in with her jacket slung round her neck, ordering her lager-and-lime in that clear Roedean voice of hers – Sherborne, actually, he'd discovered – that open-air brilliance) had been positively threatening. Dr Max standing on the sidelines, buying a jar for some punky lad he'd discovered, had remarked on her. 'So who's the blazing innocent?' Charlie thought it was rather well put. He had a way with words, had the Doctor – but all in all a nasty piece of work; and anyway,

Harriet heard somewhere, from one of her girlfriends, that he'd been struck off the register a couple of years back…

Charles had long ago finished the Sunday papers and was waiting for Harriet to call him to carve the joint. Usually they went down to the cottage for the weekend, but a Saturday dinner party had buggered that up: he'd had to cancel his golf. And Nanny was visiting her old mum in Upminster and the boys were bored as hell and driving him spare. They frequently did: golf was his weekend escape drill; now he'd probably have to take them to the Round Pond or something this afternoon… London on a Sunday was pretty grim – unless of course you were young and could pile into some old banger and whizz off to the Compleat Angler or a wicked afternoon cinema – cocktails at Kettners – the Hard Rock till all hours – *that* was the way to beat the Sunday blues.

And he wondered what Lucy Morland would be up to, at this moment. If she'd gone into the pub, he might have popped over for a quick pint… Was she lonely too? Blue Meanies? The thought of her mouldering away in that ghastly flat, dusting the shrunken heads or whatever – what a shocking waste! Sentimentally he imagined knocking on her door. 'We're both lonesome, Lucy, aren't we? So how's about taking in a movie and then playing it by ear.'

'Charles!' Harriet's heavy tread. 'Charles, do get a move on! Didn't you hear me shouting? It's getting cold and the infants are gorging themselves on crisps. For God's *sake*!'

As he plodded down to the dining room, Charles Vesey saw his moonshot. Harriet wanted them to look in on her Mama after supper. He would wriggle out of that, and, if Nanny got back as pronto as was her wont, he might just pop across and try his luck with the lovely Lucy. 'Coming dear…'

Closing the front door behind himself, he glanced at his watch: nearly ten o'clock. Nanny's phoning and asking for an extra half-hour to see an old friend had at least given him the excuse to baby-sit; now she was back, and he calculated there was still time before Harriet returned from Kew. 'Just going for a pint' was the alibi, so he must look in at the pub in case the old bat observed him from her bedroom window on the top floor. Nanny had been with them six long months: a replacement, hand-picked by Harriet, for the au pair she'd got in such a lather about – and she still didn't believe that it was Inge who'd made the running: virtually thrown herself at him.

Lucy, now, was a different ball game. The breeding was there; she'd know the rules. Waiting for his change, he looked through into the lounge to check. A tableful of spooks were present: with a bit of luck she'd be on her own at home – not that 'home' was the *mot juste* for that place she'd taken on: more like a sort of thirties cat-house, and weird with it – a combination of creepy and tarty... Just how prim and proper is she? he wondered. Suppose, instead, the safe little band of chaperones, as he saw them, the spooky set were onto a good thing... Could Dr Max, say, or Cecil, or even Dermot, be in there two or three times a week – screwing her regularly on that vast fur-and-satin sofa of hers? With naughty old Mrs V. and Estelle cheering from the side-lines... That black chap, the oddball priest, had been round there too, according to Nanny who missed very little. Wow – what a scene for the candid camera! He downed his half, surveyed himself in the mirror behind the bar, loosened his silk scarf just a touch, and went out into the square.

'Hullo!' said Lucy.

She was wearing a sort of kaftan and a lot of eyeliner, and had done things to her hair: frizzed it out and caught it back with a snaky black comb. The new look was a touch wild and dramatic for Charles's taste, but undoubtedly very off-beat, very sexy. He said: 'Goodness! Way out,' and she smiled dazzlingly.

'Do come in.' She turned and led the way to the sitting room. He could hear no other voices. Fine. Then she paused at the door and whispered: 'We mustn't break the spell: the board, you know,' and for a moment Charles wondered what weird annual general meeting could be in session.

Inside the incense-filled room, only two small lamps were on. Cecil, Mrs Villiers, Estelle and another woman – Charles recognised her as the harpy who ran the country-crafts-and-whole-food shop – were sitting in silence round a ouija board. Close to him, Lucy giggled apologetically.

'There was nothing on the telly, you see... I've always been warned off these things, but Mrs Villiers says it's only a parlour game – and Germaine's often done it, apparently, with no ill effects. What will you drink, Mr Vesey – OK: Charles? Here's a clean glass, I think: difficult to see in the cloistered gloom! Nothing much has happened yet.'

'A bit like fishing,' said Charles nervously, eyeing the rippling silver mass of hair by the half-light and scenting its musky animal smell. He thought: Inge was never like this – washing her hair with Scandinavian vigour every other day. 'You know,' he went on: 'cricket or fishing: hours of bloody nothing, but always...'

'But always a sort of tension, you mean? A feeling that anything could happen?'

'Yes,' he said, glancing sideways along the silky curve of her breasts; 'that's it, absolutely.'

Lucy was glad Charles Vesey had come: he still seemed most like the sort of person her parents dined with. At worst, she guessed, he was a charming, slightly wet, city gent, and probably happier out in the wide open spaces. Henrietta, or Harriet – the wife – had the money, according to Cecil who knew these things: the Clarence Square house was hers. Standing by him in the darkened room, watching the odd little circle crouching over the board, Lucy was aware that Charles Vesey fancied her; and that she was looking good, far more exciting than her old image.

She had tried out the hair-do earlier that week, wetting and plaiting it as soon as she got home from work, and turning up in the pub quite late that evening. Two aggressively-dressed youths – she'd always thought they were gay – had cornered her and bought her a *piña colada*; and a rather blue-chinned, byronic young stockbroker came over, ostensibly to 'rescue' her, and stayed to buy them all another while they listened to his risqué city stories. She had enjoyed being mysterious and a bit fey, refusing to tell them her name, where she lived or what she did – 'why don't you guess?' – and needling them with tricky questions for her own entertainment. Tucked away at the far end of the public bar by the space invaders, she revelled in half an hour of being someone else – that's what it felt like. She had not set eyes on a single spook; and she disappeared into the night, when she had had enough, by the simple means of going to the Ladies and then slipping out. Now, pouring herself another dram of Tia Maria, she thought: I'm diversifying, that's what. And our Mr Vesey is sick as a cat he hasn't got me on his own.

'You must join us, Lucinda,' said the peasant-weave lady imperiously. 'Oh yes: how do you do, Mr Vesey – Yes, I'm sure we've met somewhere... I insist, my sweet: you're creating a separate wave-pattern, you see: imagine *two* pebbles dropped in a pool.'

Cecil had put 'Tubular Bells' on the record-player. 'Come along, Lucy: be a sport! We need all the juice we can to get this thing moving – and you sure do look juicy this evenin', honey chile! Right, squire?'

'What? Oh, certainly – absolutely fantastic.'

'That's not fair, Cecil,' said Estelle: 'it did move a little.'

'What about you, Mr Vesey, dear?' said Mrs Villiers. 'Why don't you –?'

'Oh no! I don't think I –'

'Come on, dear: no excuses! Squeeze in there beside Lucy, why not, and let's see if we can get a reply this time.'

Charles sat down carefully, shifting the folds of the kaftan to share the broad stool. With joss-sticks and liqueurs and Lucy's proximity, he felt hot and slightly dizzy. He knew he should keep an eye on the time; but they were all holding hands now, and he could not break the circle.

'So: fingertips on the planchette,' murmured Germaine the Whole-food. 'Are you there...? Are you there?' They waited.

Lucy felt the wood under her fingers suddenly lurch and slither. She and Charles both pulled back sharply as though from a live snake. 'No! Keep them *on* or you'll spoil it!' hissed

Germaine. They obeyed. Nothing happened; it was just a dead piece of wood. 'We'll start again. Who are you? Tell us, who are you?'

Silence. No movement. Lucy was acutely aware of the warm weight of Charles's shoulder and thigh against her, his quick breathing, his eyes travelling – 'We must *all* concentrate,' said Germaine, 'and keep that concentration on the planchette... Who are you? Answer us: who are you?'

It started to move, sliding gently towards the B on the board; it wavered on towards the I, changed its mind and stopped on the L.

'Who's "BIL", then?' whispered Mrs Villiers. 'I thought it might be Bob Loren at first.'

'Right,' said Cecil; 'and it was a bit unsure of the I, wasn't it?'

Germaine took over again. 'Are you Bob Loren? Tell us, are you Bob Loren?' The planchette bucked and spun in a tight circle under their fingertips and out of their grasp. 'It didn't like that,' she announced, retrieving it from the floor. 'I don't think it is Bob Loren.'

Estelle said: '*I* know what Maisie used to say. Remember? "Are you blind?" "Are you black?" "Are you dangerous?" ' There was a small silence. 'Well, that's what she –'

'Oh come, now: that's a bit...!' said Charles Vesey, taking out a handkerchief and wiping his brow. Lucy glanced at him. He seemed to be under some sort of stress. 'We'll try it,' said Germaine. 'Fingertips on. Very lightly – Concentrate... '

'Are you blind?'

'Are you black?'

'Are you dangerous?'

'Well I don't get it,' said Cecil sitting back: 'It just says ZU to everything... Must be a Zulu, what? No wonder it can't talk proper! Eh? We've got a blinking fuzzie-wuzzie in our midst! I say, squire?'

'Charles? Mr Vesey – are you all right?' Lucy had been too busy concentrating on the puzzling parlour game to take much notice of the increased weight against her shoulder. Now she turned and saw him staring at his hands; sweat was trickling down his ashen face.

Someone opened a window and they helped him over to it. 'Thanks – sorry about that,' he said, sitting down heavily. 'Do shut it now… Thanks, but actually I'm awfully cold.' He was shivering. 'I wonder if I could have some water? So kind. Matter of fact I do feel positively ill – ridiculous: as though I was getting the 'flu.'

'Or some bug like Estelle,' said Mrs Villiers.

'Well it couldn't be anything wrong with the booze, squire,' said Cecil. 'Got it from the off-licence – been drinking it myself – all of us.'

Charles took the water greedily. 'Thanks. I was sort of – dried out. Tell you how I feel: just as if I'd had one of those pre-op jabs.'

'I know,' said Cecil – 'that dry out your throat and nose and one doesn't like to think what else – ha, ha.'

Charles was on his feet now, still shaky, and making for the door. 'That's right,' he said with a weak smile. 'I think I'll just cut along. Got to get back anyway. Sorry about the nasty turn. No, I can manage: I'd rather – only just across the square. Be seeing you.'

'Are you sure?' cried Lucy; but he was gone.

'Dried out, eh? Maybe a drying-out's what he needs, poor chap,' said Cecil. 'Wonder how he'll pass it off when Lady Harriet opens the door to him… '

Germaine said: 'Now that the disrupting influence has gone – oh I'm sure of it, my dear – what do you make of "ZU"? Not once, not twice, but three times? Shall we repeat the question?'

Lucy looked at her watch without concealment. 'I don't think I feel like starting again,' she said: 'working day tomorrow and all that.'

'Oh no – is that the time?' Mrs Villiers went into her routine fluster. 'Come along: we must – Estelle! Cecil? Germaine dear?'

Cecil left with the older ladies; but Germaine stayed on – 'Just for a moment, to gather myself together again you know.

And perhaps a small one for the road?'

She had intense eyes, arched black brows and unnaturally purplish auburn hair in coils over her ears. Lucy guessed she must be in her forties and that she both wove and tailored her own clothes. She got up from the low pouf with a sinuous grace, flinging her oatmeal shawls round her thin chest and over her shoulder to a clash of bangles, and stood by the hearth (the spot Lucy most avoided) in a fine balletic pose.

'I don't even *know* when it's late,' she said: 'I'm a sort of gipsy at heart, I'm afraid... I do think you've created a wondrous Aladdin's cave, my dear, in the middle of drab old London Town! There's a certain sulphurous beauty about the colours – and textures, and lighting – and then yourself, of course: the spirit of that cave.'

'Oh, but I didn't.' Lucy managed to stem the flow, 'I mean, it's not mine, you know. Didn't Mrs Villiers –? No: the flat belongs to a Mrs Maturin.'

'Of *course*: I had been told. A very wonderful person, I believe: very strong, very psychic.'

'I wouldn't know,' said Lucy. 'I've never met her.'

'Ah, but you can *feel* her, I'm sure – here amid all her fascinating *objets d'art*.'

'Well I'm just looking after them – as well as I can of course.'

'My dear, the perfect acolyte: that is what you are – tending the fires while the high priestess is away – a vestal virgin!'

Not again, thought Lucy. It seemed she hadn't altered her image quite as successfully as she thought. What lengths must she go to – apart from the obvious? 'Look, I'm sorry – Germaine,' she said, 'but I really do want to – I mean, I must get an early... '

'Of course, my dear. Don't want me to tuck you in? Not this time... Well, thank you for a very interesting evening. I hope you didn't mind my joining your little circle of admirers in the pub, but I felt an affinity – and they were all so full of you and your flat. We must try the board again another evening; at my place, perhaps.' She put it away in a large tapestry bag. 'Fascinating, this ZU we called up. And we did, you know.' She reached out for the telephone pad. 'Here's my number. I'll put

"ZU" beside it for you to ponder on.'

As Lucy was helping her with her cape, she froze suddenly, her finger to her lips. 'But what is that?' she whispered.

'Oh – just the cooling noises. That happens when the boiler in the basement goes off.'

'How strange: it's not so much like something ending as something beginning – do you know what I mean?'

Lucy closed the door behind her and went back to tidy the sitting room. Passing the telephone pad she looked again at the phone number, and that ZU. The writing was strong and cursive, with a curly Z that looked more like a 2. Two U. Two of you? or, to you? 'Are you blind?' 'To you.' 'Are you black?' 'To you.' 'Are you dangerous?' '(Yes) to you (I am).'

Like some obscure litany, it ran on in her head as she put the chairs and stools back into their places. It was all such frightful nonsense, and the sort you could interpret any number of ways, to fit your hopes, or your fears… Carrying the tray past the clicking radiators, the locked cupboard, she found she was trembling. She put down her load in the kitchen and stood staring at her beloved beech-wood, as though the clicking from behind it were sounding its doom: a secret, tireless death-watch beetle eating it out. To you. To you. To – the washing up could wait: clearly she was tired and foolish.

She noticed again that the sleeping pills were running low. But she took a couple – just to be sure – and went quickly to bed.

It was two months since she started work with Lees-Langham, just over a month in the Clarence Square flat, and Lucy reckoned this must be 'being established'.

She wondered about this, as far as life in the flat was concerned, when an old schoolfriend she hadn't seen for nearly two years paid her a visit: telephoned, came for supper and spent the night.

'Friend' was not quite right perhaps: Gudrun had fitted into no particular circle at school. Although a year senior, and ultimately a prefect, she used to attach herself to Lucy; and

97

once, when there had been some crisis or other at home, had come to stay in Wiltshire over Easter. She was a very bright loner: a serious, fat, rather eccentric individual, and always determined to be a doctor – 'on the research side, you know,' as she insisted. ('And just as well,' Caroline used to say, 'she's not exactly a genius with people.') Now she was at London University doing medicine, and had got hold of Lucy's number by ringing home.

On the phone, Lucy was rather more welcoming than she really felt; and proceeded to rationalise this to herself as she tidied the flat in preparation. OK, so she had perhaps been, not just too kind, but too lonely herself to say no – so: why not see it as a dry run for Nell, or Caroline, or Jenny, Jamie's girlfriend, who was coming through London in December?

Gudrun had smartened up a lot, and looked taller in a dark dress and boots; her black, too-curly hair was pulled back into a bun, and she carried a bottle of German wine. But almost immediately she said, 'Goodness gracious, Lucy – what made you live in a place like this?' All the half-remembered spikiness and bossiness of this long-distance loner, all her own half-forgotten irritation, flooded back to Lucy, and she found herself bristling with unaccustomed loyalty.

'Why – it's great!' she said heartily, opening the wine. 'What on earth's wrong with it?'

'It's – well, it's doom-laden,' said Gudrun. 'I mean: all right, it's only temporary; and as you say, it's big and warm, but – well I couldn't. Too claustrophobic… ' At least she won't stay the night, thought Lucy.

But she did. She relaxed with some of her own wine inside her, and the grilled chops for supper. Lucy did not confess that this was the first time she had cooked a proper meal: pasties, the odd fry-up, or heated TV suppers, suited her routine. Now, though Gudrun was mellowing over reminiscences and the school snaps she had brought with her, Lucy found herself resenting the disruption of that routine more even than the adverse judgement on her flat. Then Gudrun said over coffee: 'The television works, does it? I want to have a look at the programme on women's medicine if I may.'

It was not a question, Lucy observed. She said, 'But there's a Peckinpah movie on the other side.'

'Which you could see any old time, surely.'

Lucy said evenly, 'You can't boss me now, Gudrun.' She smiled. 'Fair's fair: we'll toss for it.'

Gudrun's documentary won; Lucy caught only the last quarter of her movie.

'It's too late for transport,' said Gudrun, 'all right if I doss down in your spare room?'

'Not too doomed and claustrophobic?' Lucy asked, gathering the cups.

'Oh, I couldn't *live* here,' said Gudrun as she switched through the other channels to see what else was still alive. 'But I'd be glad of a bed now.'

'Fine,' Lucy replied. She didn't say, well, I find the spare room most particularly scary, as a matter of fact. She still – even with the clicking noises at their worst – felt like defending her chosen patch.

'I'll wash up,' said Gudrun bustling about. 'No: no arguments... And you shouldn't be smoking so much, you know, Lucy,' she added, with all the clout of her extra year in age and the severity of a budding MD.

'I've lost some weight – and that *must* be good,' said Lucy tartly. But Gudrun was unruffled. She tied the apron round her thick waist and started wiping down the taps and basin – a comment in itself – saying, 'You're too thin, actually, for your height and build. You must get yourself together, you know. You see, London's probably more of a challenge than you appreciate' – owlishly, swivelling and eyeing Lucy and her Glenlivet – 'you have to decide what you want from life in a big city, and go out and get it... But this place: I see it as a sort of stuffy womb – though Lord knows just what it's meant to be hatching.'

'Oh come on, Gudrun! You always did have odd ideas – but that's ridiculous... I'll go and make the bed.'

She was absurdly put out to find it was already made up: must have always been; and realised it would not need airing in the warmth of that room. 'Sure you don't want me to remove the masks?' she called.

'I'm not bothered,' said Gudrun. 'I'm aware it's all in the mind. Can I give Simon a ring? My boyfriend. I told you about him.'

'This late?'

'Yes. He might worry.'

It was an odd little visitation – totally different from anything Lucy could have predicted. She saw herself as having so many advantages: not just good looks and a solid family (Gudrun's parents were now divorced), but a big flat of her own (Gudrun was in a hostel), what she had vaguely thought to be a potentially glamorous job, and the rather bohemian life-style. Yet for some reason the lumpy school-chum – bad at games, resented as a prefect, an oddball without the oddball's required sense of humour – seemed to pity her, to be anxious over her well-being. And what was more, Gudrun had a boyfriend (with whom she apparently spent nights), a worthwhile career and a sense of purpose. To top it all, the wretched girl slept soundly in the room Lucy could not face, woke bright and early and left at 7.30 after making herself a better breakfast than her hostess's normal supper, virtually emptying the fridge.

It gave Lucy a sudden glimpse of her own life from outside. While she assured herself it was not from a sympathetic angle – nor had she any desire to emulate Gudrun or see her as some 'successful' elder sister figure – yet she found herself some-what shaken by the encounter, impressed against her will, and left questioning. She tried to explain this to Sally at work.

'But she sounds a real bore, Luce. It's seldom one can observe them so young: you can spot them a mile off in middle age. Oh, be yourself, woman: you're different; you're lucky – just enjoy it.'

Lucy remembered that off-beat evening of the rippling hair and the ouija board; as the joss-sticks smouldered, and weird Germaine rapped out commands, and Charles Vesey pressed closer, his heavy masculine warmth weakening her concentra-tion – she had thought, but only for a moment – Is this being

100

me? Then as the planchette came alive, her question was forgotten.

At Lees-Langham, being established was a technical matter rather than an emotional one.

The arrival of a new secretary in her department of the advertising agency suddenly made her an old hand; at the same time, Sally, who had been secretly trying her talents at copy-writing, was promoted and moved into the section that handled the women's market. Two days later, Margaret, the new girl, joined Lucy to help cope with the Whizz Kid.

Margaret, who had been working for a firm of accountants, was a classic career secretary: very high speeds, together with a sort of faceless neatness and terrible efficiency – even in the way she unpacked her immaculate salad lunch – that Lucy found both robotic and threatening. She missed Sally's blatant, often ribald, competitiveness, even her bad moods, her cigarette-cadging, her off-key humming. Margaret did not smoke; now Lucy only felt free to light up when she was in with the Kid – a fifty-a-day, let-me-press-you-to-a-kingsize man. But such opportunities seemed to dwindle as he used the robot more and more. 'This is a rush job,' he'd say: 'can you drop everything, Margaret?' She was twenty-one, with a small pretty face and what Sally referred to as a 'cute butt', always encased in a dark pencil skirt. Lucy felt the world rushing past her as she stared at her straggling shorthand and longed for a cigarette, for the day to be over, for the bus, for home, for sleep.

And now, she knew, she was down to her last four Mogodon. Mrs Villiers had already given her the name of her private doctor; but Lucy had seen a health centre near the playground, and decided it would be both cheaper and more impersonal. She did not want the leisured, deep-delving inquiry into her 'problems': she wanted a prescription, and fast.

Waiting for nearly an hour on a hard bench in the bright, crowded clinic proved far more nerve-wracking than any job

101

interview; worse even than waiting outside the headmistress's study for a severe reprimand. For goodness' sake, she said to herself, staring unseeing at an elaborate crochet pattern in *Woman's Weekly*, you've done nothing wrong: why feel guilty? This guy's meant to be on your side...

'I see,' he said, taking off his glasses and rubbing his eyes wearily. 'Well: for a start, you shouldn't just take pills you find in a cupboard, given to someone, on prescription, and, no doubt, for a specific course of treatment. Secondly, coming along to me asking for Mogodon or whatever is like marching into the bank and demanding another overdraft instead of putting your business in order. *Why* are you not sleeping? Have you asked yourself that?'

Lucy stared at her hands.

'Is there something you're worrying about?'

'I think... Well, it's just that I don't like having – oh, bad dreams. And these pills seem to stop them. That's all.'

'What sort of bad dreams?' He scribbled on her form and waited. 'Tell me about them please.'

The clock ticked loudly, and Lucy thought of the serried ranks of properly ill people waiting and coughing out there in the room at the end of the passage. 'Nothing specific – I just wake up frightened, I suppose, and can't – can't get to sleep again.'

'Do you take any exercise?'

'Yes, walking – you know, to the tube. And shopping at weekends I walk quite a bit – could try jogging, I suppose, like so many –'

He cut her short. 'More exercise; some iron: you could be a little anaemic. A hot drink last thing and, if you like, a small measure of alcohol: far better for you than sleeping pills. Come back and see me if you find you need to.'

'You mean I can't have the Mogodon?'

'That's exactly what I mean. To be dependent at your age on barbiturates is totally wrong.' Lucy got to her feet and out of the door. He called to her, 'Iron, remember; across the counter from any chemist. Next please.'

So. She would have to go to Mrs Villiers' private doctor and shell out a fiver or more for the pills, and Christ knows what for the appointment itself. There are four left, she thought: I must go before the end of the week...

When she got back, Alma was coming down the steps of Clarence Mansions. At first Lucy did not recognise her with her grey flannel coat and the umbrella, her wild hair bobbed and held off her face by a thin gold band.

'I was trying to contact you,' she said.

'How marvellous!' Lucy almost hugged her. 'Goodness, and you must be a married lady now, and back from your honeymoon – wonderful: I just needed something really nice to happen! Come in and I'll –'

'No, actually – thanks awfully, but I can't. I mean, that's really what I came to say. You see, Lucy, Walter is – Walter rather disapproves of – of odd things in my old life,' she laughed. 'He's terribly conventional. Awfully good for me really... But the whole Maisie episode – well, he wants me to put all that behind me. He's terribly keen that I should keep up my painting,' she hurried on: 'setting up a studio for me – you know – please – you mustn't think he's anti-everything – but he always saw Maisie Maturin as a bad influence, sort of... ' she laughed again. 'You know how amazingly square men can... '

'Look, do come in,' said Lucy quickly: 'just for a moment.'

'I can't. I said I was just nipping out to catch the shops before before – there's one that closes at eight, isn't there?'

'You mean he doesn't want you to... '

'That's it: you're tarred with the same – Oh Lucy... I've got to go. Don't think he's – you see, he's so good – really he is: he's sorting me out. I was very mixed up, you know – it was all a bit messy and – no: not even the pub, I'm afraid. The "spooky set" is out.'

'But Alma, *I'm* not –'

'I've got to go. Sorry, Lucy. Thanks anyway.' And she went.

Fumbling for her key Lucy felt quite cold, in spite of the heat in the lobby. There was nowhere in the kitchen to put anything down, so she dropped her bag and her shopping on the floor and poured herself a warming tot. She wished, now, in spite of the mess, that she had agreed to Sally's calling in. The excuse had been that she didn't know how long the surgery would take; but the state of the flat had been the real reason. 'I can't make it later: he's booked a table for after the show,' Sally said. 'Couldn't you go to the doctor tomorrow?'

As it was, Lucy wished she hadn't gone at all. She had drawn a blank – and, for her pains, felt six inches shorter and twice as guilty as when she went in. On her way to the sitting room, she counted the pills from the bottle in the medicine cupboard. Yes: four. Then she switched on the television and turned her attention to the twice-weekly guilts and shortcomings of the good folk of Coronation Street.

That night she lay awake longer than usual, thinking of Father Sebastian. On her way to the health centre she had caught sight of him, through the thin drizzle. He was standing in a lighted doorway talking to someone inside; and she had crossed to the other side of the road and walked quickly, head down, to escape. She was not looking her best: her macintosh needed cleaning and her scarf and hair were dank with rain. I wouldn't mind meeting him socially, as an equal, she thought: he's a very unusual and fascinating man. But I don't want him peering at me and pitying me, thanks very much... And her sensible unhurried, inner voice said, in that clear, prefect's tone (sounding rather like Gudrun, Lucy realised to her disgust): Oh come on – you just want him to find you attractive; that's all *you* want.

He had not called on her again. She hadn't expected that he would; nor – she kept telling herself – did she want him to. The memory of those brief, chilling questions still humiliated her: just when she had begun to relax in his company, sitting back, watching him, enjoying him as he explored her drawing room, he suddenly cut her down to size, made her feel childish, flustered; and her reconstructions were still full of hopelessly clever retorts.

A disturbing man, in more ways than one; and clearly he had intended to disturb her with his apparently serious suggestion that she needed help – unless, of course, the 'ghouls', as he called them, were near the mark in guessing at ulterior motives. His silent observation of the pentacle – of which she had not told them – could not have been a more effective ploy. But the pentacle was a fact; and even Lucy's healthy scepticism, her clue in the labyrinth, had ravelled a little under the continual, chafing awareness of that invisible shape lurking on her very hearth.

She did attempt to remove it; but hard scrubbing with washing-up liquid, even a dash of Vim, had no effect; and she felt absurd crouching there in the infra-red goggles, and dizzied by their distorting vision. The lines seemed to be drawn with some sort of transparent glue or paint, resistant even to white spirit – the mad logic of which cheered her somewhat – and when it dried the cleaner strips of carpet only served to remind her. She pulled the goatskin back over it. Hearty hoovering might wear it away and, moreover, could be done at arm's length. Meanwhile, though she did not know – and preferred not to know – what a pentacle signified, she avoided stepping on that place.

There was of course another way of approaching the black priest, if she really wanted to – a want that sometimes felt more like a need. The Catholic Church in her wisdom conveniently provided such an opportunity; indeed, made it a duty. There was no necessity to expose herself again to the onslaught of a sermon: that had been a mistake; but she could go to confession.

She had considered it from the time of her first visit to St Mary's: her crumb of recompense for the desolation of her discovery. Would it be wrong for a non-Catholic – and, after the excess of boarding-school religion, almost a non-believer – to kneel by that secret grille – 'Forgive me father for I have sinned'? She feared deceiving the papists far less than deceiving God. And He would know this was exploitation: a crafty way of getting within a foot of her fantasy lover... But would Father Sebastian know too?

She did go, one sunny Saturday morning. Three women were ahead of her, and taking their time. As she waited, she wondered if they too were hopeless fans of the black priest. The gentle rumble of his voice alternated with their whispered twittering. The first of them waited for the second, and they walked away together silently, rapt and careful as though they were carrying candles into a draughty world. Lucy thought of the smug, closed faces of comfortable Protestant communicants returning from the altar, and saw this was a different ball game. This was about a hunger satisfied rather than a protocol observed.

She was tiptoeing out, ashamed and unrelieved, when another priest who had been busying himself with prayer books and leaflets hailed her cheerily.

'Now don't you be giving up, my dear! There's only old Mrs O'Connor to go and she's never very long, bless her – here: have some reading matter while you're waiting. Nothing weighty: it is just about the Christmas Fair.'

Smiling awkwardly in the bright sunlight of the open door, Lucy thanked him. She was abashed by the warmth and kindliness in his broad red face; she could not be rude to him. Sitting once more on the bench near the confessional, she stared at the roneoed handout – bring-and-buy, guess the weight and win the Christmas cake – and knew she was trapped. Then she was kneeling on the hard stool, not daring to look through the grille. 'Forgive me, Father,' she muttered, 'for I have – for I'm not even a Roman Catholic.'

'Never mind,' came that voice, so close she could feel the warmth of his breath, even of his body beyond the cold metal lattice. 'Is there something you wish to tell me?'

He did not use her name and she was glad. Now she was here she wanted to be humble and anonymous, wanted only the ritual cleansing that would bring comfort. Part of her hoped, even believed, he might not recognise her: it would be like the cripple touching Jesus in a crowd and being healed. Only connect.

But now she must speak. 'Father, it's this feeling that I may have meddled with bad things – only for fun, you know. And being inquisitive. And going along with what people wanted.' She was talking low and fast, almost afraid he would speak. 'Not that I blame *them* of course but trying to call up someone

106

that – someone from another – dimension… '

'With a board?'

'Yes. All that. And also not sleeping, you know – and taking pills – relying on them rather – and then feeling run down and neglecting things. And feeling so ridiculously afraid. Not sins really, but omissions – so to speak. And. And simply not knowing what to… '

She was aware of other penitents now, rustling on the bench behind her. Then the voice of the black priest.

'These are not sins: loss of self-esteem is a simple human failing. I will not give you Hail Marys to repeat unless you wish. First you must believe in yourself, then in God. Believe in your own strength; and resist suggestion. Now look at me and listen.'

She raised her head and focused on the beautiful black mask beyond the diamond mesh – and it undid her quite. She could not concentrate on what he said. She could only think: I *am* sinning. Even as I kneel here, all so pure and humble. I'm infatuated with a priest. I'm here under false pretences, taking his time, keeping others waiting. I'm only here to be near him – so I'm deceiving everyone. Except God…

'And remember,' he was saying, 'I will always help you if things get bad.'

She nodded blindly and drew back; got to her feet, and found her way to the bright arch of the doorway.

She did not go back to St Mary's; and she seldom even visited the Clarence now. It had become such an effort, somehow. Moreover her cronies there seemed to prefer moving on to the comfortable privacy of the flat; and the kitchen cupboard housed a varied selection of bottles, the odd inch or three of many sticky liqueurs. ('One day we must mix them all together and see what happens,' said Mrs Villiers. 'Right,' said Cecil: 'like going into a pub and ordering a Top Row.')

So Lucy lay awake thinking of the priest; then got up and fetched another pill from the bathroom cupboard. No danger of my taking an overdose anyway, she thought, staring at the last two lying in her palm. Tomorrow was Thursday. Friday, or Saturday at the latest, she must go along to that private chap of Mrs V's.

On Saturday morning she made herself get out of bed when the alarm went, looked up the address in the *A-Z* and walked towards Campden Hill to find it. A picture-book nurse answered the bell. 'Oh dear no,' she said: 'there's never a surgery on a Saturday.'

'Couldn't he see me if it's urgent?' Lucy pleaded.

'The doctor goes away for the weekend. Always. I do believe there's a clinic place – a health centre – somewhere down near that big Catholic church.'

'Thank you.' Lucy turned away miserably.

Mrs Villiers and Estelle were out when she called at the maisonette. This is ridiculous, she thought walking home, hungry and cold: I'm like a junkie worrying about the next fix – I *can't* be that dependent on the bloody things. But early in the evening she went across to the Clarence.

'Aha!' said Dr Max: 'The prodigal daughter! What will you have, dear girl?'

'I won't, thanks: I'm not staying. I was just looking for Mrs Villiers.' She thought: now, *he's* a doctor... And then: no – I don't want any pills from him. I can't be that desperate.

'She'll be in later,' said Cecil. 'Aren't we all ganging up at your place, then?'

'Fine,' said Lucy. 'Super. See you over there.' If she rang Mrs Villiers now she might catch her...

'We were just on our way to the Clarence, Lucy dear; and then on to Maisie's flat – if you feel you'd like us?'

'Of course,' said Lucy: 'I was expecting you. Mrs Villiers, you know those sleeping pills; d'you think you could spare me some of yours? I've rather foolishly let myself run out. I just wanted to catch you before –'

'Ooh dear – now, do I have any? Estelle was on them recovering from her bug, you know – and then of course I should keep a few for emergencies. I'll just go and see.'

Lucy found herself holding her breath.

'No, dear: we seem to be – oh, wait a mo: Estelle's got a couple put away. Is that all, Estelle? My goodness, you did (mumble-mumble). Two, dear. I'll bring them over, all right? Aster le vister, as my lovely waiter used to – yes, dear, I will. There, they're safely in my handbag.'

The general opinion seemed to be that Lucy was looking extra radiant this evening. 'Living here seems to suit you, dear,' said Mrs Villiers.

Lucy, still trying to bring some order to the kitchen – she had hoovered the sitting room and cleared away the ashtrays when she knew they were coming – caught snatches of a running conversation. 'Well, she's so strong in herself, you see.' That was how it started; and she escaped to the sink: she suspected they were talking about her again. It was a bad habit they had, as though she couldn't hear or understand. She did not enjoy being treated like a child – even a spoilt and favoured one.

'Oh, and fatal for the truly prone… ' Mrs Villiers was saying now: 'they grow thinner – fade, sort of.'

'And there's the thirst,' said Dr Max.

'Well! And that's what reminded me! Fading, thirsty, burning eyes, can't sleep.'

'That one blamed it on the cold-cures, remember?' Estelle's voice.

'Or the booze,' said Cecil. 'You know: so thirsty, must have another.'

'That's right,' said Mrs Villiers. 'And they feel the cold terribly: can't get warm. *She* used to complain her extremities were numb – ooh Dr Max! You are terrible!'

'Mark you, dear lady, that young woman was just eaten up with self-concern, totally absorbed by her own – quite: and pooh-poohed all *my* warnings, you know.'

'*I* wondered if it could have been tuberculosis or something,' said Estelle: 'you remember, that feverish sort of hungry look when we saw her, only the day before she flitted off?'

'TB?' said Cecil. 'Aargh, moi deario! And fearsome sexy it

makes you, so they do say! There's whole movies all about that.'

'Oh indeed: "Now is all we have", and emotions running high – the white-walled clinic, the snow-clad mountains, and those unnaturally flushed cheeks – not you, my dear Lucy: never fear! We were thinking how lovely you looked.'

'But there was a young woman here,' said Estelle, 'was it last winter, or the one before? A sort of lodger really: Maisie was only gone a fortnight, remember?'

'Did she leave suddenly?' Lucy asked, setting out the clean ashtrays.

'Yes, dear, she did, as a matter of fact; not that you'd –'

'The agent told me, Mrs Villiers,' said Lucy. 'He mentioned that she was a bad tenant – seemed glad to get her out. She tried to change things round; broke something.'

'Oh, she didn't fit – did she? Didn't really belong like you do dear. Well now, what's the choice this evening, Cecil? – Ooh, and the Doctor's got a half of *crème de menthe*!'

Sunday was chiefly taken up with waking late and then trying to stay awake. Lucy felt she did not have the energy to get the papers: later perhaps. Then she decided it was too late: they would have run out; they might even be closed.

She should be washing up, making her bed with fresh sheets, according to her strict routine, and getting clothes ready for the week. But more important than any of these was the need to stay awake, in order to ensure she did not lie awake tonight. At some time in the small hours of last night she had taken the second of Mrs Villiers' Mogodons: now she had none.

She knew very well she shouldn't have kept it in the bedroom. If she'd put it away in the bathroom cabinet, at least it would have been a matter of getting up and going along the passage to get it. But she knew it was there in the pocket of the kaftan, Mrs M.'s that she had been wearing; and at the lowest moment of the night, waking and lying awake – not even for very long – she had despaired, and reached out for it where it lay on the chair.

Now she regretted it bitterly. Leaden-limbed and heavy-eyed she stared at the dust, and the small sticky glasses dotted round the drawing room. I'll be wide awake later, she thought: I'll make short work of that lot – maybe listen to Afternoon Theatre with it and it'll take no time at all; and I'll sort out the bedroom. Then she remembered Estelle: 'You'll like the film matinée, Lucy: an old Greer Garson movie.' 'Ah yes indeed: a collector's piece,' the Doctor judged it: 'marvellously naïve, these early masterpieces – almost folk art, now, with all the old tabus intact: brave little women, unspoken passions…'

Cracks of afternoon sun, thin as thieves' torchlight, fingered slowly round the curtained drawing room, touching the dusty glasses and ashtrays on the small tables, on the top of the television set, as Lucy watched the little women being brave. She may have dozed, but the background music alerted her to the important moments. It was nearly dark when she found she had finished the cigarettes. That got her out; and at least, she thought, dragging a comb through her tangled hair, at least I've stayed up all day.

When she got back she made herself some lunch/tea and started to organise her clothes. At some point she must go shopping for a new skirt; must get her mac cleaned, and her coat. Sorted out, her clutch of respectable outfits took up very little space in her half of the generous wardrobe, compared with the crowded and colourful rack next to them. What else did Mother Maturin have to offer? she wondered, rifling through them; and if one borrowed the odd scarf or dressing-gown, would she have minded?

No: she might be rather flattered, Lucy thought, from what the others said about her. 'Make free,' she would have said, laughing the while, pixie glasses twinkling, 'feel *chez vous*, dear.' Imagining her, Lucy sensed, as always, that tremor of repulsion, a faint echo of her first encounter with the flat – its decor, the smell, the absent presence. Then, she would not have dreamed she might make use of these alien clothes: the sheets were strange enough. Now, her familiarity was just part of the forced intimacy with this landlady she had never met;

111

and she accepted it. As for the received idea that borrowing clothes was 'not done', she quickly dismissed that as a childhood convention; and tried on a sort of Tunisian dirndl skirt. Even cobbled together with safety pins, it was too lumpy and would not do; but the dark varuna wool dress, when firmly belted, and falling in soft paisley folds over her tall boots, was rather dashing: the layered look. She might carry it off, even at work, with lots of make-up, a bangle or two – if only as a contrast to Margaret Cutebutt.

The bedroom was in even more of a mess now; but it was time to switch on the Sunday film: a James Bond she had already seen, but entertaining, wideawake stuff; not to be missed. Then there was something after that – there must be; and about eleven-thirty she should go to bed. Aspirins might work: and she could move in here, just this once, so that the late TV, whatever it was, would mask the cooling noises while she fell asleep...

Lucy woke to the thin scream of the empty box. She switched it off. She was cold and stiff and hungry. The clicking cupboard was like a time bomb as she hunted round the kitchen for something to eat: stale bread – no time for toast – and a small tin of *paté de foie gras* left by her landlady: the sort of thing that, like veal, Lucy normally refused to eat on principle. She took it into the sitting room, with a half-tumbler of whisky – doctor's orders – and had a midnight feast at the round table with Capital Radio for company. But the flat was getting very cold; she ate hurriedly and left the tray there, unable to face the messy kitchen and the ticking beechwood again. I must get a grip on myself, she thought, looking round and turning out the lights: this place is a tip. And now it seemed not merely sluttish, but 'wet and weedy' (taunts from childhood fitted: she was behaving like a scared kid) to camp here in the smoky drawing room for fear of something creeping in through the bedroom door. Four aspirins, into bed, lights out.

Waking with all the old unremembered terror, and no great god Mogodon to hold her down, Lucy found herself out of

112

bed, shivering, heart thudding. She felt the hard glass edge of the dressing table top behind her as she stood staring through the dark at the bed, knowing that something was there.

Something was nearly visible: lumpy blackness with a dull reddish glow. Now it was a question of pulling open the curtains without turning her back on it. She allowed herself a brief glance over her shoulder – but something was there behind her too; and she spun round to see the spinning shape in the dressing table mirror: purple shadow and, pale above it, a frightened face – her own, with Mrs Maturin's gown that she'd kept on for warmth. She reached across for the edge of the curtain and twitched it back, then stood close against it, very still, gazing at the bed.

Pale squares of street light, webbed and crackled by the bare branches it shone through, lay across the rumpled bedclothes. The lumpy black thing that glowed red was not there. All she could see now was a wide deep hollow where the quilt was pressed down: pressed down into tight wrinkles, she saw as she went closer; and she watched those wrinkles shift and alter, disappearing, and others emerging as the indentation moved.

It takes a sort of lateral thinking to assess the shape of an object from the space it makes, particularly in the half-dark. Lucy was not thinking; she was moving, laterally, round the bed, as far from it as she could. Always facing it, watching the gentle shifting of that wide dark hollow, she waded through the lower darkness in the room until she stood against the wardrobe, suddenly terribly visible in the slice of street light, and having to move on. Edging steadily and silently towards the door, she became aware that her legs were impeded down there in the deep shadow of the high bed: not simply by feeling her way in darkness, but by some soft heavy pressure that dragged at her feet and skirts, a nightmare sand that hugged and sucked at her ankles. She was forced to take her eyes off the bed and look down, and in the black she saw the dull red again, a moving outline of heaping coils, slowly shimmering as it moved. She stopped, frozen; the eiderdown still crept and shifted at the edge of her vision. Then she threw herself towards the door, dragging up her feet to step high, fast, and out. And there it was all along the passage, barely visible where the wall lamp shed a little thick light, but further along in the blackness towards the kitchen, a sort of rumpled reddish motion, sluggish, like a cooling lava flow.

Now she was in the sitting room, with all the lights on, pushing a small heavy table across the door. She had no blanket; but she crawled in under the musty fur that covered the sofa, and pulled it round her. She lay there with the lights on, staring at the ceiling, wishing she had the radio for comfort. She tried to breathe evenly, tried to be sensible and think about what she had seen, what she had felt.

If these were the images of hysteria, they were quite extraordinarily precise. OK, so the light from the street lamp was dim and far away, filtered through branches and dirty window panes and net curtains; but she had drawn near and watched those shifting creases long enough to know it was not just a big, squashy quilt settling down after her own hurried getaway. Then there was the preposterous *size* of the shape she had glimpsed in the dark before the street light dispelled it – but that was absurd and not to be used in evidence – that lumpy glowing black-red shape that had seemed to obscure much of the paler wall and wardrobe opposite. No: she would not even think about it, for that way madness lay.

But there was one other thing she had seen, and remembered now, and tried to make sense of. From her position by the window, she observed a line above the bed, hanging up there in the darkness where the slanting street light did not reach. It was as surprising as those glimpses of pinkish clouds floating above a Mediterranean landscape, and that only a double-take reveals as the distant peaks of unimaginably high mountains. This pinky sunset glow hanging over Mrs Maturin's bed, only a foot or so below the frilly canopy, was, Lucy realised, very like the upper edge of some lumpy mountain range – except that, as she saw when she replayed it in her head, it moved, piling and sinking, an action-replay of waves.

I won't think about it, she decided. She lay thinking about it, cold under the dead animal's stiff skin, until she dozed and woke – almost immediately, it seemed – to the roar of the boiler and the swift, sharp clicking of a new day. She curled up tightly, and slept.

It was after ten o'clock when she woke again. She got over to the telephone and rang Lees-Langham to say she was ill. It was almost true; she felt shivery and exhausted, without even the energy to pull back the curtains or tidy the room. Smoke and black coffee seemed all she could face; but later on she made herself turn out the lights, let in the daylight, then sit down at the table and write out a list of priorities. Things have gone too far, she told herself sternly: I must have a plan of action; and tomorrow, when I'm better, I'll start to carry it out, item by item.

1. Tidy, clean, and get flat straight.
2. Advertise for lodger.
3. Open cupboard (jemmy?) and
4. Put in all Mrs M's creepy objects, photos etc.
5. Scrub carpet by hearth (solvent? chemist?).
6. Get to know nice people (evening classes? Young Conservatives?)
7. Entertain them.

I NEED TO ENJOY/MAKE USE OF THIS GOOD FLAT.

She was still wearing the purple dressing-gown; and she slept all through the afternoon, waking disoriented to a black and glassy sky. There was enough street light through the two windows to show her where she was by the table in the bay window. There was her list, her ashtray, her coffee cup; beyond them, the glint of the gilt frame on the shrine-table, shelves of dark and shiny ornaments, the slick of satin cushions, the familiar shapes of sofa and chairs, and the bulky seated figure of Mrs Maturin.

Chapter Seven

SHE KNEW RIGHT away that it was Mrs Maturin by the glasses glinting in the gloom, the high-piled hair, and by her fatness ('dear Maisie always had a weight problem'); clothed, not in a flowing robe, as Lucy always imagined her, but awkwardly in a large pale travelling suit, her handbag on her knee. She was perching in front of the fireplace on the straightbacked chair they only used when there was a crowd; and she held herself very upright, looking towards Lucy, her body turned and her legs arranged in an elegant pose that her size, and the situation, together rendered absurdly formal; grotesque.

Lucy said: 'Mrs Maturin?', and reached out for the switch of the standard lamp. 'I'm so sorry – I must have been asleep when you… ' Close to her, the light was blinding for a moment. She stood up stiffly and took a step forward, peering into the sudden darkness of the room beyond. 'I didn't know you… ' But there was no one there.

'Mrs Maturin?' She stared at the chair, then all round the room. She crossed rapidly to the door, switched on the wall brackets and stood there, cold with disbelief. She knew she should go over to the chair, look to see if… Would the small satin cushion be moving, like the quilt last night?

How long she stood there she did not know, hugging herself against the deep cold, her feet icy in socks and slippers, until she became aware of the heat of the radiator behind her in the passage. The flat was warm: there was sweat on her forehead and trickling down her spine. She remembered now it was being so cold that had half-awakened her; she had pulled the rug back over herself and dozed again; then became aware of the black glass window beside her, the street light in her eyes, and wondered where she was. That was when she had sat up and seen…

Shakily she returned to the table, safe ground. She drained the half cup of cold black coffee, and looked at her watch: after five o'clock. Someone must know where her travelling landlady was meant to be… She switched on the lamp by the telephone and, standing facing towards the small stiff chair on the hearth, she rang the agents. She got straight through to Mr Cornfield. He was impatient, just leaving. No, they had no notification of their client's early return; had she? Then why should she anticipate a change in plan? She had not actually seen Mrs Maturin? Ah: she might have done. And what did 'not exactly' mean? So, she hadn't seen her… But why should she think something might be wrong with their client? Oh. He saw. Just a feeling… No, if people wanted to contact their client, they could write, care of the agents, and they would forward it. No, they were not permitted to pass on an address: that would constitute a breach of privacy. No, no actual exchanges with Mrs Maturin to date; the agency was simply banking her rent and forwarding letters, sent to them by arrangement with the Post Office: that was the agency's brief. 'Look, really, Miss – You know, you short-term tenants give us more trouble than – first there was some imaginary electrical fault, then a window that wouldn't lock – all right, windows – then something about a funny smell –'

Lucy rang off and tried to think. She must get a hold on herself. Now, I'm definitely not psychic, she said: I'm not that sort of person; but I think I've seen a ghost – not a ghost, but the image, the facsimile, of a living person I've never met. A person who shouldn't be here: who *can't* be here – so I *can't* have seen it – her. Does this mean I'm going mad?

Now, if I imagined her, why did I see her like that? Her memory of Mrs Maturin was underlit, but it was very definite: piled-up hair, not in shining coils but a stiff, pale, lightless nest like candy-floss – and the shine had been on the pointed glasses, so that Lucy could not see her eyes, and on the heavy clasp of her handbag, like a letter, C or G. The good suit, sub-Chanel, the skirt cut a little too narrow and a little too short for those legs and thighs. And the posed look, rather tense, head up, the darkly lipsticked mouth not smiling as in the...

The photograph. Posed, like the photograph. She went to the shrine picked up the gilt frame and held it in the light. A lot of her information was there; the things she had changed must have come to her, 'found objects' – like you get in dreams, she thought, surprising yourself with your own ingenuity. Not smiling; encased in a suit, clutching a precisely imagined handbag: Lucy saw she had invented a Mrs Maturin just back from her travels, as she would be; and that perched look – the same position, the same twist of the body. It had been coquettish in the picture of that hotel lounge, but Lucy's subconscious had made it more tense; unsmiling, looking straight forward, staring – *unseeing* – at Lucy, waiting: a woman ready for a journey, clutching her bag, waiting for her taxi.

I've created an instant ghost: Mrs Maisie Maturin as she would have been in her last moments in this flat. I've used the photograph, reclothed her, sat her on a chair and placed her on precisely that spot. But the chair...

For the chair was still there, standing empty and very oddly out of place in the middle of the hearth rug. It had not been there this morning; and Lucy had not put it there.

The nearest people were the girls upstairs. Lucy went through into Mrs Maturin's mauve bedchamber, picked up some clothes and dressed herself quickly in the bathroom. She needed people: she was thinking in circles. She was thinking: if I did put the chair there, over the pentacle, and I've forgotten – or put it there in a sort of trance, unaware – then I'm going mad. But if I didn't put it there, then somebody else did: it wasn't there when I went to sleep. So – which is worse, going mad, or actually seeing a ghost (who can move chairs), or someone being about in the flat (a real person? or a thing that can move a quilt, press down the edge of a bed, and so, move

118

chairs?); someone or something about in this flat besides me?

She stood outside their door on the first floor landing even after she knew no one was in. It was too early: they hadn't come home yet. What about the caretaker, Mrs Dortmund? She lived two floors up: a square red-faced lady with several cats. Her small sad husband 'had a back', Lucy was told when she contacted them about the suitcase. Mrs Dortmund was neither helpful nor friendly then; but Mrs Maturin might have written to her, or even sent her a postcard, telling of a change in her plans. At worst, it was something to do to postpone going back into that flat.

'What is it? Speak up, do!' The door opened only a crack on its short chain, revealing a section of broad red frowning face and, beyond, a flickering screen, a blare of sound. 'Oh, you from No 2, are you? Don't remember you – can't keep up with all the subs that come and go. The suitcase – oh, I remember. So, what's the matter now? Oh do speak up, girl! What? No – I wouldn't know, would I? I mean, I'm only the caretaker. What? No: you telephone the agents, Cornfield and Thingy – course it's too late now. Here – you all right? *What?* That's it – you ring the agents then.' And the door closed. Am I like that when someone calls in the middle of a TV programme? Lucy wondered dully; and what now?

She thought of ringing Mrs Villiers, but she still felt unable to face the sitting room. Better to go round there anyway. Her coat was just inside the hall of the flat; she opened the door, reached it and her bag off the coat pegs, closed the door – gently, for some reason – dressed in the lobby, and went out. Walking briskly at first to get herself moving, she found she was too weak: her knees felt rubbery and her breath came in little gasps as though she had been running. She walked slowly concentrating on controlling what she knew was simple hysteria. You're not ill and you're not mad. One breath to two paces...

Mrs Villiers' curtains were drawn and light showed between them, but no one came to the door. A window opened in the flat above. 'Yoo-hoo down there! They're out, I'm afraid.' It was a big lady in a polo neck and dungarees. 'Gorn to the vets,

119

you know. That chihuahua's got the collywobbles it seems.'

'Thanks,' said Lucy. 'No, no message.' And she turned away.

They were nice little houses round here: Victorian semis with stained glass in the doors. Only a street away, Alma's Walter had bought just such a house and done it up 'regardless', said Mrs Villiers when she pointed it out; 'That's why they were engaged so long: he likes everything just so.' Lucky old Alma, thought Lucy, with such strong protection, *and* double-glazing, to shelter her from harm: getting rid of your past – if you can – must seem a small price to pay for that sort of security. Here am I: and what price my precious independence now? Not yet six weeks in my own big, warm, comfortable flat, and I'm walking the streets trying to find someone to talk to. But even Walter, surely, would respond to a *cri de coeur*? She walked more briskly, summoning up a smile, the right words, to seem sane and pleasant, and only a little anxious.

'Oh – Lucy! Goodness, I – It's just Lucy, darling,' Alma called over her shoulder; then she snibbed the lock and stepped outside into the porch, smiling and shivering in her pale wool dress.

'Alma, help me!' said Lucy desperately, holding on to the cold iron railings. 'Could I talk to you and Walter just for a moment? I wouldn't... '

Walter appeared in the doorway. 'What is it, dear? Don't stand out there in the –'

'Oh Walter, it's Lucy, and she's not well – she needs our help – please?'

'Come in then, Lucy; we've got a moment before friends are due to arrive.' He ushered them in past him and closed the door. 'What seems to be the matter, then?'

All her carefully prepared and reasonable openings left her: she knew now, facing Walter, that everything she needed to say was concerned with precisely those people, those problems, from which he had so ruthlessly cut Alma free. Even to mention Mrs Maturin in order to ask if Alma had had any word from her, if something could be amiss with her – and was it possible to see the ghost of – ? No.

Walter watched her as she turned from one to the other gasping wordlessly. Probably a nice enough girl, he thought, *au fond*, and certainly good-looking under the messy hair and smudged eye make-up; but gone wrong, away from her roots and her parents' firm hand. She had lost self-respect – that pillar of his faith – and was treating herself badly, just as she was treating her good tweed coat (a button dangling, he observed, and its belt trailing from one loop onto the ground). 'Get her a drink of water, dear,' he said. He pulled forward a hard elegant hall chair. 'Sit down and get yourself together,' he said. He lowered his voice. 'Please try not to upset my – Alma more than you have already. Quite delicately balanced, you know – and now that I've got her to feel more – ah, thank you, my dear. Just sip it slowly, Lucy. Now, what is it?'

'It's – it's the flat,' said Lucy, eyes down. 'It's something – in that flat. I've seen – I've… Well – I can't – go back.' She looked up and caught Walter's frown, his tiny shake of the head. 'Oh, I wouldn't dream of asking you to…' She got up quickly, holding out the glass. 'Thank you – I feel better, just talking to real people, I mean.' Outside there were steps and voices; the doorbell rang loud and close. 'I'll sort it out,' said Lucy, pulling her belt round her. 'Thank you – for seeing me.'

'But Lucy,' said Alma.

'Sure you're all right then?' Walter was smiling a firm, fleshy smile, his first as far as Lucy was concerned; his hand was heavy on her shoulder. 'Fine: that's the spirit.'

'And you must come round sometime,' said Alma quickly – 'when we have a house-warming or something.'

Now Walter had the door open. Cries of recognition and upper-crust delight came from the couple on the doorstep, tempered by sideways glances at the white-faced girl being ushered out – but no, one didn't know her and clearly didn't need to. 'Caroline! Jonathan! Great,' cried Walter in answer. 'No, of *course* you're not early – Lucy's just going so I won't introduce – All right, Lucy?' But Lucy had gone.

When she got back to the square it was after opening time. Two cars swept past her and drew up at the Clarence; she walked close to the railings of the gardens, brushing against the wet laurels that overhung them. From here she had a clear view of her drawing room windows, the curtains half open, and the dull warm glow of the lights inside. If she went in, would she see it again?

What would Walter have done, if he had decided to espouse her cause? (Be positive; bitterness gets you nowhere; let some of that cool survival instinct rub off on you.) He would rule out the 'ghost' scenario immediately; either Lucy was imagining things, or she had seen Mrs Maturin or someone like her. Next: an intruder would have left by now, but her landlady would, presumably, stay; so, search the flat. Odd behaviour, after all, was what one might expect from Mrs Maisie Maturin, Walter would point out.

Surely he was right: she might have crouched down beyond the sofa, or moved in behind the heavy curtains of the side window; Lucy had not even crossed the room to see. Now she could be hiding in the wardrobe, or the spare room – a far-fetched idea maybe, but the evaporation theory was simply absurd. She was a wildly eccentric lady who might well play pranks; might stage a dramatic, unplanned return, to emerge with even greater effect when all her cronies were gathered together.

This was not impossible; and Lucy decided she had been wrong not to think of it, and check. After all, No 2 was, for the time being, her flat, and the sudden appearance of her landlady sitting there in the semi-dark constituted an intrusion, however whimsical; an infringement that the sub-let should stand up to, good-humouredly, even heartily – but certainly not flee from. Why, it could even be deliberate harassment in order to get the sublet to leave. And Lucy knew she should be in there now, turning on all the lights, searching every room. She could get one of the girls down to go round with her – no, perhaps not, after the hairclip incident: she had barely seen them since.

Only the 'ghouls' remained. Lucy turned her steps towards the Clarence.

She bought herself a small whisky and took it through into the lounge bar to find Mrs Villiers, or perhaps Charles Vesey, or even Dermot. Only Cecil was there, leaning on the bar with two nicely suited, upstanding young men, the first of the commuters, and probably too young for wives and warmed slippers.

'Just a small one then,' Cecil was saying. 'Oh! Thanks, squire – if you're twisting my arm. Well, well, well – if it isn't the lovely Lucy herself, begorra! Come and join the early birds, dear girl: this is, er – Angus, and – Anyway, meet our Lucinda: Miss Clarence Square, by my vote – tomorrow, the Universe, what? A drink for the lady – ah, you're already equipped.'

The pink-cheeked, short-haired Angus and his companion with the small blond moustache saw the evening definitely looking up when the girl joined them; but they began to exchange glances when, after the barest of civilities, peculiar questions started tumbling out of that appealingly curly mouth: a mouth designed for laughing at jokes, to say the least – and absolutely not for all this funny stuff about some batty landlady she was getting her knickers in a twist over. But that's what was going on: Did this reporter chap know what Mrs Thing was up to? What was she really like? Was she ill, did he know? Cancer or anything? Had anyone actually heard from her? Had he? Would he know, for example, if anything had happened to her – like an accident? Well, who would? And then, if you please, she demanded a cigarette – no 'thank yous', no response to the old hand-contact that Willy invested in a Ronson for – oh no. Shaking like a bloody leaf, this luscious up-tight bird comes out with, 'Listen: do you think you can see, well – ghosts – you know, images – of people that are still alive? See them, I mean, when they're actually far away and perfectly OK?'

Hearty laughter was no longer enough to hide the young stockbrokers' embarrassment; their instinct, not only for social niceties – the precise moment of having gone too far – but for self-preservation, was well-trained and simultaneous. In unison, and perfectly smoothly, they swivelled sixty degrees: 'Saw old Hugo the other day –' 'I was just going to say, what news of old Hugo –'

(And it wasn't just the tousled maiden with her landlady-fixation that bothered them: it was the spectacle of this newspaper johnny, Cyril or something, egging her on. He was thrilled. Dammit, he was positively licking his chops. 'No, dear girl – but, tell me: did you see something? You've actually seen something, haven't you? Did it come near? Tell me now, did it – did it touch you – or anything?')

Lucy focused on Cecil's face. He wasn't answering her questions, wasn't really listening. She put down her glass unfinished; he grabbed at her sleeve, and she turned and left quickly.

Outside she breathed the clean, cold air and looked across to the rosy oblongs of light, the nice warm flat she could not make herself go back to. Why hadn't she just asked Cecil and those other people to come across with her and help flush out the – the intruder? Because she knew there was no one there.

Then she saw someone waiting on the corner by the gardens; and now he was crossing over towards her: a dark, slender man huddled up in a big scarf – and she recognised the pale poetic forehead, the black wing of hair. It was the young man from the magic shop. She had thought him sympathetic and interesting and rather romantic, like a younger, leaner Oscar Wilde, wittily turning the Doctor's taunts so that they all laughed. And then there was more laughter later, against him, it seemed, when he went off, just before they came into the flat. She had almost forgotten him: she used to hope he would come back; and she meant to go into the magic shop – quite a serious and high-minded emporium of the occult, according to Cecil – but the black priest, and her own worries, had driven everything else from her mind. Now she smiled, and went forward to meet him.

He did not return her smile. He came up close to her; his eyes were very wide, his pallid face shining moon-white as he lifted his mouth and chin from the folds of the thick scarf. 'I've been trying to find you,' he said. 'It was imperative to tell you something – but you see, I couldn't cross that threshold. Listen to me. *She* has gone.'

'But how extraordinary! You see, she's just –'

124

'*She* has gone: *It* has not. Believe me, please. And you mustn't stay there.' He looked feverish and mad. His shifting eyes fixed suddenly on something over her shoulder; she turned quickly to see, and when she looked back he was already across the road and hurrying away.

Wetlips Cecil was following her, dragging on his coat as he came.

Lucy crossed quickly to where a small lane led through in the direction of the shops, and started walking up it. She heard footsteps behind her, glanced over her shoulder and saw he was following her. She walked faster, comforted by the distant lights of the police station at the far end; then she heard him break into a run. He would catch up easily before they reached the distant blue lamp; she took her hands out of her pockets and forced herself into a run, stumbling wearily on the cobbles.

There was no one else in sight, and only the high walls of back gardens on one side and the bleak cliffs of supermarket warehouses, locked garages and timber yards on the other. She had neither time nor energy to consider she might be over-reacting, or to remind herself she had gone into the pub to enlist help. A ferret face that licked its lips, eyes that knew more than she did, a sharp nose sniffing the danger that was closing on her, and relishing that smell – these were all she could see. She ran from a prurient eagerness as menacing now, it seemed, as the unnamed horror that shared her flat; and she drove her heavy feet and aching lungs in a desperation to escape. And at last she saw and knew that, once she was past those dustbins, she could reach the blue light before he caught her.

At the same moment she heard him slow to a striding walk. He might be giving up; if he didn't, should she go on into the police station? What could she say? 'A man has been chasing me'? He would simply follow her in and explain. 'I'm a friend, officer: I was only trying to catch up, but she seemed to take fright – must have thought it was some naughty stranger!' Nor could the law help her with her haunted flat.

There was now only one person who might.

She would have to keep going. She walked fast, trying to catch her breath, and turned the corner by the shops. He was still behind her: he had not given up; but now there were other people around, late shoppers or workers nearing home. She kept on up towards the High Street, and stopped for a moment by a shop window to rest and to glance back.

He was still there, following a little way behind; he could have caught up, but now he did not choose to. Walking on as briskly as she could and heading for the busy main street, she could feel his sticky wet eyes fastened on her back – more like a mouth: like a huge leech clinging between her shoulder-blades where she could not reach it, draining her of blood. Faintly and far away the prefect voice of good sense told her she was being fanciful; that if she stopped, or walked back to him and said, 'Cecil, thanks – but I'm off to see some friends; let's meet in the pub tomorrow for a good talk about all this: I'd like to hear your theories.' But it did not have a chance: she was just a scared and weary body driven by pure repulsion. The single clear thought still glimmered: find a phone box...

Evening crowds were flowing round her now; she looked back and could not see him, but kept on till she reached the cinema. There were queues, one right out onto the pavement, and people standing about inside buying sweets and hot-dogs and hailing one another. It was tempting to go in, buy a ticket, and sit in that safe darkness gazing at an even larger screen than her own; to lose herself – and him, surely: it was the classic, the time-honoured way to disappear. Then she saw him nearby, very close, studying a poster, watching her.

She pushed through the doors into the foyer; out of the corner of her eye she saw him follow. She slid quickly through the thick queue, round the box office, through the other queue and out of the far door; ran across the street, weaving between slowly-moving cars, and on towards the old Town Hall where she knew there were two telephone kiosks in an alley. She ran steadily, a sort of shambling jog, determined not to look behind her. She found she had to slow down; she hid in a shoe-shop doorway to rest, then ran on again.

The phone boxes were empty. Safe inside the further one, and masked from the High Street, she fumbled in her bag, praying the card was still there. She found it in the compartment of her purse where she kept her library ticket and the old credit note she was planning how to spend, if it wasn't too out of date – she would have to deal with that some time... Gathering her thoughts, and clearing her throat, she rang the Jesuits.

'Alas no: Father Sebastian is not with us at this moment. Nor likely to be all evening, I gather – pastoral duties, you know. Perhaps a message would – ?'

Hastily she put down the phone and dialled the other number. It seemed to ring for ever; then an odd, rather high-pitched, foreign voice answered, pronouncing the number clearly and slowly. 'Can I be of assistance?'

'Oh – I'm sorry,' said Lucy: 'I'm not even sure if I've got the right – I'm looking for – for the priest, Father Sebastian.'

'He is here. I inform him. May I enquire who is speaking? And can you hold, Miss Morrand?'

Waiting, ready with another coin, Lucy heard the sounds of a party, and a loud burst of music and laughter. Pastoral duties? Who *was* this man, this self-styled troubleshooter?

The party noises were cut off by a closing door. 'Lucy? Can you come straight round? Take a taxi; never mind the fare: my manservant will deal with that. And you needn't write down the address; you will remember it: number ten Eaton Gardens. Lucy? Are you... ? Good; and you'll come right here, now? See you soon.'

He had not asked her what she wanted or even if anything were wrong. And then she became aware of someone in the next phone box. It was Cecil, his face pressed against the glass like a jugged hare.

She grabbed her bag, pushed open the heavy door and ran, turned right to face the oncoming traffic and kept running along the pavement till she saw the lighted crest of a free taxi. The most beautiful sight she had ever set eyes on, it seemed at that moment: the first glimpse of the pearly gates will be just like this, she thought wildly – a tiny rectangle of warm lights floating nearer and nearer, and swooping in gracefully towards your faltering feet – 'I want to go to... '

Cecil stepped off the pavement behind her. She got through the open door and slammed it. 'Go *on!*' she cried. The cab pulled smartly away.

'Damsel in distress, eh?' said the driver over his shoulder. 'Your lucky day, darlin': there's not another cab for him in sight. Where to, then?'

'Number ten Eaton Gardens – wherever that is. Please.'

'That's Belgravia, Miss. Ever so posh, that is.'

'Well, it's only a parish priest I'm going to see,' she went on, her voice coming more easily now; and it was such luxury simply to chatter ordinarily to an ordinary person, almost as if she'd been abroad. 'Anyway, whatever it's like, that's the address he gave me.'

'Funny sort of priest,' said the taxi man.

It was a tall, elegant house in a cul-de-sac rimmed with Rollses – or so it seemed to Lucy. She paid off the taxi: she did not want the priest's charity; just his advice, and, incidentally, the pleasure of seeing him again. She wondered how she looked.

'Party is it?' The cabbie grinned broadly and rolled his eyes as he handed her the change. 'Well, I've heard of pennies from heaven – but this is something else! Have fun, duckie; and if you can't be good, be careful.'

Lucy caught sight of herself in the window as he rolled it up, and realised that her dishevelled looks must be partly to blame for his hearty disbelief. She waited until he had reversed noisily out of sight, then took a comb from her bag and dealt with her tangled hair as best she could, tucking the wild ends into her turned-up collar. She buttoned and belted her coat; found her little mirror and peered at her smudged face under a street lamp. Licking a paper handkerchief and wiping away the worst of the wandering mascara was about all she could do. Then she walked up the steps and rang the bell.

A Chinese manservant opened the door, paused for a moment to look for the taxi, and said: 'Miss Morrand? This way prease.' He led her through a wide marble-tiled hall and through an open door into a room full of people.

Dazzled, appalled, and – she prayed – invisible, Lucy followed him; aware, in passing, of a roulette table, of cards, bright lips, tall men, loud voices and shrill laughter, a waiter with a tray standing aside to let them through, the wail of a jazz trombone; then they were in an echoing passage lined with paintings. She saw a floodlit garden through galleried windows, and suddenly found herself in a big, silent library.

'The Father's study, Miss Morrand. You wait here, prease.'

'His – his study?' she said. 'Is this his house?'

'Oh yes, Miss Morrand: it berong to him. Now I inform him you are alived.' The great mahogany door shut noiselessly behind him.

Lucy stared about her, very small and full of wonder like the metamorphosed Alice. Immensely high uncurtained windows looked along the length of the garden to the roomful of party people, colourful and crowded, gesturing and shouting silently in the distance. Between these casements, and filling the other walls, were bookshelves, topped under the coved ceiling with a row of marble busts. Over the fireplace and in two alcoves were pictures, the dark gold of icons, and glass shelves of small bronzes and chinese bowls and carved wooden figures: few and choice. A tapestry was draped over an old-fashioned wing chair, and fine rugs covered most of the polished floor; but otherwise the furnishing was modern: the classiest of high-tech – soft blue-grey leather and gleaming chrome and black glass. Logs burned brightly in the fireplace.

Lucy sat down near it on the edge of a deep leather chair. For the first time in that long, strange day she seemed to be at rest, with time, and growing calm, to think again; to take in and understand where she was and what she was doing. She took off her coat, smoothed down her hair, tucked in her pullover, and held out her cold hands to the blaze. You are waiting, she told herself carefully, in a very grand study, across a garden from a gambling den, to tell a black Catholic priest about the ghost of a fat lady who is on holiday in South Africa. And he is a rather unusual priest (she had to smile at that): a mysterious priest. This is his house. (His manservant had told her; why should he lie?) You're in Father Sebastian's house, in

129

his study, waiting to see him.

And she gazed round at his ancient books, his gilded icons, his computer, his video; at the glowing rugs, the brutal silver-and-glass beauty of the huge desk, the mellow Roman busts – and thought, with that saving sanity to which she still clung: 'Humble West Indian' my foot.

Chapter Eight

UNIFORMS ATTRACT; AND certainly the black soutane had been
mightily impressive. But when he came in casually dressed, and
smiled, and held out his hand, her saving sanity deserted her
quite.

It had served her well until then, tempering her surprise and
awe at finding herself here – in the inner sanctum of her
prince's palace – with a certain steely curiosity. Expressions like
'black mafia', 'the Grenada connection', and the cabbie's
'Pennies from Heaven', to its own catchy tune, had been
running through her mind as she waited. What a front, she
thought; troubleshooter or hit man.

Then suddenly he was there: the same unimaginably
glamorous creature that had drawn her gaze on the top of the
No 9 bus, and worked his magic in the lounge bar of the
Clarence, in the pulpit of St Mary's. But this was also the man
who – God forgive her – appeared in her dreams; and dreams
now seemed the closest link with present reality: with this
fantasy house, its marble silences, its party cacophony, its
Chinese henchmen, echoing corridors, the distant wail of the
slide trombone... And now the man himself, whom her
fantasies had always reclothed, subconsciously denying his
calling. In her earliest dreams he had worn a suit and tie, or
country things – anorak, cords, and boots. In others he had
been the black runner. And he had been naked with her. Now
he was the romantic hero, perhaps: the Ordinary Man She
Loves, Who Turns Out To Be Rich And Powerful – all soft dark

cashmere and suede and rings and a find gold chain round the bare black column of his throat.

So dazzling was this new, secret, private Sebastian, that Lucy's knees turned to water. All at once she was shaky, awed, out of place; and she heard herself babbling, 'I'm sorry – I tried not to come… I did come to confession – but I tried to manage on my own. Things have happened, you see, and I felt you were the only – Oh God. Look: please, I'll go. I'll be OK. I'm sorry. I'm terribly sorry.'

Gently he cut her short. 'It's I who should apologise,' he said. He took her hands and made her sit down again. 'I'm glad you're here. And you're in a strong position, Lucy: you have found me out… ' He stood up. 'You see, I am very fortunate, to move about in several worlds. And I choose to: I enjoy them all. But they're all encompassed by the world of the spirit: that's my real home, my battleground.' He spoke with a warmth that seemed genuine: he wanted her to understand. Wondering why it was so important to him, she watched him, dazed and silent.

'This house,' he went on: 'I was left it by my godfather. Ill-gotten gains paid for it and – well, you've seen the sort of people who come here.' He had opened a stainless steel cabinet. He took out two glasses and a bottle of white wine. 'So – should I sell all I have and give to the poor? No, Lucy; I hang on to it: how else am I going to catch the *rich* sinners in my net?' He poured, and handed her a glass. 'My flock, you understand – the brethren, the publicans and sinners in my drawing rooms, in the slums of Kensington or Kingston – are all desirable to me, all equally real. Whatever else I may seem, I'm a parish priest, Lucy: believe me. And I'm the very same man who offered you help. I'm glad you have come.' He raised his glass level with those dark unchanging eyes. 'To Evil!' he said: 'to its destruction, and my retirement!' He drank, then put back his head and laughed: a big black laugh that filled the high coved room and percussed down the length of her spine as though she were a mere xylophone in his orchestra of tricks.

'Histrionics,' he said, and shook his head, suddenly mild and warm and altogether charming. 'Put a man in front of a pretty girl and a glass of good wine in his hand, and he becomes a ham actor... The trouble is that all of it's true, Lucy, however corny it sounds... Tell me about you. Had a good day?' He smiled down at her. 'It's been rough, has it? What happened?'

And so he drew her story out of her: the ghost, Wetlips Cecil and his horrible excitement, the quite independent warning of the frightened young man from the magic shop. She touched as briefly as possible on her night fears, her sleeplessness, her waking illusions, the pills, and even on Walter's rejection, painful as it was to recount. 'And I was going to be so sensible and cheerful and lucid,' she said; she smiled, remembering. 'When it came to the point I just stood there gasping, then blurted out – oh, I don't know what.'

'Perhaps it was better, at that moment, for them, that you were comparatively incoherent,' he said. 'It sounds as if they've got their own problems: certainly *she* wouldn't have been able to cope as you have.'

He had been pacing up and down as he listened to her story, prompting her but never pressing her. He stood silent for a while, staring down into the flames. His face showed nothing; there was no way she could read this man in whom she had put her trust. Maybe, she thought, I am mad, and this is the maddest thing I have done. Who the hell *is* he?

Then he squatted down in front of her, his eyes level with hers as she sat in the low leather armchair. 'I'm impressed,' he said, 'because as I say, you *have* coped; you've survived.'

He told her simply that she was strong: stronger than she knew. She was pure, whether she liked it or not – he smiled – and nothing could harm her. 'Innocence,' he said, 'like Wisdom, and, Purity, is a quaint old-fashioned word; but we haven't found another. Now, the Innocent cannot, by definition, know they are innocent, or evaluate their own strength.'

'I do see that,' said Lucy: 'it's really the sort of thing you only recognise in retrospect, like having been – happy or involved?'

'That's it: if you stop to think "I'm involved", or "I'm

133

innocent", you cease to be; so you've got to take it on trust. It's a calculated risk even telling you about it – but you seemed to need reassurance: that "strong breastplate of righteousness" needed an extra rivet or two.'

She watched the fathomless brown eyes, and knew he was powerful, and wondered if he were good – but everything in her told her instinctively he was, and that she must trust him. He was saying...

'Consciously, however, you must refuse to give in to suggestion: it's a web, Lucy, woven round you by the grey people, the ghouls. Most of them are relatively harmless, but they are all lonely, unsatisfied folk, *craving* entertainment; and one or two of them are dangerous, leaning out over the abyss to look, unbalanced enough to topple and drag you with them... Now, in practical terms, it seems something is disturbing your flat. On simple health grounds, you must get away: go home early for Christmas. Get back to those strong, sound country roots: plug into that – it's a powerful inheritance – and get fit again, regain some peace of mind. Afterwards, in the New Year, I propose to move into your spare room – if that suits you? Fine. Now I'm going to call a taxi: I want you to go home and pack, Lucy.'

There was a strange incident on her way out. As they passed through the party rooms, a loud quarrel started up; a man in evening dress pushed over a table amid an explosion of broken glass and shrieking; a lamp crashed and went out. He was shouting obscenities at Father Sebastian, and the priest stopped, quite still, in front of him. His cold voice brought sudden quiet.

'It's no good, my friend: you have your choice. Keep looking, or give up. But you know you are running out of time, don't you?'

The man broke down suddenly. He crumpled, and crouched there sobbing, clutching the priest round his knees.

'And you'll get no absolution here, man,' said Father Sebastian. 'My presence does not make this place a church. No, this is a den of thieves.' And he detached the supplicant like a toddler, and moved, with Lucy in his wake, through his silent guests.

134

Everything was the way she had left it when she got back to the flat – as of course it would be, she told herself briskly, walking round switching on lights, opening cupboards, peering under beds: ridiculous, but she knew she must do it for her own sake. She closed the curtains and removed her coffee cups; then she started to pack – still uneasy, glancing over her shoulder, and carefully avoiding the trouble spots (she still had not moved the chair from the hearth); consciously busy and obedient.

What a relief it was to relinquish command; delicious, almost luxurious, to accept her own weariness, her need for direction, and even acknowledge her altogether different fear of her new commander. She realised she was under his spell (fancy words: you've got a hopeless crush on him, said little Miss Sensible inside her); but he was undeniably glamorous, rich, powerful, mysterious, attractive and, on top of all this, her self-appointed champion. Her fear was no less unreasonable: this black priest was a totally unknown quantity, like some natural force: like fire, like the sea...

Go tonight if you can, he had said. Contact your advertising agency tomorrow with a *fait accompli* – no arguments. Go home, get a doctor's certificate from your GP, then put the whole thing away from you. But go tonight if you can.

When she was nearly ready, she would ring to check the trains; there was always the last one, the slow one, after midnight, if she missed the others. There'd be taxis in the High Street, with luck.

'You must be thinking about the old midnight twenty-three,' said passenger information curtly. 'That was taken off back in May when the lists changed. No, nothing now till the five-oh-five.'

Lucy put down the phone. The sitting room, tidy apart from that lone displaced chair, seemed suddenly claustrophobic and menacing. She went through to the bedroom where her case lay open on the bed, put in her last few things, snapped it shut and stood it on the floor. The eiderdown on the hastily-made bed breathed out gently, still holding the rectangular impression, and she watched for a moment warily, then smoothed it flat, switched out the lights and put her bags in the passage. Relax, she told herself: OK, you've missed the last train – but surely you're not going to run away with only a few hours to go. She must have some supper, set the alarm and get some sleep. There was nothing here to hurt her.

She found a lone egg; she made some toast and coffee while she timed the five minutes' boiling. In this light her dried-out poster on the cupboard opposite was little more than a sinister black glade: she must remember to get a replacement over Christmas. She glanced at her watch again. Still two minutes to go: a minute after the hour her egg would be – Then dumbly she registered what the hour hand pointed to. With all her busy obedience, her packing and basic tidying, she had not once thought: if I miss the train I'll be here at midnight.

Under her feet the boiler in the basement cut out, and in the silence the clicking started.

No room was really safe now, except perhaps the small hot bathroom where unexpected reflections of reflections always seemed to dog her in the depths of the shiny dark green tiles. Feeling very foolish, she carried the tray of supper in there, but the narrow, high, overheated cell crowded her; she returned and sat herself stiffly by the table in the bay window from which she could see the whole of the drawing room.

Now the cold outside began to sidle in through the gaps between the curtains, chilling her shoulders. She put her overcoat round her, and sat, straight as a sentry, nibbling a piece of toast and thinking of the priest's words as she was leaving. 'Lucy, it's quite possible Mrs Maturin is dead: that feels like a dead person's flat. I don't think you will see her ghost again. But remember: that sad spirit could not harm you.' She thought about Maisie Maturin; had she, on her last evening, found herself ready too soon for her journey? Lucy herself had so long to wait she knew she should at least try to sleep on the sofa; but she felt wide awake. The clicking, slower now, plucked her taut nerves like a plectrum; and as, minutely, the interval between the clicks lengthened, so – it seemed – did the moment of tension, of expectation, before each one.

Dressed and ready to go, her suitcase in the passage, her handbag on her lap, she waited for the hours to pass. As she shifted her rigid spine on the hard upright dining chair, something in her position – in her pose, as she perched there expectantly staring down the room at that other chair – revealed her to herself, horribly, as the mirror image of the ghost. Even the light tweed suit, the clutched handbag, the angle of the legs. As though she'd had a sneak-preview. As though, eight hours ago, she had seen her own ghost.

She left swiftly, almost running down the passage with her bags.

She walked for nearly an hour. There were no taxis in the High Street and she felt a childish dread of waiting for one in that long naked street where Cecil had followed her so easily, even through the evening crowds; so she headed north and lost her way in the side roads. She seemed unable to get round the park, coming up repeatedly against dead ends or private parking lots. When at last she emerged somewhere near Notting Hill Gate, an empty taxi was the only car in sight.

Paddington Station was a high, echoing shell, almost deserted; the bench in the ladies' waiting room, cold and hard. She put her head on a carrier bag, wrapped a cardigan round her legs and slept a little. She bought her ticket, and drank a cardboard mug of coffee as she waited for the five-oh-five; slept again, waking with each stop on the line, and changing at Andover. From Pewsey station she rang her parents; and she watched a small silver sun creep out of the eastern clouds as she waited for the car to drive into the station yard and carry her home.

They were awake when she telephoned, Tom making tea, Alice lying low till the bedroom warmed up and she could brave it. She was wishing she was one of those magazine idols – 'A Day in the Life of ' – flitting about in appealingly ruched and quilted dimity, ministering to her family of happy morning faces. As it was, her own half-dressed state was an old track-suit of Jamie's that had shrunk in the washing machine: you couldn't feed chickens in a dimity gown. Then the phone rang. Her husband answered it downstairs and appeared with the tea.

'Here – I've got to go. That was Lucy: she's at the station.'

'Something wrong?'

'Don't think so: a bit "run down", she said, and suddenly decided to take an extra week or so on top of her Christmas break.'

'How marvellous! But why at this ungodly hour? She must have caught the –'

'I've got to go, love: all will be revealed no doubt. But she said "tell Mum everything's fine". So: drink up while it's hot and get ready for your big hungry daughter.'

Lucy spent a long time in the next fortnight marching along wet lanes and across ploughed fields with only the dogs for company. Muddy, rained on, exhausted and ravenous, she would return for tea in the big kitchen.

Those walks, at first intended as a time for soul-searching, became a mindless, almost timeless, freedom. She felt – if and when she thought about it – invisible, plastic, unbounded, not separate from the drizzle or the stones, the sloping woods or the pollarded willows down by the stream, foxy with new growth; the tangled hedgerows, looped in briony and furry with old-man's-beard; the bright, wet beech leaves underfoot, or the low-hanging boughs she stopped to ride on, just as she had always ridden. Even the clouds that raced across the red, sinking sun were hers and part of her, as they had always been. The rain that soaked her hair and streamed down her face washed away Clarence Square and the spooks and the mauve bed-chamber, the black velvet and masks and horns, the hooded madonnas and clutching hands, and quite obliterated the slimy pentacle.

'She's back to her old self,' said Alice toasting tea-cake on the open top of the big range.

138

'I think so,' said Tom slowly. It was a measure of their concern that they had not discussed Lucy's well-being for some days. 'She was a bit of a mess at first – did you ever find out what the nightmares were?'

'She didn't want to "revive" them,' said Alice.

'Very sensible.'

'She is. But it's good she took the extra time; Lees-Langham didn't seem too bothered.'

'Well,' said Tom, 'I hope that doesn't mean they don't need her.'

'Darling, I told you: and after all, I did do the phoning. And this boss of hers, Jerry, only said she hadn't been looking a hundred per cent; sent his love and looked forward to her coming back "firing on all four cylinders": that's the only firing anyone mentioned... There you are, Luce: good bath? – not that you could've got much wetter than you were! Here, this one's well buttered.'

There was shopping to do for Christmas, and decorations to put up; mince pies, and beds to be made, and the tree to dig up, pot, and establish in the hall. Absorbed and occupied helping her parents, Lucy was totally contented; but she noticed their pleasure in her was more openly expressed than the normal cool, jokey approval, and she knew that they were immensely relieved; that her sudden arrival and her run-down condition must have worried them.

Her father, whose favourite she was, had watched her covertly and said little in those first few days. Alice had tried to be quite open and hearty about it: 'Well, the undernourished look may be all the rage, my girl, but I suspect you're just bloody lazy about food – and what on earth is that smell you've brought home with you? That bundle of washing you handed over: it *reeks* of incense and smoke and booze and Lord knows what else.'

'No, not drugs actually, Mum: joss-sticks and whisky and – yes, I'm smoking too much; that's why walking in the rain is so therapeutic: you can't.'

But Lucy's brooding silence had worried her parents far more than mere booze and fags. She seemed not only exhausted – burnt out – but preoccupied; and they would catch her staring into space as though at some secret terror. All they could do was cosset her, and leave it to her to talk when she felt like it. Lucy was grateful. Sometimes, however, she would look across at her father, so busy filing down the rough edges of the lock he was mending, or her mother bending over her pile of exercise books, and think: what do *you* know of fear, or loneliness? And how would you react if I told you about the nice warm flat that seems to be destroying me gradually? But she knew she would not tell them, because she wanted to master it her own way: not alone – that had patently failed – but with the help of a beautiful, rich, mysterious, black man who wore his collar back to front.

Later they questioned her more: clearly they thought she was up to it. She told them about her working day, and the characters in the Lees-Langham hierarchy. She described the flat – even drew them a plan of it – and made them laugh with her descriptions of Mrs Villiers and the pop-eyed Estelle, late of *Come Dancing*; of Dr Max and the Colonel.

'What about – your friends, Lucy? People your own age.'

'Oh – there's Esther and Sally, and Margaret – the new one – at work; Sally's very good news, but she's been moved away from our department. And Gudrun – remember? – Of course: she phoned you. Came for supper and stayed. She seems fine. And there are the girls in the flat above me, Ella and Josie and Diane. And Alma: she's nice. But she's married now; the dread "bell jar" has descended and she's a bit cut off. I'm going to their housewarming, I think. I'm afraid I missed a party in Oxford.'

'You should keep up with your old friends, my dear,' said her father.

'Did you ever ring Nell?' Alice asked.

'I tried… I'll send her a Christmas card with my new address – OK?'

They were wondering about boyfriends, and she was well aware of the hanging question mark. Should she tell them about Charles Vesey, gay Eddie, or the Oscar Wilde of the magic shop? Or this smashing six-foot-plus West Indian, son of a drug-runner, she was going to have as a lodger?

Jamie returned from Scotland, limping slightly from an end-of-term rugger party, his ancient Triumph piled to the roof with presents, Christmas fare and sacks of washing. His girlfriend Jenny arrived on Christmas Eve; and as they were expecting a phone call from William in Canada at one-thirty am Greenwich Mean Time – his last chance to be near a telephone before he took the family off to the log cabin for a week ('And knowing you, Mum, you'll still be stuffing turkeys and stockings and things anyway') – they decided to attend the midnight service.

Lucy had announced she would not be going to church: 'I'm still recovering from the religious OD of all those years at school,' she said; but Jamie persuaded her to come along for the ride.

'It means a lot to the aged parents, you know: much more than they'd dream of admitting. Mum, Lucy's coming with us.'

Lucy had, she realised, been totally self-indulgent over the last fortnight: hard to avoid when she so enjoyed even the routine chores, the wood-carrying, the chicken-feeding, the floor-mopping. But her self-disciplinary muscles had fallen into disuse without the effort of tubes to catch, typing to finish, shopping and housekeeping – quite apart from the daily challenge of simply returning to that flat, or the nightly ordeal of counting sheep. Still – she had not been inside a church since her attempt at confession. As they walked along the lane with torches under a black, starry sky, she prayed that she would be able to pray: good and evil were huge abstractions she did not want to dwell on in this childish, mindless, blissful time out.

There was a spangled Christmas tree by the lych-gate; festive folk were gathering, their breath puffing in bright clouds as they hailed each other noisily in the streaming light from the arched doorway. Holly and mistletoe and God Rest Ye Merry – this is the good, sound Church of England Christmas Party, Lucy told herself: no bleeding saints in pink and gold, nor drug of heavy incense, nor massed ranks of candles weeping wax for dead souls. And only a cheery social message from the

141

pulpit: no hell fire, no painful self-questioning, nor intimations of mortality.

But as she knelt, head in hands, for the final blessing, trying to pray, Lucy glanced up at the plain gold crucifix on the altar. Help me! she called silently, closing her eyes; and was blasted with a huge close-up – an image she immediately recognised from her forgotten dreams – of the sleeping Sebastian with his fine gold chain slack on his black chest, the cross inverted.

Chapter Nine

IT COMES FROM me. All this sick nonsense comes from me.

She was striding home down the dark lane with her pocket torch, ahead of the others. 'Wait for us!' they called.

She shouted back: 'I'm just going ahead to put the soup on.'

That blasphemous vision still burned in her mind's eye, and she was running from it. But it's all psychological, she told herself. For Christ's sake – these are the repressions and fantasies of a rather over-protected nineteen-year-old! I could have given rise to *all* the strange happenings, even the electric faults, the ghost, the pins – like young girls and poltergeists. I must be retarded: an over-age disturbed adolescent. I thought I was being driven mad, but *I* was the cause of the harassment: a self-inflicted wound – very kinky: no wonder the ghouls were gathering.

Christmas was over and only a few days left before the return to London. Lucy's health, her looks, and, to a lesser extent, her sleeping, had all improved; she knew this. She almost resented it: now she was well enough to put away childish content and sort herself out.

First she faced up to the odd paradox that, as she had grown more attuned to her new flat, she had grown somehow weaker: more careless about her wellbeing, her housekeeping, even about her work. Once she saw this, and decided that her state had been due to a species of self-induced hysteria – hard though this was on her self-esteem – she felt much less scared of going back. Even the paradox itself was explained away: the Clarence Court flat was not preying on her: she had simply grown sluttish, then depressed (or vice versa, chicken and egg), and her budding neurosis had created the significance as an excuse. Soon Father Sebastian would be moving in. Do I really need him? she wondered. And why hadn't *he* told her she was at the root of the disturbance? Was it that he did not want to hurt her? Or that he had totally misjudged the situation, too intent on the paranormal trees to see the wood's flourishing nut plantation? Or could it be that he wanted to move into her flat for some reason of his own, and this was the only way?

Three weeks ago she had gone asking for help, he had taken her in and listened to her. He had been very gentle, had not even told her to pull herself together; and his promise to install himself as lodger and protector in the new year felt at the time like rope to drowning hands. Now that Lucy was herself again, even the pleasure she took in the prospect of his company was tinged with embarrassment: the sheer melodrama of summoning a priest to deal with a ghost. Get back early, she decided; give the flat a spring clean, ring the good father, ask him round and talk about it. Don't just tell him you're OK: show him. And his reactions will sort out any doubts about his motives. Then get on with enjoying life and working through the list. Yes, and there was something practical she could do right now: acquire a jemmy. She knew that, however else she had improved, she still dreamed, and the cupboard featured in her dreams. *That's* what is getting at me, she thought; otherwise, I'm fine.

Jamie was leaving before New Year for Hogmanay in Scotland with Jenny's family. 'Lucy's looking good,' he said to his mother on his last evening. 'But somewhat quieter than usual. Specially since Christmas.'

'Anticlimax, probably; I mean, once that's over, the business of getting back to work is suddenly close and real. I'm glad she's going to a New Year's party; she's been stuck here with us most of the time: that's what she seemed to want.'

'Well *I* don't feel like doing a thing once I'm here, Mum –

144

and from what you said about her state on arrival, I reckon that's just what our Luce was needing.'

But in the car next day, heading North, Jenny offered 'a penny for 'em,' and Jamie said: 'Nothing much really: Mum said Lucy was just suffering post-Christmas blues – but I got the impression she clammed up after that midnight service. She simply wasn't *like* that in the days before – no, I didn't mention it to Mum: she said Lucy was so much better than when she'd arrived, and I reckoned the Aged Ps had had enough to worry about without me chipping in with my penn'orth – now yours. I wonder if there's anything in London that's bugging her... '

Lucy borrowed the car for the New Year's party. Tom heard her get back just after twelve-thirty. Alice was already asleep so he did not call out. He heard her moving about again early the next morning, went down and found her making tea.

'You're up betimes,' he said. 'Good party, was it?'

'Lovely,' she said. 'Not too many, and all the old gang. Great seeing them – oh, and Nell and Alex are getting engaged! God, I'm so out of touch – I really should have done something about seeing them sooner. Dad, I'm getting a lift up to London, this afternoon. I know work doesn't start till Tuesday – Wednesday, even, for some – but I should really get back and spring-clean the flat, so I can advertise for a lodger. I think I do need company. Anyway, Nell's sister and her husband are driving back to Canterbury, and they offered to drop me in London as there are no trains today. I'm packing early so I can have a longer last day: they'll be here soon after lunch. I'm sorry to be so sudden, Dad; but in a way it's easier. And Dad, d'you have a jemmy or something you could lend me?'

Back in Clarence Square, four pm and already dark, she fixed her mind on hopeful, practical things like tea and buns by the electric fire, and put her key in the door. She was telling herself

145

it was a good way to do it: taking the dilemma by the horns, instead of counting the days, and then the hours, left her before she must return. Insomnia had been troubling her again, and she knew very well that, however straightforward the explanation, she had gone through bad times in that flat: tying on the neat label 'psychosomatic' was not an instant cure. It had been easy enough to explain things away from the top of a Wiltshire hill. Down here, back among the sounds, the smells, the things half-seen by street light, by the fringed passage light, and all transmitting minute signals of alarm to every nerve ending, she wished she could recapture that sweet reason, that confidence. And she wished she could control her pulse.

She hung up her coat, set down the bag of food from home by the kitchen door, and took her suitcase along to the bedroom. That persistent smell which used to hang about the passage seemed to be better. The kitchen, she knew, had been left in chaos; and the tray with her half-eaten egg, abandoned in her headlong flight, must be lurking in the sitting room, three weeks past its prime. She opened the door boldly to tackle it.

Though the room was almost dark, it was not empty. And she could not see the single candle set down in the hearth except as a wavering radiance: it was masked by the silhouette of a seated buddha. The candle threw its vast shadow across the room, the doorway where she stood, and clear up to the ceiling: a penumbral cloak that wagged and shivered. But the statue itself was solid and still as black marble.

She heard her own gasp as her breath came back to her, and she fumbled for the light switch. She saw the priest, back view, and naked but for a yellow loin-cloth. He was deep in meditation; he neither moved nor spoke. She turned off the lights and backed away, closing the door gently. She leaned against the passage wall, heart pounding, eyes closed; but her retina held the bright imprint of that shape – like a crude ebony cross inverted over the invisible pentacle – and she hurried to the kitchen where the strong light extinguished it. It's only Father Sebastian, she told herself: he must have got a key from the caretaker and moved in early...

Then she saw the kitchen had changed. Every surface, even the floor, was cleared and spotless: no sign of dirty cups or old toast or brimming ashtrays. On the table was a bowl of fruit – grapes, mangoes, papayas – a celophaned sheaf of blue winter irises, still in bud, and a large loaf of crusty bread.

He found her making tea. He was fully dressed now, not as a priest, but in jeans and a sweatshirt.

'Hi there,' he said. (So gorgeous; so big – she always forgot that, was always surprised by it – so close in the small kitchen. And that scent of dark skin, like black muscat grapes, like fresh olive oil over a low flame – and as addictive in its way as linseed-and-turps or grease-paint or the first breath of newly-opened coffee, fine and black in its foil packet... She had tried so often to recall it precisely. But here he was: the gleaming, ebony buddha, thinly clothed. He was saying –) 'I'm sorry if I startled you, Lucy: I didn't think you'd be back before tomorrow morning at the earliest, with the holiday going on an extra day. I wanted to give you a nice surprise on your return – and what do I do? I set up one helluva a shock for you instead! The best laid plans... Come and see: I've been rearranging the spare room, and I need your approval.'

Still dumbfounded and unbelieving, Lucy followed him obediently. All the masks and ornaments had been removed, packed in boxes under the bed; thin, striped durries made secondary curtains, hiding the black velvet and brightening the whole room. Another covered the bed; a big white lamp with a powerful bulb stood on the bedside table, where a wooden cross and a rosary lay in the pool of light. Despite the cold, the jammed windows she had never been able to move were open wide, and that stuffy, threatening room transformed to a chill, elegant, monkish simplicity.

'You *have* been busy,' said Lucy. She was still reserved, and not a little shocked at this cool takeover by a lodger she had decided to invite round and fob off gracefully. 'When did you move in? And how?'

147

'I brought crumpets for tea,' he said: 'I'll tell you while I'm preparing them.'

It had clearly been a mere bagatelle for Father Sebastian in full priestly gear to square things with Mrs Dortmund. She had been all sympathy for Miss Morland, leaving so suddenly on sick leave; all admiration for the good father who, with the blessing of Foss & Cornfield, was to rent a room, and who so very much wanted to make things nice for Miss Morland's return. 'I got a key cut and moved in yesterday, Saturday morning: I planned to see in the New Year in here, on my own. Lucy my dear… ' They were having tea, crumpets and home-made jam in the bay window – 'tell me, do you resent my high-handedness? Had you changed your mind about my moving in with you?'

Lucy was silent for a moment, gazing at the tall glass of irises on the centre of the table. Then she smiled. 'You are extraordinary, Father,' she said: 'you always seem to anticipate me: read me, if you know what I – Yes, I decided, only a few days ago, that all these disturbances were issuing from me: like a poltergeist, you know; and I came back a day early to clean the flat and get myself in order, then ask you round graciously and tell you I was OK thanks.'

'This is admirable, Lucy: you really used your break. And you look new: renewed. You've even got the confidence to take the blame and bear it. I think you are being over-hard on yourself – may I give you some more tea? – but I can't stop you from seeing your situation and running your life your own way. I'll move out the moment you ask me to; I just hope a lodger of some sort is part of the plan.'

It was so strange to be sitting there with the man of her dreams, passing the jam and discussing her 'situation': a cosy domestic scene that felt extraordinarily good, and perfectly natural. Lucy realised that, after the initial shock – due as much to her fearful anticipation as to unfortunate timing – she had quickly accepted his presence. On each encounter he was more alarmingly real than her dreams allowed; but even this solid, masculine, space-consuming entity in her flat seemed more assimilable in his new role.

148

Even that strong attraction must diminish with daily contact: familiarity, surely, would blunt the edge of her sharp physical awareness. Now she must try to see him as family: a father – as she already addressed him – or a large, useful brother; all the easier since she was genuinely impressed by his thoughtfulness, his practical skills.

This mystery man was still full of surprises: just when she had managed to absorb the fact of his conspicuous wealth (though she could not yet fit the incident with the troublesome guest into her jigsaw), he suddenly materialised on her hearth as a naked mystic, then turned into the soft-footed houseboy. He had warmed the teapot: she never bothered to; he had laid the newly polished butler's tray with a lacy tray-cloth, conjured out of a drawer she hadn't noticed. Not that there was anything servile about him: he was subtly in command – as deft and fastidious, she knew, as he would have been alone – brushing aside her apologies for the state of the flat: 'I like housework: you can see results.' And now he was the sympathetic companion, advising her on the best way to find an alternative lodger.

He went out in his priest's clothes for vespers at St Mary's. 'Don't worry about supper,' he said: 'it's prepared; and there's more than enough for two: coming from a big family, I cook real lazy – in large quantities.'

It was pork and peppers stewed in a wine sauce; and there were roast sweet potatoes, wrapped in foil and cooked in the sitting room grate.

He had returned from church with a bag of coal balanced on the shoulder of his soft black coat. 'I'm a closet miner,' he said: 'no one knows, and I don't even have to wash.' Back in his jeans, he removed the electric fire from the hearth and reached his hand up the chimney (long black hand with its single silver ring; eyes half-closed as he felt for and released the cover). 'There,' he said rocking back on his heels: 'the flue's open – yes, I checked with the girl at the estate agents: working fireplace, smokeless fuel permitted.' He brought in a box of kindling and fire-lighters ('I'm no boy scout'), and soon they had a crackling blaze that settled down to bright flickering flames and a marvellous glow. It quite altered the whole focus of the room – for Lucy, a transformation: all at once the television set ceased to be the centre, the only live thing.

Now, however, she had to step on to that dreaded spot covered by the dark goatskin to move the fireguard; she had to kneel down on it to shovel on more coal. She could not so obviously leave it to him when he was doing everything else. When later, carrying in the casserole, he said, 'Those sweet potatoes should be ready, Lucy,' and she had to crouch there, stabbing and lifting them out with a toasting fork, then peel off the foil and arrange them in a warmed dish (Father Sebastian, like Walter, had to have things 'just so'), she quite forgot for a moment she was over the pentacle.

But as she combed her hair and tied a pretty scarf round her neck in honour of the occasion, she thought how odd it was that both of them knew about the invisible scar on the carpet, but neither of them had mentioned it. Moreover, she knew *he* knew, but he could not be certain she had seen it – though he might have guessed. It was almost as if the priest were deliberately exorcising the nastiness of that spot by using it as a proper hearth: cleansing it with fire; forcing her to overcome her fear.

Or has he simply found a way of getting me into the pentacle? she wondered; and once again was confronted with the big alternative: either this man was very good or very evil. All she could be certain of was that, with him, there was nothing in between.

He had moved back the sofa and set a smaller table and two dining chairs opposite the fire for their meal. They were drinking coffee, proper coffee, and listening to Jimmy Cliff, when the bell rang.

'Oh no!' said Lucy leaping up: 'of course – it'll be the – Mrs Maturin's friends from the pub.'

'I'll clear these things away,' said the priest.

'But must I?'

'Of course you must: to some extent they're your friends now. You can't just drop them; Walter might, but not you.'

Another ring.

'Go on, Lucy: I'll make more coffee.' He carried the tray into the kitchen.

Lucy opened the door, fearful more than anything of seeing Cecil.

'Happy New Year!' they cried: Mrs Villiers, Estelle, Dr Max and the Colonel. 'We saw the light and knew you were back. Did you have a lovely Christmas? We did miss you, dear – going so suddenly like that. You do look well. We all forgathered at the dear old Clarence on Christmas Eve, and the Colonel here was saying…'

They had deposited their coats and were moving in a bunch along the passage when the black priest, six-foot-two in sneakers and butcher's apron, emerged from the kitchen.

'Hi! Happy New Year,' he said.

Mrs Villiers found her voice first.

'Oh! What a lovely surprise! Oooh, but you won't want *us*.'

'Coffee all round?' said the priest.

They could not resist.

Lucy had got them all sitting down round the fire – as good a conversation point as the TV, it seemed: they all talked at once, and rather loud – by the time Father Sebastian came in with the tray. He set it on the small central table where they had dined, and there was a silence, then another nervous burst of muted chattering, while he poured and handed round the cups. Mrs Villiers thanked him with queen-motherly sweetness and commented on the shining silver coffee jug.

'Haven't seen that for ages… Have we, Estelle? Maisie always said – she always said it's such a nuisance to keep clean. *And* her dear little cups: her best. How lovely.'

'Truly civilised,' said Dr Max who had barely uttered so far: he seemed absorbed in observation, chiefly of Lucy herself.

Another awkward lull followed the handing of the sugar. The priest was standing on the hearth rug stirring his coffee and surveying them all with an easy, unhurried gaze; and

Estelle leapt into the breach.

'Well, Lucy! So you've let the Black Slave out of the cupboard.'

There was spluttering and spilt coffee and hissed remonstrances while a cloth was fetched: Lucy white and blank, saying 'Don't worry – please don't worry'; Mrs Villiers scolding Estelle in whispers with all the harsh fluency of a bronchial parrot; Estelle crouching on the carpet dabbing it with the paper tissues she had plucked from her bosom, and the Colonel hovering, not knowing where to look. Dr Max smiled and observed, his eyes darting from one to the other; then the priest appeared with a roll of kitchen paper and mopped up.

When everything was in order again, Father Sebastian, quite unruffled, folded himself down onto the pouf beside Estelle.

'Tell me more, Miss Estelle,' he said: 'whom did Mrs Maturin have in mind?'

The colonel got quickly to his feet. 'Oh, that was just a reference to one of dear Maisie's little fancies.' He stood with his back to the fire, hands in blazer pockets. 'Probably some unfortunate illegal immigrant, we thought – didn't we? You know: one of her many lame dogs, what?' No one seemed prepared to help him out, not even the Doctor who sat there twisting his rings and watching Lucy sidelong. 'Anyway,' the Colonel went on with painful jauntiness, rattling his change: 'be that as it may – you know… Well, she used to joke about it: always laughing, she was… '

'And have any of you heard from her?' asked the priest. 'A Christmas card, maybe?'

'Well no, er – Father: not a dicky-bird, actually – Could be the posts.'

Estelle piped up. 'But that journalist man, Cecil, was saying that Lucy had seen her! I thought he said… ' she ended lamely; and both Dr Max and Mrs Villiers started talking at once.

'Our friend Cecil,' said the Doctor, 'species reporter, subspecies gossip, is hardly the individual one might, under the circumstances... ' but his leisurely delivery and elaborate construction lost to Mrs Villiers' piercingly best social manner.

'And tell us about *you*, Father: how did you find our English Christmas?'

'I liked it fine, Mrs Villiers. Busy of course: our turn for overtime, I guess. The Lord's birthday pretty well solves the unemployment problem for a few days: salesmen before, priests during and dustmen after – a blessing plus a bonus. But that's Christmas. How about yours?'

Dr Max laid his hand on Lucy's arm as Mrs Villiers got under way. 'Tell me,' he said in a low voice: 'was he simply here to dinner? Or has he moved in?'

'Father Sebastian has moved in until I can find a lodger – another working girl like me, I expect,' said Lucy. 'You see, Dr Max, I got a bit run down in early December, a bit, well – depressed; he is very kindly providing me with company: he was looking for digs anyway, you know. And I'll be very glad of the rent.'

She spoke without concealment so everyone could hear. Mrs Villiers lost the thread of her larky Christmas to listen, and the conversation became general.

'It suits me,' said Father Sebastian; 'and it suits the brethren at St Ignatius: they've got a bunch of mid-west Jesuits visiting them sometime in January, and need the space.'

'Ooh, but what will you do when Lucy finds another flatmate?' asked Estelle.

'I shall have to set out again with my begging bowl,' he said. 'So don't say I didn't warn you, ladies.' The ladies laughed merrily and accepted more coffee. Lucy noticed he did not mention his little place in Belgravia.

They left earlier than usual. Lucy had effectively avoided even a brief heart-to-heart with either Dr Max or Mrs Villiers; but on the way out, the Doctor managed to pull her aside into the kitchen.

'How do you know he's a priest?' he hissed. 'Don't you realise what he's here *for*? It's not just your considerable attractions... Ah, Father: just making a bid for the washing up. Are you sure, dear girl? Yes, yes, Mrs Villiers: I'm coming.

Sleep well, then – I'm sure you will. You look so much better, dear girl.'

Lucy did sleep well: tired and healthy; and knowing that the cavalry was at hand, across the passage in the spare room; her guardian angel. She did not dream of the black runner. She dreamed of home.

He was gone when she woke in the morning, and telephoned her at midday to say he must visit a friend who had just been taken into hospital. 'I may not be back till late. You OK? Good. And don't forget the rest of the stew.'

It was an unhurried domestic day spent spring-cleaning the mauve bedchamber, and polishing nails and boots ready for work. Knowing he would be back, she did not long for company. Everything was so spick and span she even started reading the Henry James she had brought from home, without a twinge of guilt about what she should be doing. She ate two helpings of pork-and-peppers watching television, went to bed early, heard him return some time after, half-hoped, sleepily, that he might come and see her, sit on her bed, tell her about his day. She slept again.

He knocked on her door with a cup of tea before he left next morning. It was still dark.

'I'll probably be here when you get back,' he said: 'let's decide what shopping we need then, OK? See you.'

It was easy to accept that he would lead a busy, separate life: enough that his intermittent presence – solid, dark, warm, and, so far as she could tell, serene – had apparently earthed the forces that had troubled her. Or that she had troubled. Since their first conversation on her return, she had not thought seriously about finding another lodger, whatever she told the assembled cronies. Theirs were the only eyebrows likely to be raised: and mixed flat-sharing was common enough. It seemed so natural, so convenient, that she no longer dreaded even telling her parents; and her deepest misgivings about having a crush on her flat-mate were lulled by the easy companionship she had felt that first evening: familiarity would breed content.

154

There was now only one thing on her list of priorities that must be dealt with, and swiftly: the locked cupboard. It was something she had to do alone; and on the previous day, as soon as she knew her lodger would not return unexpectedly, she had taken out the jemmy and tried it on the door. She found she could get it into the crack, but not deep enough for leverage. She needed to buy a hammer – but no tool shops were open on a bank holiday, and she could not borrow one from the Dortmunds without arousing their curiosity. She might have nerved herself to ask the girls upstairs, but they were not back yet. As it was, the jemmy had left marks on the grey gloss paint: she moved the poster across to cover them.

The priest might have guessed she had seen, and disliked, the pentacle; he did not, however, know of her obsession with the locked cupboard, or her determination to open it. She had not told him; and when he saw her taking down the seared poster and pinning up its replacement, he had only said, 'Surprising what heat will do, isn't it? But it warms my room next door very nicely.' Lucy had been tempted to warn him about the magnetic wall, but she did not want him investigating further and coming up against the razor-blade effect. She suspected that, since she was balanced and sane again, it would have disappeared; but now (she told herself) that the room was no longer hers, she had no business going in there – and this relieved her of the need to test her theory.

The apparition of Mrs Maturin had also been reasoned away: if Lucy had seen anything, it was no more than her own troubled doppelgänger. She was certain that, whatever vague notions Father Sebastian might have about 'a dead person's flat', Maisie Maturin was alive and well and coming back in March as planned. Lucy had even written a brief, chatty report to her, care of Foss & Cornfield, that last day in Wiltshire; and in a PS she had artfully set up the possible necessity of opening the airing cupboard: 'a suspected air-lock in the heating pipes'. This side-stepped the charge of vandalism, though Foss & Cornfield might not see it that way; but Lucy had decided she could not please everyone: if she did the break-in as neatly and professionally as she could, replaced the lock, and made

155

her peace with Mrs M. when she returned, it would have to do. The vital thing was to open the cupboard and put an end to her childish fears – without implicating the priest. He would have to know, of course, and might help move things in and put on the new lock; but the decision was hers alone.

Today in her lunch hour she would buy a hammer; then she must wait until the next time she had the place to herself.

For three days the new hammer and the jemmy lay in the back of the wardrobe, behind her boots. There was never time in the mornings, and each evening he had been there when she got back from work. It was so pleasant and luxurious to be welcomed by a lighted fire and delicious smells of cooking, a poured drink and chat about their very different days' work, that Lucy could not really wish it otherwise. But every time she passed the cupboard her resolve hardened.

She knew she must be patient and wait until she was sure she would not be interrupted. More than once he had come in unexpectedly; and apart from mass and confessions he had no fixed routine. When he talked about his day, the mornings seemed to be the most occupied with his official pastoral duties. The weekend will be no better, she thought: it may have to be a week-day morning, and I'll just be unavoidably late for work.

On Friday she got up and dressed as soon as he had left the flat. There'd be no time to put away all the things on her hate-list, but at least the deed could be done: this evening she would face him with it and explain.

Now that the anticipated moment had arrived, she was more uneasy than she had let herself admit to; far worse than the first try, when she had seen at a glance the jemmy would not be enough. 'I must do it,' she said out loud; 'then I'll be all right.' That would be the end of it.

Feeling like a surgeon preparing for the first incision, she spread an old dustsheet on the passage carpet in case she made a mess, took down the poster carefully, rolled it up and put the drawing pins on a saucer in the kitchen where she could find them – no (she told herself sternly): *not* from fear of their disappearing under the door... She heard the girls moving about upstairs. Their radio came on; and she thought how nice it would be to have one of them there, all hearty and supportive, handing her the implements. But it was desperate wishful thinking, ducking away from the memory of Josie's dire warnings, and Ella's collapse on this very spot. These were the very things she must keep from her mind; the reasons for opening the cupboard. She must not think now; she must act.

She inserted the jemmy into the bruised crack close to the lock, held it firm and drove it in deeper with the hammer. It splintered the edge; the wood was only deal, and not very stout. The curving tip of the jemmy was well in, and she dropped the hammer, and leaned all her weight on the iron shaft. The lock burst apart with a satisfying crash, and the door swung open.

It was a deep, narrow, walk-in cupboard: a store really, high, like the rest of the flat, and running back the full length of the spare room. The plastic toggle of a hanging light switch swung against her face; she caught it and tugged it on. Inside were rows of slatted shelves ranged with china, ornaments, trinket boxes. Below them on the floor were larger boxes, suitcases, and a cabin trunk; and huddled between them was the body of Mrs Maturin.

She had been a big lady; fat, jolly and well-preserved; pushing fifty. Now she was well-preserved in a different way: she was dried out. Her ample skin, looped on her arms, under her chin, was like rows of puckered scallopping – one of her fancy pelmets, perhaps. She was bone draped with sour leather bags, and she lay in a foetal crouch, shrunken and agape, both hands held out as though to pray, or to ward off the response to that terrible prayer.

Chapter Ten

LUCY MUST HAVE regained consciousness, crawled along the passage towards the front door and collapsed again. That is where Sebastian found her.

He came in soon after nine, intent on making himself a decent cup of coffee before his morning call on the brethren of St Ignatius. When the front door stopped against something solid yet soft, his mind raced ahead, previewing every frightful possibility in the passing seconds as he eased his way through the gap. He took in Lucy's huddled, unconscious body, the groundsheet, and the open cupboard: this brave, mad girl had beaten him to it. Had she known what to look for? Had she found it?

He bent down and felt for the pulse in her neck; then walked swiftly to the cupboard, and saw what she had seen. He closed the door, and carried Lucy along to the sitting room where he laid her down and turned her head on one side. He wrapped her in blankets; he telephoned the police, 'And an ambulance will be needed,' he said. Then he went back along the passage to the airing cupboard.

He did not touch the body. He barely glanced at it; but he muttered a prayer as he stepped over it. Now he had to search, and search quickly, before the police arrived: not the way he planned, but that could not be helped. No fear, at least, that she might have taken it away with her. What he had sensed before was simply confirmed: Sebastian now knew it was still in the flat.

He moved steadily and swiftly, opening trinket boxes,

unrolling baize-wrapped bundles of silver, peering into bags, leather cases, a small tin trunk; closing and replacing each meticulously as he went. He was sweating, but that could have been the heat of the pipes. Two cars drew up noisily outside. The priest stopped, and stood quite straight and still, his eyes closed. Then, as feet clattered up the steps, he opened his eyes, leaned across and slid his hand down between the quilted red insulating jacket and the hot water cylinder.

He took the stone from its velvet bag and cradled it in his hand. It was so small – no bigger than a hen's egg – and shiny and strangely heavy, just as he remembered, its surface laced with a pattern of fine silvery whorls like a stylised brain. In the blast of images that hit him he did not even hear the noise of the door bell. He heard the second ring and knew he must either take on this burden, or put the stone back in its hiding place. Now.

The police doctor said she had probably been dead at least seven or eight weeks. The conditions made greater accuracy impossible; and especially the condition of the body itself.

'The extraordinary thing,' he remarked, pulling the sheet up over the head, 'is that there is no evidence of normal biological deterioration: no corruption. Just dessication.'

Lucy came to on the sitting room sofa, with the priest holding her hand, a policeman waiting to question her. First she became aware of voices, then faces looking down at her; then, beyond them, the yellow head of the young Mr Cornfield back view, talking to another policeman. She closed her eyes again, and snatches of his earnest protestations came through to her.

'Only a PO Box number, you understand... No reason why she should have got in touch with us – or, come to that, why we should know if she ever arrived... One might at least have thought her friends or relatives – whoever was expecting her – would attempt to... Well no: they would not necessarily know her agents' address or even their – I concede that; but obviously a letter sent to Clarence Mansions would... Anyway

– you will appreciate that as agents for the entire block, we – and the landlords, of course – would be very concerned to keep the whole incident... Oh quite – just until some reasonable explanation... A brief and simple notice to the *Times* and the *Telegraph* must at some point – but surely, after eight weeks' delay – ? As you see fit, officer.'

The police now put a few questions to Lucy: small points mostly, to fill in the picture, so far as was possible. Clearly, they said – and Mr Cornfield agreed – Mrs Maturin had been on the point of departure; in something of a hurry (as Lucy's reports on the kitchen confirmed); and had gone to the cupboard, possibly to put in some other valuables, had inadvertently got locked in...

'But wait a minute,' said the priest: 'it's a two-way Yale lock, and you found the key in her pocket.'

'True. We were coming to that; and it conveniently rules out any question of foul play – unless there is evidence of some drug, of course. And the possibility of suicide would seem even less likely. No: we think she was overcome by the heat; that she panicked, lost consciousness and died; most probably a coronary, as the post mortem will show... ' He referred to his notes. 'She was wearing a travelling suit, the jacket over her shoulders, it seems; a short-sleeved silk blouse – suggesting her destination was somewhere with a hot climate; and the plane ticket in her handbag –'

'Her handbag?' Lucy spoke, and they all looked down at her. 'Was it – Did it have a big shiny clasp – like a C – or a G?'

'The deceased's handbag was underneath the body, Miss Morland. It was – Did it have a – a clasp, sergeant?'

The young policeman nodded. 'Yes, sir.' He turned to Lucy. 'It was a Gucci handbag, Miss.'

'So. Her handbag and her coat were in there with her. Her suitcase was outside, we understand.'

Mr Cornfield said: 'That is correct. When the sub – When Miss Morland arrived and contacted us about that, we assumed Mrs Maturin had discovered her baggage was excessive. It seemed the sensible thing to hand it over to the caretaker, Mrs Dortmund. Miss Morland suggested putting it in the cupboard; and we agreed that our client had probably intended to: tragically, it now seems she was attempting to do just that when… Be that as it may, officer, *we* had no key to her private storeroom. And under the circumstances we intend to take no action over the young lady's rough treatment of our client's property: breaking the lock and…'

'Just as well she did, Mr Cornfield,' snapped the police officer; 'and you might like to offer her alternative accommodation?'

'Oh, naturally: that goes without… We are booking a hotel room for you, Miss Morland,' enunciated slowly and clearly, as though to the disabled, 'and shall, of course, defray the expense.'

Father Sebastian spoke. 'That is very right and proper, I'm sure; but might I suggest that, now the disturbing influence has been explained and removed – God rest her soul in peace, poor lady – Miss Morland might well prefer to stay on until she has found other long-term accommodation? After all, that's why she took the flat.' He turned to Lucy. 'Do you know what I mean, child? Something like getting back up on a horse after a fall?'

Lucy nodded. She felt very tired and sleepy; but she was half aware of conflict, restrained and suppressed for her sake, going on above her still dizzy head; of the Law's and the Agency's nagging resentment and distrust of this white-collar West Indian who spoke with such authority, and some arrogance, about the psychological and practical advantages of the 'sub-let' staying on.

'Suits *your* book, friend: we can all see that.' This, from Mr Cornfield, was the only direct sally; and Sebastian's voice, deadly quiet:

'I have two other places of residence, my good man, as no doubt police enquiries will confirm – so let us not have any of that.' The West Indian accent was strong now. 'At least I was in a position to find her and call you – or, like your unfortunate client, she might have been discovered a whole lot later.'

161

A sergeant remained after the others left, and a policewoman was on her way round. The priest went out to make the most urgent of his pastoral visits: Lucy was asleep and safely guarded. He knew this; and knew he needed time to think, away from her, and the flat. Still he found it hard to go.

However thoroughly he had prepared himself for it, the sudden reality of the Belial Stone – there, in his hand, in the stuffy airing cupboard of a Kensington flat – had been overwhelming. Even now, walking along the familiar back streets to visit the needy, and breathing deep, consciously clearing his system of the dark poison, he felt weak as though he had run a marathon.

That brief onslaught of images should have been easier the second time; but now he knew no amount of anticipation, of study, or cool discussion of it with his teachers, could protect him from such naked evil. And not just the moments of contact. Never before – even when Bob Loren took it from him, even when he realised it was in the flat, even that dedicated New Year's midnight when he opened his mind to its so-close presence, and felt it stir and reach out from its cooling nest – never had he felt its pull as he had done on replacing it just where he found it. And he felt it now, dragging on him as he moved further from it, more real to him than the Friday shoppers as he threaded the busy street-market of the North End Road.

But there was another pull. A newer one altogether, and something he had not anticipated, reaching the places (he thought, as the lager hoardings shouted cheerfully down at him) that the Belial stone could not reach. That girl was getting at his heart and his loins. It was a complication; and he did not need complications just now.

Of course she was attractive: he had always admitted that; indeed, it was a vital part of his plan, the front that fooled the other seekers of the stone. He had thought it could only make the job more palatable. He had not thought he would fall for Lucy Morland.

And he only realised it now because of his pity for her. *That* was the irony. As a healthy, friendly young animal, nicely proportioned, glowing with charm and innocence, flitting round the flat, or coming home from work, pink-cheeked and happy to see him, he appreciated her. She was sweet and sexy. And safe. He had resisted temptation before, and would resist again. He was a busy man, fortunately; moreover, there were other, less vulnerable women available to him if he decided to give in to the need; and, on the principle of knowing there was a packet of cigarettes in his coat pocket – the same principle of choice – he chose to resist.

But she had got to him through pity. That moment when he laid her unconscious on the sofa, held her pulse, gently turned her head on one side and felt to make sure her tongue was forward, free – and his thoughts racing all the while over the stone's newest killing, and his imminent search for its hiding place – he registered, almost in passing, that *for this moment* Lucy was safe from him: he had experienced only charity.

Now, alone, he examined the irony of it: a moment of close, of intimate physical contact. The helpless body, the lovely, sleeping face, the parted lips and the warm, wet tongue on his fingers. And his passing thought, his surprise: I feel only pity and concern – *for the first time*.

Yet pity and concern were surely his brief. Use her he must, but protect and care for her throughout as a priest should. So: now he admitted it. I have felt protective about the girl, but never just that. Never. I have always fancied her. Lately, I've wanted her. I've gone into this situation, electing to live with her – so neat it's all been – with my eyes wide open, and not seen a thing. I had to experience a moment of purity, of pure caring, to discover I'm hooked on her… He stopped suddenly and stared at himself in a shop window.

'Oh brother,' he muttered: 'you just better watch yourself.'

Lucy made very little sense of that day. She remembered the police doctor flashing a light into her pupils, testing her reflexes, and, when the police had finished with her, giving her an injection. She knew she was 'in shock': Mrs Villiers – much later on, it seemed, and bearing grapes and magazines – told

163

her so. Lucy could remember the blue rinse bending close, that familiar sugary scent, and questions to which she could find no answering words; a small dark policewoman saying, 'Never you mind, my duck: she shouldn't have been allowed.'

Then it was evening, and she felt better: just a headache.

'You probably fell on the hammer when you fainted: you've a bruise on your forehead.' The priest was arranging cushions so she could sit up. All the others had gone. 'Here, drink this soup. You told the police you were going to stay on here – do you remember that?'

'Yes,' said Lucy. 'And I've decided I am.'

Any news that leaked out had reached the spooky set soon after opening time. They were all there, even Mr Winslow, even Germaine, waiting to hear the latest after Mrs Villiers' breathless report at lunchtime: something nasty had been discovered in dear Maisie's flat, and the police were still there.

Now she was able to up-date it: she had actually seen poor little Lucy.

'I waited, you see, until the priest went out; and then I persuaded this nice young policeman to let me make her some tea. "It's all very well," I said, "but she needs a woman's care and understanding." "A policewoman is coming round," says he; "still, there can't be any harm… " So I gave him a cup too; and that's when he softened up, as it were, and came out with it.' They all leaned closer. 'But he was ever so insistent it must go no further.' She sat back and sipped her gin-and-it.

'Dear *lady*!' cried Dr Max: 'we are a little *band* – are we not? Survivors on the troubled waters of this great heartless city: we must cling together – share all we have! Divided, we fall!'

They thrilled to his words and raised their glasses. (It was shorts all round this evening: 'Good for shock, m'dear,' as the Colonel observed.)

'Go on,' said Cecil: 'you can't stop now! And as far as *I'm* concerned, Mrs V. – reporter's honour – it's off the record.'

'And he was the one,' said Estelle: 'weren't you, Cecil? The first one of us who felt premonitions: you *said* you knew something was wrong, way back in December before she went off so suddenly, didn't – '

'Well,' said Mrs Villiers resuming centre stage. 'Well, this sweet young sergeant – so tall! – he didn't say much, mind you: it was all far too hush-hush. But when I told him – over our tea, as I said – that I was such a close friend of Maisie Maturin's, he did let slip that I should prepare myself for bad news: he even made me sit down – so charming – so thoughtful! He said: "We have reason to believe… " No: "we have reason to *suspect*… that your friend may be with us no more." '

She looked round them all, receiving their exhaled 'No!'s and 'Ah's like so many wreaths for the loved one. Then, whipping out a scrap of lace handkerchief and pressing it to one nostril, 'I suppose I was closest,' she said; 'but I know how you all… '

The Doctor squeezed her free hand, and there would have been an observed silence long enough for an angel to pass; but Cecil rushed in, wet-lipped and red-eyed.

'Why the ambulance, then?' he said in a dramatic stage-whisper.

'When?' snapped Mrs Villiers.

'This morning: quite early on – so Mr Winslow says – that right, Squire?'

The gracious old actor nodded happily, suddenly the focus of attention.

'It would have been,' he said slowly, 'towards nine-thirty. And the two police cars. I felt I should not loiter: it smacked somewhat of sensationalism. On my return, some dozen minutes later, only the police cars remained.'

'Oh, that,' said Mrs Villiers. 'They probably thought at first that poor little Lucy would have to be taken in. For observation, you know.'

'But suppose,' said Cecil, 'they did take someone away… ' He licked his lips, glancing round. 'Suppose – just suppose – dear Maisie had been there all the time.'

Mrs Villiers let out a little cry.

'I think she feels faint,' said Dr Max.

165

'I'll take her off to the Ladies,' said Estelle: 'get some nice cold water on her face.'

'No… no,' said Mrs Villiers: 'I must be strong. But I do think Cecil has gone a little far this time.' She sniffed and drew herself up. 'We must banish such thoughts; and concern ourselves with the living rather than the dead. I mean, think of that poor child – so pale, so weak – and with only that weird black priest for company: no kindred spirit to turn to… '

'But I thought you saw her and spoke to her,' said Estelle.

'Quite, dear; until I was hustled away, wasn't I? – by some little jumped-up police-woman no bigger than a traffic warden… '

'Where will she go?' asked the Colonel. 'Back to her people, I suppose.'

'Ooh, no! That's just the *point*, Colonel, dear,' Mrs Villiers cried: 'she's *staying on*! The young constable told me! And it was all that priest's doing, according to him. Yes: that's right! As good as insisted she shouldn't run away!'

'*Well*!' said the Doctor: 'with friends like that, as they say, who needs enemies?'

'Exactly! As the constable said, it suited that holy father's book just fine.'

'Implying that he had some sort of power over her,' said Dr Max nodding sagely. 'Yes indeed: he would want to stay there… I tried to warn her.'

Estelle said loudly: 'We must give her our support.'

'One of us should phone her, perhaps,' said Mrs Villiers.

The Colonel got up to buy another round. 'I don't mind going over there later on,' he said. 'I'd like to. Just to speak to her, you know – not to go in.'

Mrs Villiers nodded briskly, quite in charge again. 'I and the Colonel and Estelle will go across and talk to her.'

'Perhaps I should see her alone,' said Cecil. 'After all, it was me she came to when –'

The Doctor interrupted. 'Supposedly I myself am the best qualified to assess… '

'I think not,' said Mrs Villiers: 'not today. Lucy has been very poorly. Just a close friend or two with a warm word of goodwill and advice… Thank you, Colonel, dear: mine was gin-and-Italian, since you insist.'

Lucy's mother telephoned just before supper. Handing over the receiver, Father Sebastian murmured, 'Don't worry her, will you?'

'And whose lovely deep voice was *that*, then?' asked Alice.

'That's – oh, that's my new lodger,' said Lucy. 'He's a priest, actually: very kind and domesticated. And just about to cook me an omelette.'

'Oh darling, how lovely! Then I won't rabbit on – just wondering how you were, you know, and what it was like going back to work.'

'Fine, Mum; absolutely flourishing. Driven up in style, with all my lovely goodies from home.'

'But you sound a bit muted, darling: are you really all right?'

'Yes: I just had a bad – well, a headache today, as a matter of fact, and I've been lying low.' She realised it had to be all or nothing; and she was enough herself again to appreciate how catastrophic 'all' would be. One day soon she could tell her the whole story. Now she said work was going well, and she had had a raise. 'Mum, I'll come home for a weekend soon, OK? Yes, I'll go now: my omelette's ready. Love to Dad. And you. And thanks for everything. Bye.'

Half an hour later the phone rang again. Lucy took it; it was from a phone box, and when she heard Cecil's voice, she hung up quickly. About ten o'clock the doorbell went. Lucy answered it herself. It was Mrs Villiers, Estelle and the Colonel.

'Should you be up, dear? Are you really better?' They stood huddled together in the lobby and would not venture in; instead they beckoned her out, and she put up the catch on the door and followed them. 'Listen, dear: we just wanted to say that we're all thinking of you.'

'I'm all right, really – but I can't tell you anything, because I don't know exactly what happened.' The priest had primed her. 'It seems I just passed out.'

167

Glances were exchanged as Mrs Villiers reassured her. 'We wouldn't dream of asking you questions, dear. No, Lucy: *we* just hope and pray it isn't going to be out of the frying-pan and into the fire. I mean, are you sure he's a genuine priest? According to what the Doctor's heard, he's got some very strange friends – well, dear, as long as things get better, all well and good; but if not, then we'll know who's at the bottom of it, won't we? I mean, it's just so odd that he only started looking for a room after he'd heard of this one – Ah! You didn't know that, did you dear? And now he's insisting on your staying here and not running away... '

From the time her supper plate was empty, all through that evening and late into the night, Lucy was cross-questioned by the priest, interrupted only – but considerably disturbed – by those calls; and the censored chat with her mother had been far easier to take than Cecil's voice on the telephone, or the cronies' dire warnings in the lobby.

Even when she was planning her break-in that morning, a hundred years ago, Lucy had anticipated a confrontation with Father Sebastian. She knew she would have to explain; and there were some explanations she would like from him as well. The priest, however, had been very quiet: content even to watch television over their supper. He had looked after her without fussing her, and she was grateful; she still felt weak and curiously numb, but perfectly clear-headed. Then, quite suddenly, he had switched off the TV, taken her plate and fork from her, stacked it with his, and turned to face her.

'Now you're rested and you're fed, Lucy; and you seem to be out of shock. It's time to sort this thing out – OK?'

Never, not even at his Belgravia house, had she experienced his total concentration like this, nor felt his power to this extent. The gentle, self-contained lodger, the easy companion, the house-proud West Indian – even the enlightened darkie he sometimes played for Mrs Villiers: all had disappeared. This was the chief inquisitor behind a carved black mask. And he grilled her.

This time round she told him everything: first, all the strange occurrences – every one; and he wanted to know when they happened and in what order. Then her fears: of being haunted, of being taken over, of causing the disturbing phenomena, of going mad. Then her dreams, her illusions, her fantasies; he forced her to distinguish between them, so far as she could. When she admitted to her feelings, and the consuming guilt they gave rise to, he made her examine and explain the guilt. As his great relentless millstones ground finer, he forced her to describe the individual images, from her childhood nightmares as well as from the recent past – even when, like her guilty fantasies, they involved himself. He did not seem shocked; nor even surprised. Perhaps he was used to it.

It was late when he stopped the pacing and questioning. Untended, the fire had burned out. He poured her a small drink; and he lit them each a cigarette.

'And is that all? Are you *sure* that is all?'

Lucy nodded.

For a full minute the priest sat with his eyes closed. Then he leant back in his chair.

'So be it... Well then, it clearly wasn't your "influence" that's been disturbing things, was it? Now we know for certain of Mrs Maturin's death, and where, and how, we can reasonably assume you were being haunted: you really did see her ghost, Lucy – though I can understand how you convinced yourself it was some sort of doppelgänger emerging from a time-slip. But the handbag was conclusive; so precisely observed. An elegant proof... Now she has gone, poor lady; and all should be well.'

'But was she – was she *bad*?'

'Possibly. More likely just bored, I think; and inquisitive: involved in so-called "alternative religion": rather messy necromancy. The pace got too hot for her, I guess' – a grim smile of apology – 'anyway, she decided to quit; but, probably scatty and careless with some big fear by then, she managed to get locked inside that cupboard... '

'Did *you* feel anything wrong here?'

'I am not strictly speaking a "sensitive" by birth – simply well versed in these matters, as any responsible parish priest must be: so I recognised the symptoms, felt the vibes, spotted the pentacle; and, more than anything, observed you. You, *and* the ghouls, the grey people. The sort that gather round... '

Lucy was silent; then she said: 'Do you think it's gone?'

'Don't *you*? Go to bed now, child.'

She went: but she had observed, throughout these last exchanges, that Sebastian was only half there. She tried to sleep, but she had been unconscious for so many hours, it seemed; and, though she felt worn out, the day's grotesque images kept scattering the sheep she counted. So she turned on the light, and read.

Some time after midnight, and even through the clicking cooling sounds, she heard his swift, soft-footed tread along the passage. He knocked on her door

'Saw the light,' he said, sitting on the edge of the bed. He took her hand. 'Lucy, you haven't told me everything, you know. I didn't want to prompt you, or I'd be giving something away. But I've decided you simply didn't realise it was important. Now I'll tell you, so you can tell me.' He was very grave; and she knew she must concentrate. She drew her hand away and sat up, consciously exorcising the spell cast by his touch. This is a holy priest, she told herself: he holds hands professionally, to comfort the sick, to break bad news. 'I found Bob Loren's stone: it was hidden in the jacket of the hot water cylinder. In the cupboard. She must have been putting it there. So: tell me about it.'

'What, the ju-ju thing that's meant to sit on that little stand in the Shrine? *That* was important?'

'It could be a little matter of life and death,' said Sebastian.

Chapter Eleven

MRS VILLIERS HAD related titbits of the odd affair to her on so many occasions; now Lucy tried to piece them together.

The first version had been a simplified one. In the expanded edition, with helpful interpolations from Estelle, it emerged that Bob Loren had been terrified of the South African police – or the 'authorities' or the 'state': Mrs Villiers could not remember which. 'They wanted something he had; mind you, he was rather a highly strung young man – ever so good-looking.' 'And such a lovely skin!' said Estelle: 'always so tanned.' 'I mean, he could have been imagining the whole thing. But that's what he said, according to Maisie. "It's kind of powerful, for good or ill; they don't like me having it: afraid of who else might know of it – dangerous if it fell into the wrong hands – the black community, even." Anyway, he persuaded her to keep it for him "while the heat was on". They arranged to meet in Nairobi when the South African tour was over; but by then, you see, she'd grown very attached to it.' 'She used to do that, didn't she?' said Estelle: 'remember when she got so attached to that scarf you lent her?' 'Yes, dear; but this was different, wasn't it? This was special. I mean, no question of popping into Jaeger in the High Street and picking up another...

'Well, he just laughed at her: "Oh, you're 'rather fond of it', are you?" he says. "People would kill for this, and you want it as a *keepsake*?" She'd served her purpose, I suppose – and after all she'd done for him, nursing him and caring for him and

looking after his blessed ju-ju… She loved him, you see: she
wanted something to keep, something to bring him back to
her, him and his funny stone – well, more of an artifact really…
So she nicked a little snap of him; and she seemed to know
he'd come back one day: so sure of it, she was.'

(Here the priest nodded. 'Classic,' he said. 'A powerful lady,
Mrs M. And he came back?'

'Yes,' said Lucy. 'Actually I heard the rest later, though of
course I knew already how it ended.')

'Oh, he came back, dear. She said he would and he did:
Maisie was never wrong about things like that… When he did
come, well, it was like visiting royalty – quite a turn up for the
books! Oh yes, most of the regulars can remember two
members of the group walking in, asking for Maisie Maturin –
Fancy that: pop stars in the Clarence! They said the drummer,
Bob Loren, wanted his fortune read. Well of course, like I told
you, she'd done fortune-reading for famous people in her
time, politicians, artists, TV personalities – ' 'Only a news
reader,' said Estelle, 'and only for the deaf. Don't see him at all
these days, so maybe… '

('They argued about that,' Lucy said; 'but later on the others
were talking about "gifts" – foresight, and seeing auras,
healers and seventh sons of seventh sons: all that; and Mrs
Villiers came out to the kitchen with me… ')

'Let's leave them to it,' she had said: 'sometimes it's better
not to be too inquisitive about the future, perhaps. I mean –
what about poor Bob Loren? Well, it seems Maisie took one
look at the cards and was reluctant to go on. So she started
making all sorts of excuses. But he insisted; and in the end he
promised her the stone as payment. So she made up something
about a spell of bad luck – beware of Thursdays and a tall fair
stranger from the South – *you* know. But he wasn't impressed:
said it wasn't good enough for that sort of prize, put down a
tenner and walked out. "Quit screaming," he says at the
door, "and you can have the bloody thing when I've finished
with it." "That'll do nicely," says Maisie. But still he didn't
twig… Well, there it was, a fortnight or so later, packed in a
jiffy-bag and stuffed through her letter-box. No name. And

she knew right away: she'd forseen his death, you understand.'

'She could have been responsible for it.' The priest was thoughtful. 'She knew so much... Did Mrs Villiers tell you how he died?'

'She said something about a car accident; and that the coroner had dragged out the inquest before deciding on accidental death. "Must have been a bit fishy," Mrs Villiers said; "but the oddest thing of all was Maisie coming over at lunch-time and telling us. And then the papers. She *knew*." '

'There was even a question of suicide at the time,' said Sebastian. 'Mrs Maturin was never questioned by the coroner, or he could have put two and two together: that the stone was delivered some time during the morning – it *was* a Thursday – and Bob died later that day. For him, surely, it was just a question of safe-keeping, "while the heat was on" again. Probably a contract was out on him, and he got word. But we'll never know how far Mrs Maturin was responsible for putting the finger on Bob; all we can be certain is that she went across to the pub and said he had "passed on", and he was dead by evening. So: either she foresaw the future, or she rearranged it.'

'And *I* thought all along it was just more gossip, the sort they live on, the Clarence regulars: Maisie's big affair... '

'She was a virgin, actually,' said Sebastian.

'But Bob Loren... '

'He was gay: a great charmer. I met him once... She had to be a virgin, Lucy: a prerequisite for the job. And the post mortem will prove me right.'

Lucy was silent. Then she said, 'The stone: where is it now?'

The priest frowned. 'I put it back.' He stood up and walked round to the window; he twitched back the curtain and stood looking out into the street. 'There was so little time to decide, with the police breathing down my neck. It's safest there. The people who want it – you saw one of them at my house that evening: a powerful and very dangerous man – they already suspect it is in London somewhere. The only way is to destroy

173

it, if I can. But the time is not ripe: it has to be caught at its moment of maximum growth and before the moment of spreading, of dispersal. Imagine a seed-pod, Lucy; all that potency must be trapped and contained, must be wiped out, before they can get it. If I had it, they would know. It changes people, you understand... Yes, it's safer there. But – God forgive me – now I can guess how Jesus must have felt when Lucifer offered Him the kingdoms of the earth, the principalities and powers – handing Him a stone like this – what a pity, eh? that He didn't just turn it into bread... Yes indeed: it's in the records. One of these consecrated, these *unholy* – little – stones – was there, in Galilee, in that year... '

It was as if he were talking to himself: brooding, remote, eyes half-closed. He believes that the stone is magic, thought Lucy watching him; and I suppose it could be if you believed in it enough. But her straight, practical mind stopped short, a horse refusing a jump: if it was a matter simply of keeping some precious object safe from the bad men who wanted it, like a thriller on TV, then all there was to fear was some mafia character forcing a window, surely. She said: 'Sebastian, won't the people who are after it suspect you are guarding it? After all,' she added slowly, 'that's why you're here, isn't it? Why you persuaded me not to move?'

He stood at the end of the bed, and smiled. 'You read me, girl? Yes, I did suspect the stone might be here, particularly when I found *you*: just the sort of "keeper" Mrs Maturin would have chosen for it, to serve, to be taken over. The poor lady could have no conception of *your* power, you see... But I was genuinely fearful for you; and when an "unspooky" individual like you started seeing ghosts, well, it looked like she – it – was getting to you. I moved in because I felt I could support your – your innocence; and to find the stone. As it happened, you opened the cupboard first. I wanted to save you from that: I failed to guard you from your own curiosity. But to answer your first question: no, they don't suspect that's why I'm here. They know of you, and at least one has seen you. You are my cover: the man I'm talking about would assume I was visiting my mistress; that's how his mind works – and for our security

174

from his circle, it's a great front. Have I shocked you?'

He stood beside her, looking down at her. She studied the counterpane, silent. His mistress, she thought. A simple con... Then: 'I believe I'm rather flattered, Father,' she said.

Sebastian laughed, roughing up her hair, a sort of blessing, and went to the door. Thin ice. They were both behaving beautifully. 'Sorry you had to hear of the stone: I'll tell you the whole history one day. Now, the less you know the better. It doesn't tempt you; and its physical manifestations have stopped troubling you.'

'Maybe that's because of you,' she said. 'But the trouble hasn't actually gone away, has it.' It was not a question.

'Well, we seem, together, to have insulated it: it's better now, maybe different, a mere hobgoblin. You know, I did consider bell, book and candle; I've done it before. But it's strong stuff: can stir things up, particularly if it doesn't hit the target. So I want to consult my old teacher in Brixton. He wouldn't come here; but with all you've told me now, he will know what to do. And Lucy, don't worry about this stone. Don't be afraid: it can't affect you: *you* haven't changed.'

'But might you change? Are you – good?'

'Who can say he is good? I cannot answer that. I believe I am a force, or the channel for a force. By their fruits ye shall know them.' Inscrutable and withdrawn once more, he nodded and closed the door behind him.

The priest was involved in church and parish over the weekend, and his old teacher had a family gathering in the early part of the week; so the visit to Brixton was arranged for Thursday evening.

Sebastian left after vespers.

'I can't tell how long I'll be,' he said to Lucy; 'but this will take some time.' It was the jeans, sneakers, and an old baseball jacket this evening: a becoming garb, and she smiled. 'Hey, you're looking for my rasta bobble cap, aren't you, white gal? You always think I'm playing a part now, eh?' and he feinted a slow left to her jaw.

She laughed. 'As long as *you* keep track of who you are, it's great – just hard sometimes for a simple girl to keep up. I find myself imagining this scene... '

'Zowie! (as I say when I'm wearing my baseball jacket) – a brand new one? X certificate?'

'Sebastian, that's not fair – that's a rotten –'

'Tell me your scene. Please. I'll shut up my big mouth – OK?'

'Oh, I don't know: just wondering how you'd cope. Like, there's you in the Bentley.'

'I *never* had a Bentley.'

'Hush. Your limousine, and the cashmere casuals and the shades, swanning along to a party in Mayfair, and you get a call: Action Stations: trouble in Lewisham: one of your old parishioners is being held for ransom by three vampires and a rabid werewolf – right? Sebastian to the rescue – But you've gone out in your wrong ego – and down Lewisham way the limo and the cashmeres are considered threatening.'

'So: I park the limo and get my collapsible thousand cc Norton out of the boot. All right so far? In a vandalised phone box (no lights, Clark Kent never thought of that), with a *roar* of velcro, I tear off the suedes and the cashmeres. I step out, leap on to my throbbing Norton, and erupt in Lewisham High Street: the Black Runner to the rescue – da-dah! No? Tell you what, Lucy: I'll have a tracksuit tatooed on to me – just the welts at neck, wrists and ankles – OK? And then some fighting slogan on the front, like: "Satan Sucks"? Perhaps not. Don't worry: my old teacher will think of a good one. Come to that, he'll also know the very best private tatooist... See you, gal. No worries?'

'No worries.'

'OK. Don't let in any strange men.'

'Oh, I wouldn't.'

It was after eleven, and Lucy was in her dressing gown and nightdress cleaning her teeth when the bell rang. He's back early, she thought – and must have forgotten his key.

176

Usually you could see recognisable shapes through the frosted glass; but the light in the lobby was already on its time-switch, and all she knew was that someone was standing there in the dark. That was strange in itself. She called through the front door, 'Who is it?' Sebastian would not just stand there silently.

A quiet voice said: 'It's only me, dear girl: Dr Max, you know.' And Lucy was so relieved she opened the door swiftly, almost glad to see him.

'Oh Dr Max – goodness, it's so late! Is anything wrong?'

'Not at all, Lucy: just a friendly call to see how you were recovering.'

'How kind. Well actually I was just going to bed. D'you think you could make it another time?'

'Oh come, my dear: it's only just after eleven! And your friends have been kept away for nearly a week: we were beginning to fear the worst! Lucy, I *am* a doctor after all, and I've been sent along to see you – just for a moment – so I may set their hearts at rest. You can imagine how fussed they are! But really, child, you can't keep me talking out here... That's better.'

He closed the door behind him. It's all right, she told herself; he isn't a strange man: just an all too familiar bore. And that soft soothing voice she found so irritating went on:

'Well well – and it was in the drawing room, was it not, that you saw the, the manifestation?' He produced the word with the lowered eyelids and voice, the slight grimace, used by the fastidious for subjects like hysterectomies and head-lice. 'But the poor lady herself? Not another word, dear girl... And you've quite recovered, have you? No after-effects? Concussion is not a thing to be taken lightly, you know. It must have been highly traumatic.'

'I don't remember much,' said Lucy, staying pointedly near the door. 'But I still seem to feel tired easily, so really I'd like to...'

'Quite right: rest the great healer. Of course, you'll have to cope with it psychologically one day: you're suppressing it now, you realise; and, as a psychiatric practitioner, I might be

177

able to – oh, not now, dear girl! But it's extraordinarily interesting, is it not? – the whole phenomenon of suppression and its root cause. As for that, dear child, and while I'm here – unencumbered by Maisie's old pals, eh? – there are one or two small points I would very much like to investigate further.' He was taking off his coat.

'Sorry Dr Max, but you must go: I don't feel like any – '

'Why of *course* not, Lucy! Don't worry – I have absolutely nothing I need to ask of you – goodness me, you *are* in a state, aren't you? You really shouldn't let yourself get so over-excited, you know; perhaps I should give you a little sedative injection. No? Well, you can run along to bed; and I'll make a few quick observations round the flat and have a word or two with our dear Father Sebastian: so knowledgeable, so articulate.'

'Father Sebastian isn't – He isn't up still, I'm afraid. He's asleep. I think.'

'Oh dear. I rather wanted to have a brief look in the spare room – that is where he sleeps, I assume,' and he smiled at her over his shoulder as he moved off down the passage. 'If I'm quick I might just catch him still reading the Good Book.'

'Please *don't*!'

But before she could stop him he tapped on Sebastian's door and opened it swiftly without waiting.

'Dear me,' he said, switching on the light. 'Perhaps he went out through the window! He's an odd man, isn't he, my dear? But I must say... ' he was pacing round the room, picking up the priest's belongings – his books, his ivory-backed brushes, his cufflinks – peering at them and replacing them – 'I must say, I didn't put him down in my private diagnosis as a night prowler! Come to think of it, our mystery man might well have to flit off under cover of darkness: how else would he lead his double life?'

'Please, Dr Max – will you go now? You can see – '

'But perhaps you didn't know he led a double life, Lucy? Oh yes indeed.' Now he had stopped in front of the warm wall. Very lightly he placed his well-manicured finger tips on it and closed his eyes for a moment.

'Dr Max! I insist – '

'Oh yes indeed,' raising his voice and steamrollering on: 'our humble priest is in reality a very wealthy man with a circle of equally wealthy – and equally interesting – friends: a species of underground jet-set; a "sub-set", if you will: gun-runners, gamblers, drugs millionaires, a sprinkling of deposed dictators and exiled royalty too hot even for established society to handle – and all with the most extravagant taste in companions. Oh yes, he's got that long – black – finger of his in a lot of pies, has our Sebastian. I've been doing my own tiny bit of detective work, you see, and now I'd like to make sure precisely what… '

'You knew he was out, didn't you? That's why you came.'

'Just so, Lucy: that's why I came. As I tried to tell you, there is some very good reason why he wants to be here, in this flat; and I intend to find out – for your sake as well, dear girl: I will not stand accused of mere idle curiosity.'

'Suppose I don't want you here. Suppose I shout for help, or telephone the police.'

'Go on, sweet creature. Do both if you like: whatever turns you on, as they say. Personally, I should welcome the opportunity to ask the neighbours, and especially the police, a question or two – and I'm certain the law would be interested in some of the juicier bits of information on the extra-curricular activities of our absent friend. Surely it could not have escaped your notice that they were not merely puzzled by your dusky flat-mate; they were downright suspicious. Be honest now, Lucy – and you've known me for a while now: far longer than your, your – association – with him. Be honest, my dear, and tell me: don't you wonder about him, just a little? I mean,' the soft hypnotic voice flowed on, 'I admit, we *all* admit, how attractive, how eloquent, how charismatic the good father can be; and we've watched you, dear girl, falling under his spell. No, hear me. First you turned him down when he showed interest in your spare room: we were all there, remember. Then he moved in – what a flutter in the dovecots *that* caused! – but only till you found a girl instead. Am I right?'

179

Lucy opened her mouth to speak but he stepped close and laid a finger over it. She backed away as though he had stung her.

He smiled. 'Very exclusive, I see,' he said. 'And the room? Still no nice working girl has answered the advertisement you did not put in the papers... Then, shock-horror, as they say: something nasty comes to light in this lovely home. Police, ambulances, the sub-let in a state of collapse; she is offered alternative accommodation, right? I know I'm right.' His voice, still quiet, was harsher now. 'But you turned it down and stayed here, on the advice of that same tinted gentleman, your so-called *lodger*!'

He almost spat the word. Then he laughed and crossed into the kitchen.

'Got any of that good malt, my dear? Perhaps we could both do with a wee dram. Ah, here it is: the medication that requires no prescription. I'll pour you one while you ring the police: I should genuinely like to see them, you know. For example, apropos Mrs Maturin's mysterious death – and my dear, I play golf with Cornfield senior: I probably know more about this business last Friday than you could ever hope to put together in your concussed state. The police are aware that you came to Clarence Mansions on the evening she died; and they haven't ruled out murder – drink your whisky, dear girl – if, as I was saying, they discovered you had come into the flat – '

'But Dr Max, I *didn't*!'

'Be quiet. Let us suppose she was here, and she let you in and told you she had changed her mind, and you killed her and locked her in the cupboard and went off, all innocent.'

Lucy burst out with an angry laugh. 'But it's not a motive for *murder*! Losing a four-month let, for God's sake! I mean, it's just ridiculous! And anyway the girls upstairs knew I couldn't get in.'

'Come come, now: you could so easily go upstairs and establish witnesses after the event – as easy as leaving the Yale key in the pocket of the corpse – there's not much I don't know, you see: golf is a very edifying pastime. And as for motive – well... ! You know and *I* know there is a motive for

180

murder – indeed, for *mass* murder, at various times in its long life – concealed right here; and what is more, I believe,' he said, moving to the cupboard with its shiny new lock, and laying the palm of his free hand flat against the wooden panel, 'I do believe I may be getting warmer…'

'But *I* didn't know about the –' Lucy stopped short, and reached for the whisky she had refused. 'I'm perfectly innocent,' she said. 'And I want you to leave. Now.'

Dr Max strode back into the kitchen and grabbed her with one hand by the neck of her nightgown, squeezing her back against the wall.

'*What* didn't you know about, Lucy? What precisely was it that you didn't know and do now? *Ah* no.'

His whisky glass crashed to the floor as he snatched her hand away from the knife drawer. Holding her neck and her wrists he forced her down until she was on her knees.

'Well well!' he breathed, letting her go and stepping back: 'who would have dreamed our dear little Lucinda could even think of such things! Is it too much Hammer Horror on the TV, or could that sweet innocent face really be hiding a murderous heart?'

Lucy coughed weakly, holding her throat.

'You were hurting me,' she said. 'I was frightened.'

Dr Max felt safe enough to get himself another glass from the cupboard.

'Come, my dear: get up. Forgive me – I forgot myself.'

She could see he was still shaking as he lifted his glass to his lips. He's mad, thought Lucy; and what's more he knows about the stone. But his reasoning and his threats had been clear enough: if she brought the police in, it could be dangerous for herself – and how dangerous for Sebastian she could not even guess. And yet – and yet: to explain their presence, their interest in the flat, the doctor would surely have to abandon his own designs on the stone; and daring her to ring the police was a bluff he had convinced her she could not call.

Was this one of the powerful, dangerous men the priest had warned her of? Would he not have named him? Lucy felt

181

instinctively that the psychiatrist was simply not in that league: when he spoke of the underground jet-set it was with all the awed and prurient disapproval of the outsider. All she could do now was to pray that Sebastian would return, or that this nutter would make his investigations, whatever they were, and leave quickly.

'Seriously, Lucy,' he was saying, 'let us at least agree not to act hastily: we both of us have so much to lose. I should not have been so rough; and you would be most unwise to summon help: I think you can see that. Moreover, if you should decide the only other way to stop me is to put a kitchen knife between my ribs and plead self-defence – and I hope I don't misjudge you when I assume that bungled attempt was pure impulse rather than the result of such cold planning – then it would very swiftly become obvious, from the coroner's questioning of old Cornfield if from no other source, that I was onto something very odd to do with our friendly neighbourhood priest and his so carefully selected lodgings. You would be facing, not "manslaughter in self-defence", but "murder of a key witness". Do you understand? Go on: finish your drink and toddle off to bed, dear girl. Neither of us dare do the other any mischief.'

He was in the passage now, opening his doctor's bag. He took out some sort of meter, quite small, like a surveyor's hydrometer.

'So, on that understanding, I will presume to turn my back and get on with my inquiries. I have wasted time as it is; but if we have achieved some sort of truce, it may be time well spent – for both of us.'

He was examining the new lock as he talked. Lucy backed away down the passage, sore, angry and helpless. She saw him go into Sebastian's room. And I can't do a bloody thing, she thought.

'Don't worry: this won't take long,' he leaned out and called softly after her; 'Oh, and don't try climbing out of the window, will you? I'd hear – and I might get even rougher next time.'

Down in the cellar the boiler went off. But there was no question of bed or sleep while he was there; she put the electric fire back in the sitting room hearth and switched it on to keep herself warm. Through the clicking noises she could hear the psychiatrist moving about in the spare room. Now it sounded as though he were shifting the furniture around: a faint bumping and scraping. If he tried breaking open the cupboard or picking the lock, surely she should ring the police: he couldn't talk his way out of that. Or could he? She felt too bruised and weary to work it out; but for some reason she was fairly certain that he would not take the stone; that he would not dare.

She went over to the window and gazed through a crack in the curtains at the empty square, willing the priest to appear... Her neck was sore where the mad doctor had held her. He'll go soon, she told herself: he's just got to make sure the wretched ju-ju is still there – that Sebastian, or even the police, haven't removed it. She realised that, though the Doctor was only a small time villain – a ghoul at heart, a fringe person who had struck lucky – and did not even qualify for the priest's blacklist of searchers, yet his most serious threat lay in what he knew and could tell the others, the people powerful enough to buy his information and use it. This place was no fortress; as Father Sebastian had pointed out, its strength was in its anonymity. Once the Doctor had sold his secret to the highest bidder, it would be only a matter of time.

She glanced at her watch. The flat had been very quiet now for several minutes. Perhaps he had finished his investigations and gone. Instead of getting rid of him, should she not have tried to keep him here till the priest returned?

Lucy went along the passage cautiously. She saw the meter by the door; then she saw his legs. He was lying face down on the carpet close to the magnetic wall, and he was unconscious.

She had not thought of the razor-blade effect as a line of defence.

Dr Max looked terrible. She must not let him die here in the flat. If only he could get up and go and die elsewhere, she thought, and felt gingerly for the pulse in the pale muscular neck. As she did so he grunted and half-opened his eyes.

'Help me, girl,' he groaned. 'Help me out of here – no: don't call anyone else.' He was holding her wrist and would not let go. 'Don't want anyone else,' he smiled lopsidedly. 'You know why.'

He clung on to her with surprising strength. 'Help me stand.' Still clutching her he dragged himself to his feet, almost pulling her down, and leaned heavily on her as he hobbled along the passage. He collapsed on the sofa. 'Whisky,' he said, 'get me some whisky.'

This is my chance, she thought – but the sensible watchdog voice said, 'What, more ambulances and scandal? Come, dear: can't you see that just at present it wouldn't do at all for this address to hit the headlines? No: play for time, and your priest will be here… '

When she got back with the whisky he had a small phial of pills in his palm.

'Two,' he rasped: 'give me two.'

He swallowed them down with a gulp of malt, grimaced as it burned his mouth, and then exhaled noisily. 'Har – that is better. Bad luck, little girl: I haven't died yet. I'd better not, eh? Embarrassing for you… Christ, but I did think I was dying.'

Lucy watched, disgusted and fascinated. His firm white flesh had a damp sheen; his abundant wavy grey hair hung limp and oily behind his ears, straggling over his open collar, the protuberant pale eyes staring down at the trembling hands.

'Something cut me,' he said, 'and it was like hundreds of knives slicing me to the bone.'

'There's no blood though,' said Lucy evenly. 'What were you doing?'

'I'd found a gap between two pieces of skirting board. I wanted to get my geiger-counter in there, and I was trying to prise the short bit of skirting off and suddenly there was a frightful – assault… '

'Like knives in your hands, you said.'

'Knives all over my body. I felt it in my hands first and then all over me, even in my neck, my face – and I remember

184

holding my hands over my eyes and still feeling those blades striking through... Extraordinary – and when I tried to call out – to scream – my throat seemed to be paralysed... ' He put down his glass and massaged his throat, then felt carefully all over his face and neck. 'No marks? No blood? Most extraordinary – hard even to remember it, now that I'm better, much less describe it; but the shock, the *pain*... You knew! You *knew* about it – didn't you? *Didn't you?*'

'Please – You're hurting me – let me go – I didn't know – how could I know it would – ?'

'You knew. And you didn't say – you just bided your time. My Christ! You vicious little tart!' The slap he laid across her mouth and cheek did not feel like the parting shot of a dying man. He gripped her by the shoulders and pushed his face close to hers. 'So you set me up – then you toddle back when you reckon I'd be good and dead... And now, dear me! How unfortunate for you! I've recovered – completely recovered – an interesting phenomenon, eh dear girl? Almost as if I'd been recharged!'

He held her with one hand and with the other he started undoing the ribbon at her neck. His full, wide lips kept on talking, spraying her face with stale whisky. 'Magnetism – that's what it used to be called, my sweet: Dr Mesmer and his Rejuvenating Magnet' – tearing open the front of her nightgown. 'He could make the dead to rise – did you know? – and feel *that*, dear creature.' He grabbed her hand and pressed it against his crutch: 'Alive-alive-o!'

You don't hit out at an invalid; and Lucy started fighting a moment too late. Stunned by the slap, she still did not realise what she was up against. Now, as she wrenched her hand away from his bulging flies, twisted free and ran for the door, she knew she was running from rape: that staple of horror movies and jokes in bad taste, of the *News of the Screws* 'Exclusive' and the therapy centres where you could go and talk about it; the violence that was closest to murder, and only happened to other people. All this she knew in the seconds it took to reach the passage. Looking down the long shadowy path to the distant front door, she thought she saw something moving –

185

then he grabbed her by her hair from behind and wrenched her head back until she was on the floor.

The fall winded her. She hit out and tried to scream, but it came out as a gasp; and he stuffed his silk handkerchief into her mouth with one hand, pinning down her wrists with the other. Dr Max's indecently muscular body was heavy on her, sweet-and-sour with malt and acid sweat. His strong legs held her firm while he tore at her nightdress, opening it to the waist and then, arching up and pulling at the tangled skirt. 'You can soon stop fighting,' he hissed: 'you'll like this, dear girl.' His coarse lips and smooth hands were all over her. 'A welcome change from your black stud,' he mumbled into her neck; and she felt him rummaging to reach his trouser zip. Then he was forcing his fingers between her tightly clenched thighs.

'Christ!' he said and lifted his head to look at her; and he laughed. 'Stone me if you aren't a fucking virgin after all!'

But the rictus of laughter seemed to freeze, as though the reel of film had stuck. Slowly he started moving again. He dropped her, drew away from her; and all the while his eyes were staring at something just beyond her line of sight. She wrenched her head round to see. There was only the open door, the dim passage light and the mottled black and red carpet, all swaying slightly with her own faintness. She dragged the stifling gob of silk out of her mouth, rolled over and vomited. She heard and half-saw him going: hurried, stumbling, still unzipped; no parting shot, nor explanation – just a rasping version of the heavy breathing she had felt hot against her breasts and neck and stomach. The distant door slammed and he was gone.

She lay still for a while; but the floor was swaying, and she got to her feet, found her way along to the lavatory and was sick again; then she crawled into bed. And it was only as she was going through to the bedroom that she registered: the carpet in the passage was brown and grey and orange, not black and red.

Chapter Twelve

SICK AND SHIVERING she lay in bed, unable to sleep.

Her body felt trampled and mucky. The chill sheets seemed to stick to her, the blanket rasped her sore skin. She could still smell him on her torn nightdress, on her hands; and the taste of whisky and vomit and Dr Max lingered in her mouth. She dozed off and dreamed he was there and woke strangling, gagging. Her hair, pillow and neck were wet and slimy. She got up and washed all over at the basin, fearing herself too weak to climb out of a bath. She found a fresh nightdress, crept into the priest's bed for safety, and fell asleep.

Sometime towards four he returned. She thought it was a dream. She woke, felt warmth, and found him there holding her close and chaste. She tried to tell him what happened, but she broke down, weeping desperately; and he stroked her hair and calmed her shuddering till she drifted off into a dreamless sleep.

It was at 7.05 am that the police rang the bell. A newspaper reporter, one Cecil Scarfe, and a retired colonel who lodged in the same boarding house, came along to show them the way. So, this was the flat where all the excitement had been on Friday... They rang again, peering through the ripple-glass. Inside, a door opened, a figure approached and pulled back the bolts, unfastened the latch.

It was the girl. She was rumpled and sleepy, and wearing a

man's dressing gown: good quality dark blue silk.

'Miss Morland? Sorry to disturb you; may we come in and ask you a few questions?'

Unaccustomed to the closeness of the noise in that room, Lucy had been woken at six by the central heating. The priest was turned away from her, fast asleep. She dozed, woke again and lay very still for fear of disturbing him; lay thinking about the long extraordinary night that was now over. And I never dreamed I would sleep in this bewitched room, she thought, or sleep so well; or sleep with – yes, I have dreamed of that. She knew she must get up and deal with the mess in the drawing room and the bedroom; also that her bruises and stiffness, now only a dull ache, would hit her when she moved. Five minutes more basking peacefully in the priest's warmth, and then she would get herself up. Or perhaps he would wake; and everything would... That was when the bell went.

The police had been back more than once since Friday; she was only surprised to see two new faces, and that they should call so early, with Cecil and the old Colonel in tow. Now the constable thanked them for their help. Lucy could see they were disappointed by this clear dismissal; but she was relieved: it was the first time she had seen the journalist since the evening when he chased her and frightened her so. How relatively harmless that eager, ferrety face looked now.

As she led the way along the corridor to the sitting room, she apologised for her state of undress, the untidiness of the flat; and took them to the table in the window where she opened the curtains and glanced anxiously round the room. Apart from a cushion and a whisky glass on the floor, and the electric fire still burning, there was nothing untoward, no signs of struggle; she could deal with the carpet later.

The constable brushed her apologies aside. 'Miss Morland, we understand you were acquainted with Dr Max Gassman; is that right? And when did you last see him?'

Lucy knew she had jerked her head round on hearing the name; now she must be very careful what she said, what she suppressed. Something had happened. But there was no sense in denying his late visit: Cecil and the Colonel would certainly know of it.

'Here, last night; sometime after eleven,' she said. 'Maybe eleven-thirty. He called to see if I was better. Why, is something wrong?'

The priest came in, dark-suited and dog-collared. It was clear that the police knew about him. They explained their early call, checked that he had been out: mere confirmation, it seemed. Then they turned back to Lucy.

'Dr Gassman is dead, Miss; at his apartment in West Kensington. A lady who – who also lives there came home at about five this morning and found him. It was she who put us in touch with Mr Cecil Scarfe, a journalist, and he told us the deceased had planned to call on you. This means, Miss Morland, that you could have been the last person to see him alive.'

'I understand,' she said.

'May I ask if you know the cause of death?' asked the priest. She was glad to have him there; grateful for time to collect her thoughts.

'Well now, sir... ' These policemen seemed both more embarrassed by the situation and more respectful towards Lucy's unconventional lodger than the others had been. 'The doctor who examined him was somewhat puzzled, to tell you the truth. It looked like suicide at first: razor wounds, you know; but then it emerged – Well, it seems an odd sort of way to take your own – I'm sorry, Miss Morland. I do hope this may not upset you; a shock, I know, so early in the morning – but I understand he was only an acquaintance; and if you can throw any light... He bled to death, you see, from what, as I say, appeared to be razor wounds: fine deep incisions all over the body and – Miss Morland? Miss, are you... ? Get her some water, sergeant.'

Lucy had sat down suddenly and covered her face with her hands. The constable pulled over a chair and sat beside her.

'I'm sorry, Miss, but I do have to ask you some questions – all right? When did Dr Gassman leave?'

'After twelve,' she said between her hands, 'about twelve-thirty – maybe a little earlier.'

'I see. So he was here for an hour or so. Can you tell me what sort of state of mind he was in when he left? Did he seem depressed, or – ?'

'Not depressed – certainly not that.' She laughed harshly. The priest put a hand on her shoulder.

'Take it easy, Lucy,' he said. 'Officer, the good doctor tried to rape her. Then something frightened him off and he left quickly. I don't think she can tell you much more than that.'

'I'm so sorry, Miss Morland: what an unfortunate experience. Did you call for help?'

'He – he –' she broke down sobbing.

'Here, drink some water, Miss. Try to answer, please.'

'He gagged me with his handkerchief,' she whispered.

'I see. Now, do you know what could have frightened him off?'

The girl sat up and opened her eyes wide at the policeman.

'Maybe he saw a ghost,' she said flatly.

'Officer, I think Miss Morland should be allowed to rest now,' said the priest. 'As you know, she has had another bad experience very recently, and we shouldn't put too much strain on her.'

'Very well, sir. Now, you say you were out last evening… '

They went off down the passage; and after a few minutes, Lucy heard the police leave. The priest came back.

'You OK, Lucy? They're just going to ask the people in the other flats if they heard anything,' he said. 'They'll probably be round for more answers this evening. They'd have to, considering the other interesting piece of information they vouchsafed on leaving: the police doctor said the wounds appeared to have been inflicted some hours before death occurred.'

They stared at each other, silent.

'Seems like the devil, too, moves in a mysterious way,' said Father Sebastian.

News of the psychiatrist's demise hit the Clarence lounge bar at lunch time. By evening, all the various rumours had been drawn together, from what the police asked Cecil, what they told him, and what could be gleaned from hearsay and neighbours. Even Germaine was involved: she had been forced to put up a 'Closed' sign on the whole-food shop while the Law questioned her; and it was she who disclosed that before Doctor Max died he had assaulted Lucy.

'Attempted rape,' she said, still out of breath; 'and something scared him and he ran off home and there he met his fate – a most bizarre retribution, don't you think?'

This was strong meat indeed; and the spooky set spent a happy hour worrying at it. Mrs Villiers kept saying, 'I'd never have *dreamed* – would you ever have dreamed, my dear? – that our dear Doctor... '

Cecil's theory was that the Dark Force – his collective term for whatever had caused all the strange happenings in the flat – had objected to Dr Max's attempt on Lucy.

'It's obvious, isn't it?' he said, lowering his voice so they all leaned closer, and glancing nervously over his shoulder: dark forces, after all, could get around. 'I mean, she's Its *handmaid*! And It wanted her pure and unspotted – don't you see? It wants her for Itself!'

There was a silence, and 'last orders' was called up at the bar.

'What about the black priest, then?' asked Germaine. 'I thought you said that when you and the Colonel here went to the flat this morning with the police, you were quite certain she came to the front door from the priest's room – *and* that she was wearing a man's dressing gown – isn't that right, Colonel?'

The Colonel was shuffling his beer mat around. 'Oh I couldn't be certain, m'dear – couldn't swear in a court of law.'

'Well,' said Cecil, 'I was close to the glass door and I got the clear impression that a door opened on *that side* of the passage, and then there she was,' his tongue passed swiftly across his thin lower lip, 'all untidy, you know, and still tying the sash of this... '

Germaine cut in. 'There you are. So, I repeat: what about the black priest?'

191

'Oh dear,' cried Mrs Villiers: 'you don't think?'

'He must have,' said Cecil.

'But would – I mean – a *priest*?' Mrs Villiers was quite pink and a little tiddly; it had been a long session.

'The Borgias did,' said Estelle darkly. 'You saw on the telly.'

'But that lovely man!'

'Just so,' said Germaine, rather tart. 'But there's only one conclusion, you see – don't you?'

'No,' Mrs Villiers was shaking her head lugubriously. 'When I think of that poor, sweet, innocent…'

Cecil was smiling. 'Come on, Mrs V. – you'll have to face it – call a spade a spade, what?' (Only Estelle laughed at that) 'He's had her, and survived to –'

'*Ergo*,' Germaine was triumphant as the one who always hides the last piece of the jigsaw, 'Father Sebastian *is* the Dark Force.'

The priest made breakfast for them both when the police had gone.

'You get dressed,' he said. 'You must go to work, you know – for your own sake, Lucy.'

She did as he told her; and she put fresh sheets on her bed. She cleared up in the sitting room and found the damp silk handkerchief. Sebastian took it from her, wrapped it in newspaper and burned it in the grate.

'No, girl, you're not going to be sick again: you're eating your melon and your poached egg, and then you're away.'

So life went on, and Sebastian kept the wheels oiled. He was glad now he had insisted on Lucy's long break over Christmas; without that reserve of strength, she could not have taken the double crisis of the last few days. Now it was vital for both of them – for their safety as well as their sanity, to find a status quo, and establish normality; mix with people, go to the pub, entertain: to live and be seen to live their own routine, busy lives.

192

As far as outsiders were concerned – the neighbours, the police, and especially the seekers of the stone – life at No 2 Clarence Mansions, London W8, must look as safe and boring as rice pudding. Sebastian had to keep it so, day by day. And only he could know what his teacher had told him: for the next thirteen days, until the change of the moon, nothing must happen. Then, everything. Then, and not till then, the stone must be taken. That would be the moment to destroy its powers. Meanwhile, the seekers also were very well aware that time was short.

It was pass-the-parcel with the music running out: and he who held it then would be the winner – would take all, for better or worse – and the odds were on the latter: 'For this stone has gone too far,' his old teacher said. 'Everything you tell me only proves that which has been suspected, feared, foretold in the distant past and throughout its latest cycle: that too much evil has been invested in it over the recent centuries; and in the hands of one more evil man it could bring disaster. This time it must be destroyed. Sebastian my son, you must be strong to destroy it; and strong to wait, knowing all you do – but wait you must. There is a right time for everything. Clear your mind and see that it is really very simple: a stone egg that will be ready to hatch out in thirteen days; and you must cull it then. But how? The oldest ways are best, my son. Tell me, how did they break up the big rock-stones when they were digging the foundations of your father's house? Do you remember?'

'Heat and cold, master.'

'That is right, my son. You will find the way. But harken well, Sebastian: should you fail, or be tempted to fail; should the stone still be in your care when it "hatches", then – the Lord help you. For you, even you with your great strength, will become its creature; and I – even I, an old man – and all those who take on as their duty the care of the future, will be bound to hunt you down, you and the stone, and destroy you both before you destroy us. Alas, my son; for they say: in that evil day, chance and destiny will favour the keeper of the stone, and many people will die: six million was its last score – numbers so great they became mere abstractions... More real, more

193

imaginable to us mortals, is the individual death. And it has killed two recently, has it not?'

'Two, my father? Only the woman who was its servant, surely?'

'And another tonight – soon – no, calm yourself: it is not the girl. She is strong; and she does not threaten it. No, this is... ' He closed his eyes and sat silent for a moment. 'This is a dabbler, a grey person, who knows something and is eager to know more, and profit from it. He is, it seems, afraid of the stone; but he has meddled. He has presumed too much; and is even now shot full of the seeds of death which will grow and flourish and blossom red before morning. I am sorry, my son: it is no clearer than that. Yes, you must go. But she is safe. The stone kept her safe. It wants her, my son. It is only waiting.'

The weather was mild for early January. It made the dark morning walk to the underground much easier to face; and on Saturday when Sally and Eddie came round, it was warm enough, though muggy and sunless, to drink outside the Clarence. The priest was busy all day and did not join them, but Lucy provided a snack lunch in the flat, and showed them round.

'I don't *believe* it!' Eddie cried. 'My dear, you didn't tell us the half of it! This is a collector's piece, no less. You know, my TV producer friend would go *mad*! He'd commission a *Tale of the Unexpected* or something late-nightish to be written round it – he *would*!'

'Right,' said Sally: 'this is vintage ghastly: you should have a party, Lucy, to show it off.'

'I was going to – but it seemed a bit heartless, so soon: I told you about my landlady, didn't I?'

'Oh yes of course, poor soul. She died on holiday, didn't she? Wasn't it all a bit odd?'

'Well, nothing much has been made of it; her solicitor managed to contact a sister in Canada – who didn't seem greatly concerned, except about the will. A notice was put in the *Telegraph*. But no inquest yet. The police seem to have got it

194

under wraps for the time being.'

She did not tell them that Father Sebastian wanted to delay the coroner's inquiry, and that the police had agreed on the understanding that he would be able to provide some new information from Johannesburg within the fortnight. She had noticed that the law was far more prepared now to listen to the priest.

'Only because I have some useful friends,' he told her; 'they're not *all* publicans and sinners, my child. What's more, apart from that first funeral I told you of in the pub – remember the missing head? – when I overacted wildly, I have in fact sorted out various mysterious deaths involving black magic of a sort; so my credentials, though unconventional, are fairly sound. The police can't stop rumours, but they have fairly effectively concealed the fact that Mrs Maturin died *here* – and that is the most important thing for us. I'm afraid that when the coroner reveals all, reporters will try to get in on the act. And the agents may have trouble in selling the lease of this place; but your continuing presence here – '

'And yours.'

'And mine, will be recognised as a blow for good sense; Foss & Cornfield are prepared to let you live here for free, the police tell me, until they find a buyer: that's how good it is for them, you see. Cecil was the weak link, and they've put the frighteners on him. As a matter of fact, I think he was so shaken by Dr Max's sticky end he's unlikely to cause trouble. And now we seem pretty well trouble-free here, don't you feel? Whatever it was that caused the Doctor's multiple stigmata... '

'Hey, isn't that blasphemous?'

'Not strictly: not if you use it in the commonly accepted sense, a term – and I quote – for wounds psychosomatically or supernaturally induced (depending on whether you're a sceptic or a believer), usually associated with religio-hysterical awe and dread – right?'

'If you say so.'

'But whatever caused it is not concerned with us. I tried putting my hand in there – yes, I should have told you, I suppose: sorry, Lucy. Anyway, not a spark did I raise.'

'But then you're very odd,' said Lucy. 'I remember that first time I made you coffee, and you laid your hand on the kettle.'

'Come – not all *that* odd: mild electric shocks, like heat or cold, are quite resistable, you know, if you've learned to control your – your mind, for want of a bigger word: it's your being, really – but that sounds pretentious. How do you think people walk over hot coals?'

'They're sort of hyped up to do it, aren't they? Religious fanatics? You're not like that.'

'Oh yes: I'm a religious fanatic all right, since you put it that way. But you needn't let it bother you, gal.'

It was as far as he could go in preparing this fresh-faced girl for the strange happenings that lay ahead. She was no longer a mere helpless bystander: she was involved deeper than she guessed. Installed there as an acolyte, all unknowing, she had been in danger by the end of the first month of losing her identity to that power; another sacrifice. He longed to remove her from its force field, and from any fear of the seekers, but she was a vital piece in his endgame, like a lone white pawn capable of holding black knights and bishops at bay... Some pawn, thought Sebastian, standing at his bedroom window and watching her walk back across the square.

She had accompanied Sal and Eddie as far as the tube, and had clearly been waylaid by the window of one of the smart High Street florists on the way home. Now, as she drew nearer to the watching priest, her face and hair seemed to be lighted by the reflection of her armful of daffodils. Rapt and gilded, like some processional icon, she bobbed swiftly closer in the mild afternoon sunshine, her eyes narrowed against the light, half-smiling over the wealth of her cargo. And also, he thought, over the prospect of surprising me. Then she looked up and saw him; smoothed back her hair, suddenly self-conscious, and brandished her flowers, smiling up at him with her whole being, as though it were spring; as though she were in love.

It was this that made the enforced period of waiting so

painfully complex, so bitter-sweet. The strain of his task would surely have been enough, together with the anxiety he felt for his dying friend in hospital – and it was clear now he would die soon. The girl, whether he considered her a partner, a pawn or a goat staked out, was no longer merely a diversion to ease his vigil – though that, however cynical, was the way he had first seen it.

But it turned out to be far less simple. Ever since those illuminating moments of pity, it became clear that living at close quarters with an intensely attractive nineteen-year-old, and one, moreover, who had taken something more than a shine to her lodger, was a situation for which even Sebastian's colourful career had not prepared him. He had faced it: his own weakness; and he had mastered it. After all, he had expected, as he often reminded himself, to be drawn, physically, and to resist. But not that he would relish her company to this degree; nor that he might find her so familiar and sympathetic as to be thrown off his guard; nor – strangely enough for a man whom many women had loved – that she might fall in love with him. Perhaps that very innocence he rated so highly had lulled him into a false security: he had warned himself only against his own desire. And of this he had learned to take due care: he knew how easily he could forget this was just a job, a temporary position; could relax, as though accepting their life together as right and continuous. Moreover, he had, off guard, made one mistake. He remembered it all too well – and that in itself was dangerous. A chance remark: such a little thing.

It had been late one evening, and they were both tired; but reluctant to leave the crumbling end of a good fire. Or each other. They had been talking long, as they did on the odd evenings when they were both at home: talking about their respective childhoods – the first things they could remember, their favourite toys and games, their early fears, their special treats, their passing passions.

'Would you believe I was horribly horsey?' Lucy said yawning and tucking a fallen cushion under her head. She laughed at the memory. 'And not in the proper "English gel" –

the county way – at all, you see. I was simply in love with horses: with their faces, and the way they moved. I drew them hopelessly all the time, all over my exercise books; and I cut out adverts for White Horse – one of my special heroes – and carried them round with me – when my friends were having crushes on Mick Jagger or the games mistress.'

'I guess I was more like them. Girls. I was in love with girls – ladies generally – from way back – just as hopelessly: the kindergarten teachers, film stars, my mother's friends… Sneaked into *West Side Story* six times for Rita Moreno, I remember. But I did have a passion for octopusses at one stage: baby ones, you know.'

'Sebastian! How *could* you?'

'There you go! That's what they all said. But I just happened to encounter one, all translucent and solemn, with those great eyes… Like a tiny subaqueous owl clinging to my hand and gazing at me. One of my first dives – so I must have been very young – and in quite shallow water, all sea-grass, and a few pipers. I always looked for octopusses after that; and I used to think they knew I was friendly. I asked for a book about them when my birthday came around; and I learned how clever and how elegantly evolved they are – as my passion, of course, had already told me. Cephalopod. Head-foot. It was my magic word… But people used to be horrified. "If you bring one home, child, it's him or me!" That's what my mother said. So at least I didn't try to keep them captive.'

'You must have been an extraordinary little boy, Sebastian. Not just that – but to grow up and become what you are. All the things you've been.'

'Not at all: I played cricket and fought and looked forward to meals like any boy. I was lucky to have folks that didn't laugh at my silly questions; and especially in having a Wise Man for a godfather: not just witch-doctor wise, but well read, too.'

'Was it that godfather who gave you the house in London?'

'His brother was the man with the money; but yes, that's the godfather who inherited it and passed it on to me when he died a few years back. The house is nice; but it was poor compensation for losing him. He was the most important man in my life.'

'Not your father.'

'No: my father I simply loved. And wasted many years disapproving of. Almost like a younger brother, sometimes, when I had to go bail him out of trouble.'

'But you must have inherited quite a lot of his nature.'

'You on about my wild streak again, gal?' He laughed and stretched. 'Yeah man, the fighting and the jazz... He was a terrific piano player – did I tell you? Not just the grand piano he imported for the crazy big house he built: even when he was in the money, all respectable, he used to escape down to the rum-shop and meet his friends for late night sessions round the old battered upright there. Yes, I got some of that from him.'

'But what made you give up all that and study philosophy? Was that your godfather, the Wise Man?'

'Indirectly, yes. Travelling the world as a young man with introductions from him – and from his wealthy brother – so I had a way in to the oddest circles: Maxim's and Mount Athos. Monks and millionaires... And in the end, the monks won – though I tried everything else on the way, I guess.'

'And it's – it's still millionaires and monks. Isn't it?' Sitting up now; watching him, her chin in her hands.

'Hedging my bets? Running with hare and hounds? That house of mine really shocked you, didn't it, Lucy? Not so odd maybe to meet up with me in other folks' houses, the token darkie at some smart gathering. You know, I believe you could accept me as the hep black parson – or even the nigger jazz player, if that's how I'd decided to stay – but a wealthy society host simply is not part of the stereotype you people can... '

'Oh Sebastian!' She was on her knees beside him, holding his hands and smiling up at him. 'Don't start on stereotypes – you *know* you don't fit any – and you know I love you exactly as you are.' She was suddenly abashed; she sat back on her feet, serious now. 'You're great. Just somewhat mysterious... Perhaps you are my Wise Man. And you don't mind my asking about when you were a child, do you? I try not to cross-question you – but is it odd of me to be a little curious?'.

He shook his head and smiled; but he knew from her face that she could sense his withdrawal. Better she should think it was the black man in him resisting the white liberal, than let her know how far that affectionate gesture had thrown him off balance: how nearly he had pulled her close and kissed her to the point of no return.

She was standing up now, saying: 'I'll turn the record over, OK?'

'Fine. There's another couple mugfuls of tea in the pot,' he said, reaching down for it where it sat on the hearth. 'Lord, it's late. We're getting into bad ways, aren't we? like some old married couple.'

It just slipped out. In the silence there was only the fall of a coal, the click of the record player starting up. Then the girl said: 'Well no, not quite.'

She went out to the kitchen and he heard her washing up. He followed her and stood in the doorway.

'Don't you want your tea, my child?'

'No thanks, my Father,' she said.

Fortunately she did not turn round, for the black priest was watching the nape of her neck bared by the forward swing of the heavy hair; watching her shoulders and her waist, and those well-worn jeans framed by the edges of the butcher's apron, bisected by its dangling tie; watching in a way that bore no relation to his cool question.

The sight drew him, and he found himself suddenly close behind her. She stood quite still and straight, her head up as though listening, while he breathed in the scent of her hair and her body under the thin sweatshirt. She spoke, and it came out almost like a sob.

'Know something? You make me homesick in a funny way. We've got this big, black kitchen range – silly isn't it... ' She leaned back against him. 'I love warming myself on it.' Then the pressure of her bottom and thighs, fitting close; and he buried his face in her hair.

'Oh Lucy.' He was laughing weakly. 'So I'm just your Aga, not your guru, after all.' In the silence the radiator's staccato cooling was as shocking as a machine gun. He stepped back. 'God help me, but between that stone and you – it's the devil and deep – blue – I forgot myself, Lucy.'

Already she was busy washing up again; silent and busy. She paused for a moment, head up; she said, sweetly and clearly: 'It doesn't feel sinful to me, you see. But you know best, Father. As always.' She turned round, for the first time. 'Just no more cracks about old married couples, OK?'

Talking sensibly (for oh, she was eminently sensible, thank God and alas) might have defused the moment; but he had been in no mood to talk. Later, he thought about what might have been said – and there had been ample time for thinking: one long sleepless night... No, Lucy: not quite like being married. Agreed. More like an extended, old-fashioned engagement – OK, plus the irony, the awkward anachronism, of sharing a flat. But right and continuous (the phrase would not go away); and like an engagement since it seemed just the beginning of something. Old-fashioned because of the simple, unsatisfied and almost constant desire for each other... And the 'old married couple' remark, though so nearly disastrous, was no less true and relevant, springing as it did from that deep, almost comfortable, familiarity: a sympathy he had failed to anticipate, and that now he must consciously avoid. He must detach himself, be busy, leave early, stay out late...

Appreciating the complexity did not help one jot, he decided that night; and he had got up, dressed, worked on at his studies until the sky grew light between the striped durries, and it was time to take the girl a cup of tea. Another night had passed. There she was, warm and sleepy, still sane and safe, untouched by either the guardian-priest or the ancient evil she so innocently served.

Never – whatever happened between them (it mustn't; but it might) – could he let that sympathy betray him into revealing the full extent of the danger.

201

Sebastian had played down her garbled account of being 'saved by the red-and-black thing', as she had described it to him later on the day that Dr Max died. 'You were in no state to report on the arrival of a No 9 bus, much less some paranormal mercy-dash,' he said. 'Forget it, kid and eat your patty while it's hot: Brixton's best, that is.' But, however muddled, her impressions had only borne out the parting words of his old teacher, and it was better for her peace of mind that she should not know. Nor could he tell her of the thirteen days: the change of the moon and its special significance would sound like the stuff of fairy-tales to this bright, safe, comfortable, English miss.

Fortunately, she seemed happy to accept that the less she knew the better; and Sebastian realised that her attitude sprang not from dread, but from the same healthy scepticism she had shown all along. What she could see, she could believe, and fear. So, when he produced a dark bottle stoppered with newspaper, of some secret solution given him by his guru, and got down on his knees, and washed out the pentacle from the sitting room carpet, she dashed round to the off licence and bought a bottle of champagne to celebrate.

'That thing really bugged me, you know?' she said over their evening meal of curry-roast lamb and fried green bananas. 'It's fantastic – I feel really good now it's gone.'

In the headlong, heedless beauty of this girl at ease – glowing, laughing, relaxed and fond – the priest saw how simple it would be to forget all those admonitions: just to reach out for her. Lord have mercy on me, he thought – getting up quickly to clear the plates; splashing his face with cold water in the kitchen – Lord, try not to lead me into temptation... And you know, Lord, that I'm safer when she's low and helpless and needs my pity: but don't go putting her down into that dark valley, oh Lord, just to keep my thoughts pure – OK?

For Lucy, life was good: disturbing in a new way, perhaps – but still good. It was as though she had been becalmed, and now she spread her sails and began to move again. Poor old Mrs Maturin's inquest was still to come, and Sebastian would have to decide what to do with that wretched stone. She knew he must be troubled about it, if he really believed it to be so special and powerful, and that bad men were after it. She had watched him fix the catches on all the windows; he had even fitted a chain inside the front door. 'It's basic,' he said: 'I'm surprised the agents don't insist on it.'

But she found she was easily lulled into forgetting these things by his quiet, easy-going air of wellbeing. Once more he seemed the caring, busy lodger; always up first with the cup of tea in the morning, always good company when they were home together in the evening. It did not happen so often these days; she was out more, and he spent a lot of time at the bedside of his old friend in hospital, visiting him at all hours between his pastoral duties. Lucy knew he was under great stress. Not from her presence: enforced celibacy must be merely an inconvenience, for him. The 'devil' disturbed him far more than the 'deep blue sea'. However inactive the old trouble in the flat might be, he was concerned ultimately with some force that had caused it. She wished he could just forget it; let sleeping dogs lie: the next owners could sort it out...

He never even spoke of it these days. And though Sebastian had enough small change, it seemed, for endless social give-and-take, back-chat, gossip, or tales of adventure, Lucy knew by now this was a very private gentleman indeed, with enormous gold-reserves of inner thought. A philosopher, a scholar, a mystic, a moralist, a man of letters, a self-confessed religious fanatic – all these; and none of them did he impose on her or her friends.

When her brother Jamie passed through briefly on his way to ski for the university, he took to Lucy's black lodger in a big way. They went off to the pub together while she finished some typing she had brought home. After supper, when he was leaving and Lucy walked him to the High Street through the mild, damp night, he said, 'Mum told me about him, but she never said he was black – Oh Luce! you didn't let on, did you? Admit.'

'I've forgotten. But, no: I think I considered it was enough to inform her about his sex and calling – and then I forgot afterwards that was all she knew.'

'Well, she sounds a lot happier knowing he's there. And you'll tell her about your various nasty adventures when you see her, will you? I agree, it's much simpler to do it that way. And you seem to be flourishing in spite of the dead landlady and the lecherous psychiatrist. Make sure you keep me up to date, won't you? I'd hate to miss out on anything.'

When the priest was fixing the window catches, he had also put a lock on Lucy's bedroom door: 'So that whether I'm here or not you can feel you have your own stronghold,' he said. 'I don't want you to think I'm developing a siege mentality, Lucy; but – just in case these bad guys get in – I'd be happier if I knew you were secure in your own room.' It crossed her mind that the priest might actually mistrust himself. Since that moment, late one evening, when he had so nearly… Then she ticked herself off sternly, with a slap on the wrist for wishful thinking. Keeping her fantasies to herself was the very least she could do for him; but, for her own sake, she saw she must resist even these.

Ever since his visit to Brixton Sebastian had seemed more withdrawn, more preoccupied. Now, as the second week went by, he was showing signs of strain. Lucy could not know that the time of reckoning was drawing near. For her, this withdrawal, this edginess, was entirely explained by his preoccupation with his friend in hospital. 'He likes me being there,' Sebastian said: 'it seems to amuse him. He's a rich sinner, Lucy: a playboy to the last. But I want to save his soul. I love that bastard; and each time I leave him I realise I may not see him again.'

He spent all the free time he had there, returning late at night, drawn and subdued. Lucy liked to get up and make him some tea when he came back; but she saw he wanted to be on his own. She left him sitting there, staring at the dying fire; she longed to comfort him, and felt she knew how, and that it would not be wrong. He could do no wrong in her eyes. She was, she realised, in love with him. Her dreams reflected this; and they told her so much more about her desire for him than she had cared to admit to herself.

Now that she acknowledged her love, she also knew there was no future in it; and all those hoarded moments – travelling, or lying in bed before sleep, or after waking, or simply waiting for the kettle to boil – moments she had been filling with daydreams that, at their most fanciful, involved Sebastian's abandoning his vocation for her: all these times she now attempted to spend on self-improvement.

She had started, one lonely, burning bedtime, to recite all the poetry she knew; and went on to learn more. She was reading voraciously: all of Dickens for a start, she decided. She would teach herself Italian. She joined the library and got out *David Copperfield* and Russo's *Practical Grammar*. She joined a dance-and-exercise class just off the Strand, where she could go for an hour twice a week after work; so she bought a leotard and, while she was in this constructive mood, some knitting wool and needles. Since, to meet her own strict requirements, the pattern must be too difficult to day-dream over, she started making a rasta bobble-cap on an elaborate Patricia Roberts formula from the little shop off Holland Street – and even that erand had borne its own bonus. (But that's the joy of positive thinking, dear: it creates its own opportunities. So said her sensible voice, more bossy than ever under the new regime.) For, in Holland Street, she had bumped into the young man from the magic shop; and they had had a drink together.

His name was Gil Martindale. He was formal and reserved to begin with, as if to repair the damage caused by their last, hardly conventional, encounter. He began to explain over the second glass of wine in the old-fashioned cellar bar in Church Street.

'Please don't think that was typical,' he said. 'I was in such a state largely because I'd resisted coming to warn you for some days – and, of course, because I thought it would sound crazy.

When it finally came out, it certainly did – and when that creepy journalist seemed about to join in, I decided I couldn't face it: he'd have made such a meal of it. Those people are – well, they seem to sort of live off *your* life, Lucy; and Dr Gassman – But I heard he'd had some sort of accident.'

'Well – yes,' she said looking away. 'He's dead. And I was probably the last to see him. I – I still don't understand what could have killed him.'

' "Self-inflicted wounds", the paper said. But dear Lucy: that's all over now, isn't it? I mean, you're out of that particular wood? You're all right?' He smiled. 'I'm sorry. I shouldn't stare.'

'Go ahead,' said Lucy sweetly: 'I rather like it.'

'Well, it's just that you seem so different from when I last saw you, in the square that night. I suppose the real trouble was that I'd fallen for you at first sight in the Clarence – so all these bad dreams, the things I wanted to warn you about, could have been just an excuse to see you again.'

Lucy was silent. She was thinking, No, Gil, they made a sort of sense actually, though it's still a mystery... But she did not want to break the spell. He was saying:

'I kept hoping you'd come into the shop – but I should have known you were too sceptical for that.'

'Still, I nearly did. I would have, sooner or later.'

'Then it's a good thing I bumped into you in the street – or rather, to be exact, saw you go by and came after you. You see, I'm leaving that job, and going to work on *Time Out*. I think I only landed the Occult Boutique, as the owners call it, because I looked right, they said. Hardly complimentary. But I thought it might be interesting.'

'Weighing out all that eye of newt and toe of frog.'

'Exactly. With a sideline in party-tricks and prestidigitation, which I've always loved: used to bore the pants off my family and friends. But it turned out to be tarot cards and astrology manuals and the odd Dennis Wheatley; people like that arty-crafty lady who sells organic food in the Earls Court Road, coming in to check some finer point about werewolf lore in Alister Crowley: "Don't *move*, my sweet: I know precisely where – just browsing, really." ' He made her laugh: the voice was perfect, and the pose, with a sudden thrust of the shoulders – she could almost see the shawls and the flash of Oasis bangles. 'But that's ungrateful of me,' Gil went on: 'it was she who told me I should get together with the cosy little circle at the Clarence Arms; we even made a date – yes! I must say I rather took to the old birds and the Colonel. I went again. And you were there... Then – tell me – weren't you away for a time?'

'Yes, I had three weeks at home, just after I saw you in the square, actually. Look, I must go. But this has been nice.'

'So when can I see you again, properly? I'm off skiing in Italy tomorrow – Cervinia – Why, do you know it?'

'No, but my brother's there now with the Edinburgh University team.'

'That's extraordinary: an elegant coincidence, don't you agree? I'll find him. And can we make a date now for when I get back?'

He would look even better tanned, she thought; and, walking home, she realised she had not thought about Sebastian for over half an hour; that she had in fact been busy doing just the sort of thing her parents and friends imagined she did all the time: having a couple of drinks with a charming, attractive young man.

By now on a Saturday Sebastian would be back from confession and shopping. Striding briskly, she permitted herself the luxury of looking forward to seeing him; and Gilbert Martindale's white Anglo-Saxon protestant features dimmed, grew hazy: a pale and gibbous moon in the daylight of that hot, black sun. And even while, with eminent practicality, Lucy saw that it was just such individuals as Gil who would, when the time came, help to console her for the loss of her dream-lodger, her well-polished boots (Sebastian had polished them) seemed to sprout wings as they turned into Clarence Square.

Deliberately she slowed down. Dickens and dancing classes were all very well, and had come about as a deliberate antidote, for mind and body, to her priest-fixation; but these activities were designed to enrich her *own* life. She must make sure they did not degenerate into just another way of trying to impress her hero (Aren't I fit? Aren't I bright? And aren't I quick at knitting?); she must do them for herself alone. Must plan for Life After Sebastian...

She did not know when that would be. Now the agents had actually asked her to stay on until they sold the flat, it might be summer before she had to move. Sebastian did not talk about his future. 'May I live here for now? Fine. After that, well – I go where and when I'm needed, as a rule,' he said. 'But with a home in London and my roots in Grenada, those are two places I'll always come back to.' Then he laughed. 'So you see, Lucy, I can still be godfather to your first-born – right? Shall we pencil that in?'

Lucy could face the fact that this peaceful coexistence she was so happy with must come to an end, maybe soon; but while it continued, she must use it, to get strong, to grow up. And show him she was doing so – surely she might do that? And he would admire her so much more, see her as a partner, even, if she could only demonstrate how far she had evolved – and she felt sure she had – into a wise virgin, at least, instead of just a pretty face, or a mere victim, to be sustained and guarded. If only I could do something quite on my own, she thought: something that he would not know about – until afterwards. Somehow I must prove myself to him... So that even if he must go – and he will, she thought, trudging up the steps – so that even if he goes, he will never forget me.

And all this time the very weather observed the status quo. It stayed mild and muggy: bulbs sent up green shoots in the square gardens, and the clump of polyanthus opposite the portal of Clarence Mansions flowered gaudily in the false spring. Inside, the flat was peaceful, the disturbing influence dormant, perhaps dead.

Chapter Thirteen

NOW JANUARY WAS dying, in snow and bitter cold: the pit of the year. And Sebastian's friend, the rich sinner he loved, was himself at the point of death.

That night the priest telephoned Lucy from the hospital to say he must stay until the end. He knew, however, the time was critical for her too. Only this night remained of the thirteen; tomorrow evening, before midnight, he must destroy the stone. And, whether it was the extreme cold that had disturbed it, or its own imminent readiness stirring within, Sebastian had sensed its power round the flat these last two nights. It had not, he thought, troubled that lovely girl: she had not spoken of it. But she mustn't be allowed to sleep there alone.

He was determined not to alarm her; she should not know how close they were sailing to the roaring edge of the known world. Cool and businesslike, he instructed her to leave and take a taxi to his house in Belgravia. She was expected; Jim the Chinese manservant, would be awaiting her; there would be food if she wanted it and a bed ready aired for her. 'I suggest you take clothes for work in the morning; I also want you to take with you, and read, an account I've written out for you: a sort of explanatory letter.' He waited while she found it in his top drawer. 'Good. Take it, Lucy, and go now,' he said. 'I'll see you there.'

She had been having a big bath while supper was heating up: Prawn Creole that Sebastian had cooked for her. When the telephone rang she was pouring herself a rum-and-coke, relaxed and warm at last in nightdress and dressing gown, looking forward to a peaceful domestic evening crowned by his return. But now?

Now she must turn off the oven, climb back into her street clothes (smart for Belgravia, too) and face the snow and bitter cold she had battled through on her way home from the city. Knowing Sebastian would not be back till late, she had worked on over a project with Eddie, then unwisely waited half an hour for a snow-bound bus rather than face the walk to the tube and then the length of the High Street at the other end of the journey. Now taxis would be even thinner on the ground. Surely there was time to have her supper? After that would be soon enough to leave. But he said, 'Go now,' she thought; so I'll ring in comfort; if there's a minicab free I'll gather myself up and get out.

'Hope you're not one of the ones in a hurry, dear: waiting time's anything up to an hour this evening. It's not us: it's the weather, isn't it? Try again in half an hour – you may be lucky.'

It was not even ten-thirty. The heating wouldn't go off for ages yet: that was the time she would like to be away from the flat. So – just my Prawn Creole, OK? she said to the absent Sebastian; and while I eat it, I'll read. It would be the next best thing to having him there.

'Lucy: now I know you are out of harm's way (Well, no, not actually; but I soon will be. Don't fuss, dear: I'll cope) I can tell you about the stone; and this won't be a well-rounded monograph, I warn you, as I'll write it in snatches sitting here at the hospital; and give it to you when, as I plan, I have got you out of the line of fire – or maybe after the stone is destroyed. In case I'm not around to tell you the whole story. Incidentally, my old teacher confirmed it was right to leave it there. Another of the seekers has arrived in England, he tells me. If I had taken charge of it, they would know. But putting it back was the hardest thing I ever did: that thing is strong – irresistible, almost.

'Remember I said there was one in Galilee? I wasn't just

talking foolishness, Lucy: there are records. Books – albeit very secret books – have been written down the ages about these stones. There is a whole network, small and eclectic, patient and scholarly, of astrologers, historians, scientists, magicians, saints and villains who have tracked the stones, described and analysed them when they could. And not just in the past, or by "religious fanatics": one, in fact – possibly this one – has been carbon-dated quite recently (so my Master tells me) by a very eminent Oxford don in his very private laboratory; and he made it sixty-five million years old, give or take.

'The wise men's conclusions have always carried the implication that the more these objects of worship have been used for self-interest – for destruction – the more powerful, dangerous and desirable they become. It is what man has done with the stones, not what the stones do to man: for, in themselves, they are no more than tangible symbols of that vast integration, the serene harmony of the universe: metal plus stone, fused by fire and air and water. Truly marvellous objects, misused.

'I haven't told you about the visions, because I was afraid that the knowledge might make you curious – and curiosity has already put you at risk. It is these visions that make the stone addictive in the first place. They are powerful and beautiful and frightening, like LSD, only more so; like – I don't know, Lucy, but something like a year's television viewing crammed into ten seconds and taken intravenously – if you can imagine that. All of it: news flashes, Cousteau, battlefronts, opera, horror movies – the lot; flashing past inside your eyelids, not as a blur but as distinct images, many of which stay with you for ever.

'It seems that by holding this stone you release a violent electrical charge; and too many seconds of it can literally blow your mind. I have only held it twice; the first time was for so-called research purposes – purely academic interest: I had read so much about it by then. But I have wanted, almost needed – a *hunger* – to repeat the experience ever since. I could no more have resisted, when at last I found it again the other day, than I could have spread wings and flown away. I knew what it was, what it did; but I had to take it out of its bag and hold it; and what I witnessed was so terrible – as I knew it must be – that it haunts me continually in the way that only very strong visual images can: as though it had burned into my very retina. For, you see, it shows you its past; and its long life has been a history of extraordinary cruelty and bloodshed in the hands of the various keepers who have used – misused – its power.

'This one, they say, has been worshipped, since long before the coming of Christ, as the god Belial; it has become the monitor and hiding place for one of fallen man's greatest devils – named by Milton, as you will have read: the last, the most sensual and slothful, the "lewdest" of all Satan's crew. And this is the "brain" that has been lying hidden away from the world in the corner of an airing cupboard in Kensington. Perhaps we should be grateful for the slothfulness, at least.

'Stones like these can disappear, of course, for centuries, going underground, literally, or kept dark in private hands. One of them – and this is it, judging by what I saw on the two occasions I have held it in my hands – turned up in Spain, in the early sixteenth century, brought back, it seems, with other treasures from Brazil, and already powerful from use in brutal rituals. During the course of the Inquisition, as the "truth-stone" of some notorious test-cases tried *in camera*, it was treated with awe and dread. Rumour reported it had been destroyed by fire, and there are no more sightings of it until it appeared in Russia briefly, adorned by Fabergé; then stripped of its jewels and lost after the revolution and the division of Czarist *objets d'art*.

'Whoever its keepers may have been over the next decade, it is reasonable to assume financial ruin in the depression, or death, or both, must have parted them from the stone; for it next appeared in the ledger of a Belgian pawnbroker: a very accurate description, and the comment in the valuation column simply "Try offers?" No record of who bought it; perhaps he grew "attached" to it even as he weighed it in his hand assessing its dubious worth. Perhaps it was stolen. All we know is that it turned up in a Neapolitan junk shop in the early thirties and there was a flurry of interest in it during which it is referred to as "the relic" involving a commodities dealer, an amateur alchemist and even an internationally acclaimed astronomer-prince. It was weighed, tested, even "bitten" (sic) – and *that* must have been some encounter! But it was "acquired" in a pre-emptive bid by a big Mafioso. Within months he died violently; reports of the circumstances vary, but they all agree on the ensuing vendetta; after which no less a protector than *Il Duce* himself had to be paid for services rendered – and he demanded the stone. (And as soon as she knows you know, the great-niece in Oberlin, Ohio – last of the Mafioso's line – will recount the tale with pride.)

'This desirable "relic", you must understand, made no public appearances as such: its reputation travelled by a sort of powerful, high-speed underground; I have seen its workings. But there is virtually nothing in writing from this busy period: a crucial one, approaching its cyclical "high"; and we are fortunate in having those few scientific and pseudo-scientific notes to go by. Anyway, its next keeper was not so reticent.

'The underground network had carried the word; and now the stone was demanded as a token of esteem, a compact of good faith, by the little Austrian who was currently doing so much to restore Germany's full glory. "And how much more I can achieve with its help!" – this from the fulsome letter of acknowledgement found, though not understood, by later biographers, in Benito Mussolini's personal files. The German text goes right over the top; first in its praise of the unknown craftsman, "he who inlaid the living rock with silver... like the brain-pattern of some god"; and then, lacking only the Wagner sound-track: "It delights me to grasp that godbrain" – literal translation – "in my manhand" – ditto – "and know all it knows; for then, my friend, I am indeed all-powerful: not merely part of the eternal plan, but creating it. Furthermore, if I should ever die, I shall not be extinguished as other mortals are. You understand, do you not? that my power and indeed my image will pass into the godstone and my mighty work will go on, ever-increasing, all-triumphant.''

'This, I need hardly say, is as good as a sighting; and there is also the word-of-mouth report, unofficial but fairly convincing, from an SS officer after his trial at Nüremburg, that the Führer's "toys" (objects of sentiment) were divided among his household favourites. So after four centuries, the stone almost certainly returned to Brazil in the briefcase of some hastily-emigrating minor Nazi; it was viewed there in a charity auction of so-called "curios", and mysteriously withdrawn before sale – then disappeared completely until it turned up in Hong Kong heavily disguised as a handsome pottery elephant, fresh from Red China.

'In this form Bob Loren purchased it, he told me, for around £90 after haggling; and as perfectly ignorant of its true value, he swore, as the stall-owner himself. He was travelling in the Far East with the band; and he found himself becoming inordinately fond of the thing, keeping it with him, bulky as it was, when the rest of their acquisitions were being shipped home. So it was that his elephant, something of a mascot by now, accompanied him on the South African tour; and it was there he discovered its real worth, alerted by the sudden interest from more than one source. First, from his host at one of the many impromptu, dazzling parties, there came a very handsome offer to buy; then more offers – one from a man who just walked into the hotel lounge and accosted him. He could have sold it several times over. But now he was intrigued; and anxious enough about its safety to inquire the size of the hotel safe – but they politely refused to divulge its measurements, or to take the elephant.

'It was a black man, a seer, who approached him after one of his concerts and told him what the pottery figure contained. He warned him against it; both blacks and whites were after it now, he said, and Bob's life was in danger. "But to keep it, that is the greatest danger," he said: "the longer

214

you have it in your possession, even so the greater the peril for your immortal soul. One way or the other, it will destroy you like a little bug: to the great god Belial, that is all you are, pop-star."

'Unfortunately for Bob Loren, this talk of gods and immortal souls was not his scene: Eastern mysticism had touched more than one member of his entourage, but not him; and the quip about bugs simply riled him. On the way back he stopped off at an all-night garage on the edge of town and acquired a high-speed drill and some plastic padding. That night in his hotel suite, he opened up the elephant.

'It was easier than he'd anticipated. These figures, so popular in the Victorian conservatory, traditionally carry a raised, table-like howdah on their backs, joined to the body with a strip of unglazed paste before firing. He started drilling it there and after two holes it came apart in his hands – a natural break, as it were. He found the stone strapped inside the body, bound up in oilcloth; and that was when he first held it in his hand and saw its terrible, compulsive visions. Then he wrapped a brass hotel paperweight in the oilcloth and put the elephant together again, sealing it with Araldyte from the band's repair kit, and touching up the chipped edges with plastic padding and nail varnish.

'He was even tempted to contact the party host and take up his generous offer; but next day the elephant disappeared from his room. Judging by the harrassment of the following days, it was a BOSS agent who had taken it, and his masters had been seriously disappointed. In self-defence, Bob threw a well-publicised fainting fit sufficiently impressive to convince even his mates: at this point he felt he could not trust a soul – everyone was suspect. Well, the next link in the chain, none other than Maisie Maturin, was there in the hotel bar when it happened; and so efficient, so masterful – he told me – was the good lady in applying first aid that he feared she might discover he was faking. But she stopped them getting a doctor – "I've handled epileptics before now," she said; "help me get him to his room: I'll look after him, poor boy."

'Once they were alone there he was free to tell her a little of what was going on: he had to trust someone now, though he realised he knew nothing of her, and that if she were the least unscrupulous she could blackmail him for all he was worth. So he turned on the charm.

'As you know, it worked. Bob put a lot into it, by all reports: she was "seen around" with him by the gossip columns; for those few days he openly lavished attention on his mature groupie and – to be fair – gave her a holiday to remember. But BOSS's frighteners were still out for him, and now he was confident enough in her loyalty to hand over the stone. "This is what they're after," he told her – and that was all he told her. "I just want you to do this one more thing for me: keep it safe and meet me in Nairobi after the tour." He used her quite ruthlessly.

'The authorities trumped up some charge, and took him in; searched him and his rooms, and all through his drum kit – and right along the line: all the rest f the band. They found nothing. It made quite a stink, and the group left two days early for Kenya in high dudgeon. Meanwhile, Mrs Maturin, with the stone snugly packed in her sponge bag, could have gone anywhere the fancy took her. But dear Bob had played his cards well: it was only because she was so infatuated with a man some twenty years her junior – because maybe life seemed at last to be blossoming – that she followed him to Nairobi. She was certainly "attached" to the stone, but she wanted Bob too: Love is greedy as well as blind.

'So it was pretty devastating to lose both at one throw; to find he'd quite finished with her once he got the stone back. He did not suspect – even when I met him some months later – that he'd picked on a powerful lady. She made very sure she would see him again: one of the oldest tricks in the book. Nothing he could do would stop him turning up in London one fine day and seeking her out. She had fixed it; she just had to wait.

216

'One can only speculate about the timing. Maybe he came because the pressure was on again. Maybe he recognised one of the seekers, or the new dogsbody taken on by his manager turned out to have a face he felt he'd seen somewhere – and that was his own reason for coming just then, ostensibly to have his fortune told. But he would have turned up sooner or later.

'You know the rest. On reflection (and there is plenty of room for that: I'm in the hospital again, finishing this screed – a useful way to spend the times when he is sleeping), I do not think Maisie Maturin caused his death – though Lord knows she had reason enough to hate him for the way he treated her. I think his "accident" was arranged by the seekers – someone clever and rich and patient enough to ensure it was no worse than "a bit fishy", as Mrs V. put it. But they didn't get the stone: they couldn't know of that session over the cards and Bob's parting promise to let her have it when he'd finished with it. I think in the end he did her proud – and may the good Lord let him be forgiven for that at least: even if he knew he was going to die, passing on that stone as he did, voluntarily, was quite a thing to do. Maybe I'm giving him the benefit of the doubt (watching death come creeping seems to have mellowed me, Lucy): maybe he would have demanded it back had he survived. But I think the message had got to him, literally and figuratively: he heard of the contract on him, and he realised Mrs Maturin had foreseen his death, and there was no escaping. So he packed his ju-ju in a jiffy-bag and put it through her door. And here it is, in your flat: as effectively hidden as it has ever been. It has gone to ground again.

'Meanwhile, however, the word had travelled, and the seekers are gathering. They see me as an arch-rival; they know I am in London, that I am attached to this parish, maybe that I am onto the stone. They are aware that its new cycle is nearly complete.

'So: the pod is about to burst; and Mrs Maturin's worshipping care of it, concluding with her literally – however involuntarily – feeding herself to it, and giving it all *her* power, has fattened its strength; and will have increased its physical manifestation: a "body" we could perhaps see, and that you have certainly felt. The presence that has been disturbing you.

'Now that you know about the stone (and depending, of course, my dear Lucy, on the extent of your "healthy scepticism") you have, as it were, eaten of the Tree of Knowledge. It has been dormant of late: it has not harmed you because you have not threatened it. Now it is moving again – has been these last few nights. But if you have got this letter and obeyed my instructions, you are no longer in danger. Don't resent being shifted from the field of battle, will you? You have fought it well and truly, with your tough innocence (there is still no other word for it); now I hope to finish it off – or, indeed, to *have* finished it off – with my knowledge. See you. S.'

Lucy finished reading and sat staring at the letter. She came back to reality and present time when, with a bump and an expiring shudder, the boiler cut out beneath her feet, and she heard the clicking start. So here I am, she thought – and felt herself smiling at the irony: his letter had delayed her. Here I am, and my guardian angel fondly believes I am far away. He wanted to keep me out of it – but I'm here, and it's too late.

This could be my chance.

She stared unseeing at the congealing remains of supper, appalled at her own bloody nerve. It isn't too late, she thought: I can take my purse and go now just as I am. The priest's story had impressed her deeply; and she knew she was afraid: the worst sort of fear, more terrible even than her nightmare monsters – the fear of the unseen. It was like that foul pentacle: knowing it was there, invisible, as she dusted round the sitting room had always been far more of an ordeal than that first moment, when she had put on the infra-red glasses and seen it there.

The glasses. She took them from the mantlepiece and went over to the door, where she stopped. What did she expect to see,

for goodness sake? The so-called 'physical manifestation' of
some Old Testament bugaboo? The 'body' of one of Milton's
fallen angels, elaborately muscled, softly treading, like Blake's
Flea?

(But you've seen it, Lucy, haven't you? The inner voice had
never been so even, so careful, so clear, so near the very edge of
controlled hysteria. You know it glows red in the dark and
disappears in the light of the street lamp. That it is sluggish in
movement and very big. It drags at your feet. It presses down
the counterpane. It has sucked a big fat woman dry, hasn't it?
And it sliced a man all over: bled him and frightened him to
death. That's the creature you will see – won't you?)

She ran down the passage looking straight ahead. Even when
she felt something pulling at her skirts and slowing her naked
feet like heavy, tepid water, like wet sand, she kept on, not
daring to look down. She could see her coat, and her
wellingtons there by the door: safe, ordinary, and very far away.
And now the terrible, slow-motion gauntlet was run. She
crouched, shaking, close to the wall, dragging her boots on
over her bare feet for protection: protection against –
Protection against... But knowing she was safe now. She
straightened up and stared back the way she had come.

The bright light from the kitchen showed nothing; further
along the corridor in the darkness, before the area reached by
the fringed lamp, the carpet seemed to be glowing a dull red.
Then she put on the spectacles.

Something was emerging from the cupboard. It seemed to
be made up of millions of threads of fine, almost colourless
slime or jelly. They glistened as they moved like a series of
slow, sticky waterfalls, oozing through the cracks round the
door, joining together and forming a dark glowing mass on
the floor and along the passage and disappearing into the
bedroom. It must be looking for me there, she thought: the
pipes are cooling, and it's looking for warmth.

Now that she had the glasses on and saw clearly, Lucy found
she could accept her fear. It made sense. And just to *see* –
instead of wading through that invisible horror that clogged
her feet and clung to the hem of her nightdress: sight was a

219

revelation, like the first time she had put on a diving mask and instantly lost her dread of deep water. Now she stood watching, fascinated; amazed by the sheer fact of its existence: her night fears, the priest's warnings were all justified. And then there was its size, its extent – and still increasing as she gazed: was this one creature, or many? What would one of those seeking, sliding tendrils look like cut off and put under a microscope? Could evil have a physical form, with weight and mass? An idea taking shape, filling space, like ectoplasm, or a phantom pregnancy? And she thought of the sprouting potatoes she had found in the cupboard under the sink. Surely all growth sprang from a nucleus, a mother-body. But what sort of nucleus must it be to mother this infinite monster, this infinity of monsters?

Concentrate on answers now, she told herself. This, then was the 'body', as Sebastian called it, of the thing that lived in the stone. (And still the slow, relentless increase continued, and never wavered.) It was ripe to be destroyed, so he and his Master had said. This was the thing that had entered her room, had pressed down the edge of the bed and flowed round her, heavy as a large dog; but then – Christ! – then had invaded her very body, sliding and sipping, seeking out her living warmth.

And her horror hardened and became disgust and wild anger. She didn't give a damn if it was Belial or Mrs Maturin or some sickening, insidious, fungal growth. She just wanted to wipe it out. Shift her from the field of battle? Is *that* what Sebastian intended? *I'll show him.*

Now. Now I must be calm: I must be cool and cunning, she thought. Yes: just so – for it hates cold. I shall attack it with extreme cold – oh God for some dry ice like we used at school for the witches' cauldron in Macbeth... Should she try it with ice-cubes first to see what happened? But she would have to pass through it now to get to the fridge; for already, in the couple of minutes since she ran down the corridor, a second flow had started, tentatively, towards where she stood. She must move, and move quickly; it was growing and spreading as she watched.

Snow, she thought: there's all the snow I could want outside.

And Sebastian's plastic coal-buckets, and his rubber gloves (blessed methodical creature that he was – everything just so) were all there in the corner of the hall. She was dragging on her coat when she thought, Surely I must be cold as well: then it won't 'see' me. 'Are you blind? Are you black? Are you dangerous?' they had asked it. She must make herself very cold to hunt it, and not to be hunted.

If any of the fine upstanding householders of Clarence Square, W8, chanced to look out over the gardens very early on that Thursday morning in January, they might have seen – but hardly believed – the figure of a fair girl in a long white nightgown by the frozen pond, apparently filling buckets and plastic sacks with snow.

Lucy made three journeys to be sure she had enough, stockpiling in the lobby. As soon as she had shifted her load into the hall of the flat, she hurried to put on the infra-red spectacles and see whether the creature was still there; wondering, as she fumbled for them with the rubber gloves, whether she had not dreamed up the whole impossible, multitudinous monster out of her own… But it was there.

It was there all right. And now the lava flow along the passage was thicker, nearly knee-height; and still countless threads oozed from the cracks of the locked cupboard. Nerving herself, she went up close to it. She prodded it gently with the toe of her snowy rubber boot, and it shrank away. It had not perceived what she was – its favoured heat source – inside her armour of radiating cold.

She took a handful of snow from her bucket and sprinkled it out over the sluggish mass; and watched it shrink, lose its sheen, and buckle into tight coils, curling back and shrinking, crumbling, trickling away like a wave on the sand. Boldly now she cleared a path for herself all the way to the bedroom; and, looking back to make sure it had not closed up again behind her, she saw that the panic message had been passed along – or so it seemed. The cascade from the cupboard had become a thin trickle, the coils along the edge of the passage were

221

crawling the other way; and remnants she had cut off from the main body, wriggling with a rapid urgency quite unlike its steady outward flow, were slithering back along the carpet and disappearing under the door.

Shifting her buckets forward with her boots, and spraying great double handfuls of snow round her, she moved into the bedroom; then emptied the rest over the filthy load of glimmering jelly that lay there on the quilt. It reared up like a breaker, then separated into tight, bunched coils, clusters of blackish-red snakes, and she stepped back in sudden terror that they might strike; but they poured over the edge of the bed in tangled heaps, past her, and out into the corridor. She watched them retreat: watched them flatten and ooze in under the cupboard door; then she went back for more snow.

It was a holy war, with victory in sight. Lucy was no longer afraid. Surreal in infra-red glasses, rubber gloves, and white gown, and starred with a melting confetti of snowflakes, Belial's intended bride stalked his glowing black-and-red coils round all the rooms, attacking the extremities with cold, watching them shrink and lose their lustre and seep away into his cupboard-lair – until the last thread had disappeared.

Shivering, exhausted and triumphant, Lucy crept into the kitchen; and even the glory of surprising that bossy black priest with her victory was nothing at that moment to the thought of a cup of tea…

She took off the gloves, filled the kettle with numb hands, warmed the pot and spooned in the tea; she poured some milk into a jug – his high standards had so changed her ways – and chose a large mug for herself. She pushed back the glasses on to her forehead and waited; and hugged her cold body, smiling, almost laughing: God, if only the great Father Sebastian could see her now! The kettle boiled noisily. Behind her the cupboard bulged and strained; but she did not turn her head. And now she relaxed. Sitting on the table, breathing in the fragrance as she clutched her mug in both grateful hands like a child, she could feel the shivers abating and the blessed warmth returning to her.

Then with a crash the door burst its lock, and she spun

round to see the thing she had attacked but not destroyed; this time it was the great mother-mass, the magma itself. Huge, bulging, filling all space with its glistening coils, it towered over her, enfolded her and sucked her inside its lair – a piling wave of glowing dark jelly that crushed her softly and clammily: accommodating her; ingesting her. Her last conscious image was of a vast bulky shape, pixie eyes and mound of hair, and a red female mouth – a bloated monster in woman's form, of which those writhing coils were extremities merely – as it bent over her to snuff her out. And there was only the slow clicking-cooling, and a gentle, breathing, sucking sound of contentment, in the nice warm flat.

Chapter Fourteen

IN A PRIVATE room of the great hospital, the priest sat beside
his dying friend. There was only a green-shaded lamp low on a
table beside him, and he had pulled back the curtains from the
wide, heavily-glazed window so he could look out.

Up here, the snow-limned treetops and white, quilted roofs
seemed a world away from the infernal glow of street light:
cold and clean, and utterly still except when a winking airliner
swam silently up through the huge, starry sky. Inside, there was
only the quiet hum as of some vast machine idling, and, from
time to time, the quick quiet tread of a night-nurse, pausing to
look in through the glass of the door, then moving on.

Sebastian could do little now for the sleeping man beside
him, drifting slowly and imperceptibly towards death on the
small hours of a January night. This was the very trough of the
circadian pattern, as the priest was aware, when life runs low
even in the strongest men. He felt in himself that fragility of
tenure, and such melancholy accidie – a sort of false and weary
wisdom born of shallow breathing and thinning blood – as
almost amounted to envy of his friend: a half-wish that he too
might slip away painlessly and disappear between the cold
stars, rather than face the ordeal ahead.

He knew it must be over, either way, within the next
twenty-four hours. In choosing to watch beside his friend, he
was leaving the *coup de grace* perilously late; and he had been
torn in two the last few nights by this dual loyalty, to the girl
and to the dying man. At least he knew she was safe now: he

had done all he could. It was nearly two o'clock, and he did not think his vigil – little more now than a formality he needed to observe – would last through another hour. Then he would go home to Belgravia and sleep, and gird up his loins for battle. When night came again he must destroy the Belial Stone.

He closed his eyes, willing himself into passive meditation, the surest way of finding the strength he so badly needed. To use fatigue, to exploit it as a natural tranquilliser, was one of the rare and ancient skills Sebastian had learned on his travels from an old bushman in the Gobi. He called on it seldom and only in the greatest need, for its power was incalculable. But now he sought it and submerged in it like a thirsty man at a water-hole, laying himself open to those limitless reservoirs of energy and vision that some men call God.

So, behind shuttered eyes, and fed by minimal oxygen, the two men in the hospital room travelled parallel paths to the very edge of existence. One went on.

Sebastian was ripped from his trance with all the violence of a second birth.

It seemed to him that he had been struck by an invisible body-blow so powerful that it jerked him back in his chair like a sudden spasm, and left him weak, gasping, sweating. When he was able to see again and reach out for the pulse, his friend was dead.

As he closed the cooling eyelids he knew that, as a friend, he had failed: it was not the passing of this spirit that the priest had suffered, but the fearsome attack of something far greater, something cosmic, evil, and continuous – for there was no ensuing sense of peace. Holding the chill hands in his own, he bowed his head and closed his eyes, reaching out to the swiftly travelling spark of the man he had loved, asking it, even as it faded, to help him; to show him what it could perceive from out there.

He had a brief X-ray vision: the central body of a huge city laid out beneath him, criss-crossed with the pulsing bright arteries of streets and highways; traffic-light valves, winking nerves and switchboard synapses; and he could see down through these to the broad, dark intestines of the sewers beneath. He recognised a western extremity he knew like the palm of his hand, and saw the black-red hole in it and felt the huge ache of that nail driven deep…

The nurse looked anxious, feeling his forehead as he sipped from the glass of water.

'It's always a shock,' she was saying, 'even when you're expecting it.'

'I'm all right, sister,' said the priest, and smiled to reassure her. There was no time to explain he was closely acquainted with death in all its forms, and seldom in such comfortable circumstances as this high-class robber had been able to purchase, God rest his soul – but that something had happened, something disastrous he had seen in a vision, something he should have prevented.

'All I really need,' he said, 'is a telephone.'

The private phone had been removed from the room so as not to disturb them in those last days. Now Sebastian walked to the one at the end of the corridor, and was alarmed by the terrible weakness of his limbs as he tried to hurry.

In the Belgravia house the call was taken by his manservant, still up and waiting for his master's return. No, Miss Morland had not arrived; and there was no message. Inside No 2 Clarence Mansions the phone rang loud, unanswered.

(There, all was quiet and dark; not even the clicking now, and all the lights had fused. Above, voices, and doors opening. Torches were being found, and candles were lighted. But in the flat, only the soft breathing and sucking noise…)

Sebastian listened to ten empty, echoing rings, then put down the phone. He must get there.

The black runner threaded his way through the snow-bound streets.

There was a charcoal brazier burning outside a night-watchman's cabin. 'Fight heat with heat: for first you must

226

beckon it and then you must trap it, my son. I will teach you the words; but you will find the way.' So had his Master spoken. Sebastian crossed over to the brazier, and lifted off the upper section that held the fire, glowing and dark with topped-up coal.

For a moment he closed his eyes, centring his whole being to receive the pain correctly. When it came, it was more like a mighty weight that he must balance delicately; no searing: just a numbing burden that deadened his hands and crept up his arms – and he thought of the blocks of ice they used to carry out to the fishing boat as children. He moved forward slowly, holding it away from him – for his body felt the heat – and swung into his long, even stride again.

Through the black and white winter streets he ran with the brazier like a chalice in his bare hands; and then into the square.

There were people gathering on the pavement; more were in the lobby and crowding down the stairs. No one had entered the flat. Those nearest had heard a crash. Some thought they had heard a scream. The lights went out all over the block. Mr Dortmund made his way to the basement, with a torch, to look at the fuse-boxes. An emergency electrician service was called. Mrs Dortmund came down in her dressing gown with duplicate keys; but the lock seemed to be fused to the frame. Then they called the police.

They heard the excitement outside and crowded forward to see; but they fell back huddling together in alarm when the tall black runner came into the lobby carrying his burden of fire. He only set it down to break open the door into the ground floor flat. Then he picked up the brazier and stepped inside.

At first, in the dark, and blinded by the glare and the reek of the flames so close to him, Sebastian could see nothing. Slowly it took shape in the blackness of the corridor, its glowing red coils spreading out like a Scylla, its power sucking, like Charybdis, into a vortex of annihilating evil.

He had often imagined it. He had seen crude woodcuts and

artist's impressions of it; he had studied scientific diagrams of such anti-matter at its moment of reversal when – so men said who had observed it and lived to tell the tale – the ancient evil in the sacred stone was bodied forth in most terrible flesh. Here it was: the original slime of creation, and the moving jelly of first life fused in that slime; but growing and reduplicating at hideous, hot-house speed that telescoped sixty million years' growth overnight, and without the grace of evolution. For only its power had evolved; its motive force was still that of the original scrap of life: survival. How – the sages had wondered through the centuries – could evolving man fight such a singular power? And was it not more probable that he should use it? Find it a title and a sacred, hidden resting place; worship it, serve it and ultimately be corrupted by it, caring only to destroy and to survive with that same deadly singleness of thought?

Now the great god Belial – as man had named it – felt the fire and reached out for it. Since the long blazing journey through the skies, that descent from Heaven, and for ever after, fire was his element. He towered above the priest filling the whole passage with his mighty coils. Now they bunched and writhed towards the hot coals; and their dull red glow flared and rippled as they crowded close, a boiling wall of translucent rubbery flesh, and thick tendrils that homed in on the priest's trap.

They touched it and whipped away, recoiling from consecrated fire; but it was too late, and they were drawn inexorably into the brazier by a greater power, contained and subsumed in that mightier heat. Not Latin but the words of some far older tongue charmed them in; and the priest seemed to gather up the coiling masses, harvesting and destroying the devil's crop as he moved down the passage to where the cupboard stood open.

There in the red light of hell he saw the creature itself from which all those coils sprang and grew and multiplied: the vast and terrible image of a woman, its host and sacrifice. It filled the long tall lair right up to the ceiling, against which its shoulders bulged like cumulus, high above him. It seemed to be crouching, with its huge head lowered over its prey, and grotesque pixie eyes glaring out at the rash intruder. Below, towards the back of the cupboard, the white body of the girl lay limp across a dully glowing mound, as though across its knee; and the creature's red mouth was fastened to the whiteness: monster and body arranged in the form of an obscene Pietà.

The priest moved steadily forward with the brazier held out, driving himself on; and he hurled the sonorous battery of ancient words before him like covering fire.

But the extremities had informed the central mass of a sacred heat that consumed, and the warm stone at the heart of it felt the icy blast of exorcism. For a moment, the vast multiplicity of tendrils, even the towering body itself, seemed to bunch down, dark and knotted, muscle in spasm; then it exploded outwards, flowering like some giant sea-anemone, trapping the man in its petals, contracting, and squeezing the life away.

His head was wrenched back. He gagged on live jelly; his eyes were sealed open by it and staring into its smoky depths, his breath crushed out of him by the weight of encircling coils. He clung to the brazier and forced his head down enough to see the coals still glowing ahead of him through the slick, distorting gloom. He could feel that his hands were untramelled on its rim, and that there was a space about the fire, as though the creature could only encircle it, but feared to touch it. Now his voice was stopped; the fire was his only weapon, and he drew it closer to his chest, suffered its heat as the heavy, throttling bonds sizzled and melted away. He dragged it a little higher and the clammy shroud ravelled and fell away from his face. He could breathe.

He was inside the mass, surrounded by it. Cut off from retreat, and pressed by the great weight of bunched membrane over his back and shoulders and round his legs, he managed to clear a space and move forward. Now a familiar red shape at about chest height was visible beyond the brazier. It seemed to be guarded by a smooth wall of smoked glass; but this glowed and blackened and parted under the blow-torch heat.

Here, beneath the homely quilted jacket of a water cylinder,

lay the brain, the stone itself. Sebastian reached out one hand
through the burning stench and crumbling, blackened coils,
and plucked the small heavy velvet bag from its hiding place.

He knew he must not hold the stone: he must thrust the bag
and all in among the coals. But was it there? Might it not have
been replaced by a counterfeit? How could he be sure? To his
numb hands the velvet pouch seemed to have no weight at all
after the burden of the brazier. He juggled it into his palm,
attempting to feel its shape – and the stone rolled out and
crashed to the floor. He stretched down and picked it up. An
unthinking, reflex action.

The cupboard, the imprisoning membrane, the looming
Pietà: all were gone. He was plummeting through burning
ether – he was buried in a mountain – marvellously at rest:
cool and alone. Then violently ripped from that womb and
handled and peered at, kissed and anointed, set on a high altar
in the noonday sun, bloodied and washed and oiled and gazed
upon – hands, lips, eyes; crowds, jungles, jewels, surrounding
him; ruined cities, wings, waves, skies exploding with light
from volcanoes, from battle, from triumphant fireworks. But
this time those fearful tableaux that had so haunted him were
more elaborate, more real; for he was part of them: he was the
centre of it all, the sacred thing that caused blood to gush and
limbs to burn, mouths to gape and crack in pain.

And the priest knew he had held the stone too long. Father
Sebastian himself was trapped in it, had become part of its
history; was now, even now, involved in its imminent
flashpoint, the moment of destruction and dissemination – for
the last image was of a naked black man with a thin golden
chain round his neck where the veins stood out, tendons like
buttresses of ebony, carved ivory eyes rolled up into the
sockets. He lay in his own hand: a smooth, black-and-silver
grenade with the pin out.

Then he saw the man's mouth open. There was a shout of
doom: sacred words that blasted him. The hand that held him
thrust him into the alien fire; and his veins boiled out silver
blood that hissed among the white-hot boulders; and he was
back again in the far-distant moment of his creation.

Sebastian forced it deep in the spitting coals; and prayed that the humble vessel, too frail a property for this apocalyptic drama, and tempered only with the consecration of its calling, might contain the brain-stone of a fallen angel long enough for the completion of the task.

Now at last he turned towards Lucy where she lay.

He could see her only dimly, as though through intestines of that same smoked glass. She was crushed and mis-shapen, like pale, plucked chicken in a thick plastic packing, suction-sealed. But now the creature had lost its monitor, and was no more than a writhing heap of senseless extremities with one remaining instinct: to follow the stone. All around him it seemed to curdle and fall apart. The smooth muscular walls of his prison shivered, and corrugated, and became a crumbling slope of fine, translucent threads: the raw material, the very stuff, of organic life; and they reached out only for the fire. As the magma flowed and was drawn seething into the coals, the girl's shape slowly came clear, sinking gently down.

Above her, the huge mask of Mrs Maturin started to twist and blur as the heat dragged on it, distorting the smooth bulging features into bright barley-sugar coils and sliding strands and wriggling tendrils, undoing the image till it was only a great slithering smear with a glint of glasses, a wisp of hair, a stain of red, writhing mouth – all melting down into the receiving fire.

The huddled crowd in the lobby backed off as he appeared in the doorway. There was a great throng out in the street, and a police car came screaming into the square; but nothing stood in the way of the black runner as he carried the brazier, flaming now like an Olympic torch, across the snow to the frozen pond.

He raised it high above his head and hurled it down through the thick shell of ice – then threw himself flat on the ground. There was a crack like a direct lightning strike; and a searing explosion of boiling black steam that mushroomed upwards and outwards, bowing the trees with shockwaves, felling the nearest onlookers, and breaking glass all round the square. In the closed space, echoes came smacking back in a series of secondary explosions. The pool continued for nearly a minute to froth and boil; and there was a rumbling – no mere echo but felt through the soles of bedroom slippers on the icy pavements – as though a rogue tube-train were tunnelling through the square. It grew till it seemed to fill all space with its maniac drumming, unbearable – then getting faster and higher as it began to diminish, a sort of doppler effect, tuning up through a rising howl and fading away in a thin scream that disappeared off the top register.

In the silence, all the dogs of Kensington started barking. The people in the square unfroze; there was a babble of voices as they helped each other up. Someone started screaming hysterically.

The ambulance was there now, and the police. Most of those who had fallen were back on their feet; and before they could be moved along, they were picking their way through the broken glass, crowding into the lobby of Clarence Mansions, and up to the door of the flat; but the policemen held them there.

'Is the girl inside? – Is she all right?'

'Keep back please: she must have air.'

'He says get back she must have air.'

'So much smoke – and the smell!'

'Black smoke – could have been a chip-pan fire. We once had – '

'Did you see the smoke outside though? Did any of you – '

'Yes – from the explosion itself.'

'Sort of mushroom cloud really, wasn't it? – You saw it.'

'Right. And that coloured chap – '

'He was still flat on his face in the snow. But I saw he was moving – and then the police were there helping him up.'

'And the ambulance men?'

'They were checking to see he was all right – '

'Oh concussed, yes – must have been: right next to the blast, wasn't he?'

'What was that?'

'Was it a bomb? Sounded like.'

'What are they saying?'

'What happened?'

'Don't rightly know. Seems like his girlfriend was cooking chips in the middle of the night and the pan must have caught and he runs out mother-naked and throws it in the pond – OK, a gold chain round his neck but I still call that… '

Back windows were opened to let out the clinging black fumes still issuing from the ruins of the airing cupboard. The police had torches; another two had been provided by neighbours, and there were candles in the sitting room where the girl lay. Ella from upstairs, and a doctor who lived across the square, were there with her. Two more police officers had arrived and stood waiting as the doctor carried out his examination.

The girl's narrow, etiolated body was wrapped in rugs, with one arm in a bedraggled white sleeve lying uncovered for the doctor to take her blood-pressure. At least you could see now she was breathing: after a few weak gasps it had settled down to a shallow but steady rhythm. The doctor gave her an injection and put her arm back under the blanket.

'She may be all right,' he said straightening up. 'But we must get her on a drip.'

'Good. The ambulance men are just bringing their stuff in,' said the police officer in charge.

'The sooner the better: she's by no means out of danger, that one – but there's not much more I can do. The adrenalin shot should keep her ticking over – but she's chiefly dehydrated, it seems. And in shock – as is only to be expected.'

There was a ripple of excitement, like the arrival of a film-star, as the crowd fell back for the black priest to come through. And some hysteria as well: they would have touched him and idolised him, had they dared – but he was too powerful and strange, and they were afraid.

233

He was rubbing a clutch of snow in his hands. He came into the candlelight of the sitting room, and the snow and his teeth and the whites of his eyes were all they could see at first. Then they saw it was the black runner clothed only in dark shorts and a thin gold chain and the sweat and melting snow that streamed down his chest and legs and over his long bare feet. He was breathing hard.

'Is she alive?' he asked.

'Yes, she's alive; but she's in a bad way. She'll go into intensive care, naturally, and it may be something of a battle for the next twenty-four hours – what with dehydration, and massive shock. Perhaps you can shed some light... ?'

But the priest had moved to where the ambulance team were bending over the stretcher. They had covered her in red blankets and set up a drip feed. He knelt beside her and laid his black cheek against the cold white face.

'Not now please, sir.'

'I only want to speak to her.'

'She can't hear you, mister,' snapped the driver pulling at his shoulder.

'She can hear me and understand me, my son.' The voice was soft, but the eyes shifted the ambulance man back a pace.

'Only for a moment, then,' he muttered.

The black man turned back and cradled the girl's face. He mouthed his question silently. He watched her. They all watched. And her lips moved, shaping words.

He smiled. 'Yes, I'm impressed all right,' he spoke quietly. 'But just wait for me next time, OK?'

He stood up and turned back to the ambulance crew. 'Thanks,' he said. 'Thank you, Doctor. I reckon I should go and put on some clothes... Then all the questions, of course.'

'Let me dress those hands,' said the Doctor. 'Come over here where I can see.'

The priest spread out his broad pale palms. There was no mark on them.

'But they told me you were carrying a brazier of coals.'

'Yes. I'm afraid they may be a bit grimy,' said Sebastian.

He came out of his room in his jeans and sweatshirt, and looked into the cupboard. The ceiling, walls and shelves were singed and black, and Mrs Maturin's precious ornaments lay in pieces.

'Quite a mess,' he said to the policeman flashing his torch round the scene of destruction.

'It is indeed. Did you see what happened, sir?'

'I did, constable. It's a long story, and may be difficult to explain.'

The boiler went on in the basement beneath their feet, and the slow clicking started in the blackened pipes round them. It was six o'clock, and the start of a new day.

Outside in the square gardens, a mist hung over the pond.

A selection of bestsellers from SPHERE

FICTION

HOOLIGANS	William Diehl	£2.75 ☐
UNTO THIS HOUR	Tom Wicker	£2.95 ☐
ORIENTAL HOTEL	Janet Tanner	£2.50 ☐
CATACLYSM	William Clark	£2.50 ☐
THE GOLDEN EXPRESS	Derek Lambert	£2.25 ☐

FILM AND TV TIE-INS

SANTA CLAUS THE NOVEL	£1.75 ☐
SANTA CLAUS STORYBOOK	£2.50 ☐
SANTA CLAUS JUMBO COLOURING BOOK	£1.25 ☐
SANTA CLAUS: THE BOY WHO DIDN'T BELIEVE IN CHRISTMAS	£1.50 ☐
SANTA CLAUS: SIMPLE PICTURES TO COLOUR	95p ☐

NON-FICTION

HORROCKS	Philip Warner	£2.95 ☐
1939 THE WORLD WE LEFT BEHIND	Robert Kee	£4.95 ☐
BUMF	Alan Coren	£1.75 ☐
I HATE SEX		£0.99 ☐
BYE BYE CRUEL WORLD	Tony Husband	£1.25 ☐

All Sphere books are available at your local bookshop or newsagent, or can be ordered direct from the publisher. Just tick the titles you want and fill in the form below.

Name _____

Address _____

_____

Write to Sphere Books, Cash Sales Department, P.O. Box 11, Falmouth, Cornwall TR10 9EN

Please enclose a cheque or postal order to the value of the cover price plus:

UK: 45p for the first book, 20p for the second book and 14p for each additional book ordered to a maximum charge of £1.63.

OVERSEAS: 75p for the first book plus 21p per copy for each additional book.

BFPO & EIRE: 45p for the first book, 20p for the second book plus 14p per copy for the next 7 books, thereafter 8p per book.

Sphere Books reserve the right to show new retail prices on covers which may differ from those previously advertised in the text or elsewhere, and to increase postal rates in accordance with the PO.